Potentially Yours

Potentially Yours

Franklin White

A STREBOR BOOKS INTERNATIONAL LLC PUBLICATION
DISTRIBUTED BY SIMON & SCHUSTER, INC.

Published by

Strebor Books International LLC
P.O. Box 1370
Bowie, MD 20718
http://www.streborbooks.com

ISBN
978-1-59309-027-2
LCCN 2004100836
This book is a work of fiction. Names, characters, places and incidents are products of the
author's imagination or are used fictitiously. Any resemblance to actual events or locales or per-
sons, living or dead, is entirely coincidental.

Distributed by Simon & Schuster, Inc.
1230 Avenue of the Americas
New York, NY 10020
1-800-223-2336

Cover painting: © André Harris

First Printing June 2004
Manufactured and Printed in the United States

10   9   8   7   6   5   4   3   2   1

Synthia
Things definitely have changed.

I had on a skimpy leather skirt, a designer black blouse with knee-high boots and the audacity to stand outside in fifteen-degree weather in freaking New York City. The possibility of catching the flu was a thought but the balcony was the only place I could clear my head and come back down to earth. I was in a zone and it felt good. I was more relieved than a sista who hadn't had an orgasm after ten tries with the finest man alive.

Finally, I conjured up enough strength to reveal what had been on my mind for months to the guests; mostly my friends who were lounging about in my place. I was sure that what I'd told them had knocked them completely off their feet. There were gasps, bewildered looks, and shuffling feet moving toward the hired help I had tending bar. Their shocked voices asked for straight shots, hoping to ease my stunning revelation.

The black blouse I was wearing sure did look good. It was my favorite. I wore it especially for the night's festivities. The openness of the cuts in the arms made me feel special—like I could fly away. At the time, I really wished that spreading my wings and going off to someplace like the Bahamas and sitting in the sun like a model on a book cover was an option. But it wasn't so, I continued to stand alone and think about what I had just told everyone. Was I too brash? Did I come off like a bitch? I wondered if they all understood. If they didn't, I couldn't care about it. I had to do— what I had to do.

When I rushed my glass of Cognac up to my lips, hoping to get a blast of warmth into my system, my eyes couldn't help but look in the direction of the party going on inside my condo. I have to admit, from where I was standing about twenty feet from the inside, my place looked fabulous; especially the oil painting of James Baldwin that I'd purchased during my fourth visit to France. It was perfectly lit under track lighting and sitting directly over my white baby-grand piano.

My place didn't always have such flare. It took a while to decide on redecorating. I didn't want my daughter to let go of the family atmosphere it represented during her childhood. After all, it had been where her father and now my ex-husband had spent a good part of our lives. I knew that changing the place around was not the only thing I had on my agenda but after it was completed, it would without a doubt spark the signal of change in my life that I felt was needed. I can't even lie and say I thought it was going to be a simple process. I had major issues I was dealing with and they scared the shit out of me. I wanted to beat the game before it began to beat on me.

I give the night and my announcement a nine—only because I didn't let my best friend Byron in on what was going on. When I saw him opening my sliding-glass door leading out to the balcony with a concerned look on his face, I knew he was about to let me know exactly how he felt. I have to admit I didn't feel like explaining myself to him. He was part of the problem.

Byron
How you gonna' play ya' boy?

At first, I wasn't sure how to approach Synthia when I saw her narrowing eyes piercing over at me after I slid the door open and stepped out onto the balcony. The way she was staring at me, you would have thought I had done something to her. But I hadn't. I'd been the one blind-sided and, hell yes, I was mad about it. I replaced the frown on my face with a fake ass smile and decided to see what was going on with girl.

I know one thing. It was cold as hell outside and the first thing that came to mind was that my friend of all these years was having a breakdown or something. The Synthia I knew would never stand uncovered in cold weather. I already had my hands deep down inside my pockets when I got within arm's distance from her. She looked at me, then turned toward the slick gray stone ledge, outlining the balcony into the direction of the bright city lights. The cold air hampered my ability to get the words out of my mouth as fast as I would have liked.

"I'm going to tell you right now, Synthia. It's too damn cold for small talk—so out with it. What's going on?" I asked her. "How the hell you gonna say something like that without even telling me it was coming? Motherfuckers inside are asking a billion questions and I can't answer nary a one."

She kind of smiled; like she knew what I was going to say. Her eyes were wondrous. They were glaring and I thought that maybe she'd had too much to drink; rather than a breakdown. Synthia didn't answer me back as quickly as I would have liked and the wind began to cut through me like I wasn't a respectable five-ten, a hundred eighty pounds. I flipped up my overlarge turtleneck, moving it up over my chin and as close to my mouth as possible.

"Damn it. I'm not catching another cold this winter, Synthia. What's that you're drinking?"

She was blunt. "Cognac."

When I reached out my hand for a sip she gave up her glass. I took a healthy sip and waited to get a feel from the drink, then asked her if she was okay.

"I'm fine. Cold, but fine," she answered.

I took off my jacket and placed it around her shoulders. I'd do anything for Synthia and she knew that. That's why I was hurt that she didn't have the balls to let me in on what was going down before she stood up in front of everyone at her gathering, literally telling them all to leave her the hell alone because they weren't doing it for her.

"Synthia, everyone inside thinks you must've had a really bad day or something. What's the deal?" I gave back her drink. I could tell Synthia was thinking about what to say to me. She was such a heavy thinker.

She said, "Looking back at it, Byron, it's been a very good day." She toasted her glass. "Here's to you." She studied the confusion on my face. "Well, Byron… I've finally opened up and let go of what's been on my mind and what can I say? I feel good about it." Even though she was shivering, Synthia was at ease. She even managed to smile a bit and her bright eyes and confidence reminded me of how she was able to work her way up to the top as one of the publishing industry's leading agents.

BACK IN THE DAY, Synthia was a mere babe when we met. I was working my very first job down at the bus terminal in Manhattan. I was a twenty-year-old youngster. It was 1984. I'll never forget those days because I'd just moved into my very first apartment in Harlem. I was sub-renting from a sub-renter and thought I was God's gift to women twenty times over. I'm talking the original *Mr. Biggs*. I wasn't making much money. My job at the terminal was custodial and when I didn't have anything to do, which was very rare, I stood in the information booth and gave directions to those trying to find their way.

I spotted Synthia out of a jam-packed terminal ten minutes before she even walked over to the information booth. If I had been a crook she would have been a mark and I would have taken her for everything she had. Her eyes were huge and she was like a puppy chasing her tail trying to figure out which direction to go. Synthia was so naive to the big city that when she approached me for directions to the nearest YWCA I could tell she didn't know the East Side of Manhattan from the West. I didn't hold that against her. Something about Synthia told me she was special. She was aggressive and had her mind set that she was not going to fall to the obvious pressure of moving to the big city while trying to keep track of everything she owned. So, not only did I tell her where she wanted to go, I sneaked off the job and walked with her and then gave her my number. That's how we became friends.

I found out later that Synthia had originally come to the Big Apple to become an author. I remember she kept asking me, while we were walking, if I had ever heard of all these great writers she'd read when she was younger who'd come up through Harlem. She wanted to be just like Zora Neale Hurston or James Baldwin and even had a destined look of accomplishment in her presence.

At fifteen she'd finished her first novel. It was three-hundred thirty-five pages. I found out she was born and raised in Jackson, Mississippi. Many times we would sit down to discuss the South. Mainly because I'd never been there and all I'd ever heard about those neck of the woods was to stay the hell away if I didn't want to be lynched or beaten by the police. Synthia's stories about living there were grim, but she never talked about many bad things going on outside of her home because she was sheltered coming up. There was just too much going on inside her childhood. Synthia's mother died when she was eight and her father had the task of bringing her up all by his lonesome because he refused to have another woman have a hand in raising her. That's why she enjoyed the books of

Zora so much because she was allowed to hear a pure woman's voice reach out to her. From what she told me, her old man was pretty damn good to her. He practically gave her everything she wanted and was very supportive, even encouraged her when she turned down journalism scholarships from colleges all over the world to move to New York to become an author.

I was kind of surprised when she told me her father was footing the bill for her living expenses while she pursued her dreams. In fact, after we got closer—it was one of the reasons I invited her to stay with me as a roommate. I knew her part of the rent would never be late. It wasn't two months after we were roommates that her father died. Synthia was stunned and grieved for the longest, but refused to let his death deter her. She realized she had to make it in the big city just like everyone else—on her own now. Her father had a healthy insurance policy, but I don't think Synthia ever touched it. The policy he left for her was Synthia's remembrance of him. Synthia went on to land a job as a secretary at a boutique literary agency in Lower Manhattan and worked there for years until deciding on becoming a literary agent.

SYNTHIA HATED WHEN I STARED at her and I hadn't taken my eyes off her since coming out onto the balcony.

"You think I owe you an explanation, don't you?"

"You do and you know it. Look, we've been friends for entirely too long for me to have to stand out here in this wind and guess what the hell is going on, don't you think?"

"You're right, Byron, it's been a long time."

I moved a little closer to her. "Damn right. So out with it?"

"Okay, but this has to do with me, more than anyone else."

"Understood."

We stood silent. Synthia positioned herself in a defensive mode. Her eyes narrowed, lips became tight and then she crossed her arms. When she noticed me arch my eyebrow and slightly bend my neck trying to pull out what was on her mind, she knew that I was ready for a stare down if need be—no matter how cold it was.

"Okay, here it is. I meant what I said inside there tonight, Byron. I think it's time for me to cut all ties with everyone in my life because I don't feel like anyone that I'm connected to at the moment is really helping me to become a better person."

I felt my eyes narrow. I was truly confused. "Become a better person? What're you talking about, Synthia? You're the best!" Synthia soothed a bit and she looked out over the city, then looked back at me. She took my hand and began to walk. She opened the sliding door, we walked through her condo among all the stares of her thirty or so guests and the next thing I knew, Synthia had her coat, I had mine, and we were in a taxi headed toward lower Manhattan.

WE HAD A VERY LIGHT CONVERSATION in the cab. Synthia skimmed over the fact that forty-eight had come entirely way too fast and she was not prepared for her daughter Clarke's senior year of high school. We ended up in Synthia's office. I could barely see Synthia when she took a bottle of Cognac from her fur coat and then a sip from the bottle. There was just enough light from the city to see. She reached over her desk and handed the drink to me. She sat down behind her desk, exhausted.

"Do you really want to know why I said what I did at the party?"

"I've already asked you more than I think I should have to? What's the deal? I thought everything was going okay with you?"

"See, that's the problem, Byron. Everything is *just* okay and I believe it's time for a change." Synthia paused for a second. "I'm just saying, at the moment, the people in my life including myself, mind you, are not living up to our potential. I think it's time for me to be truthful with myself about that."

I was surprised at her words. "Living up to potential? Synthia, look at you. The way I see it, you've surpassed whatever you were meant to have in this life. Have you forgotten you're one of the top literary agents in this city? I know people that would do anything to have your job."

And they would. I knew firsthand because Synthia always asked me to accompany her when her ex-husband and live-in roommate, who had been my best friend for many years until I'd introduced him to Synthia years ago, couldn't make her engagements with the city's literary elite. She loved the way I was able to move around the rooms and hype her authors for her. I usually didn't read any of the books; except the one that had something to do with how women could love a black man. It took me a while to stomach through it; mainly because I saw myself. The only thing I let myself get from the book was that after all these years, black men still were treated as some sort of species who need specialized attention to be understood. The literary gatherings had their perks though; especially the ones I paraded myself around as a book doctor who had the ability to whip any book into shape and sell well into the hundreds of thousands of dollars at a drop of a hat. I met so many fine sisters and a few white girls, too. I even met a sister who happened to be at a book launch party mingling and networking looking to break into the industry with her for-sure bestseller. She turned out to be a hit in bed for six months until she found out I couldn't get her book in the front door of a vanity publisher.

Synthia and I were silent, except for the few times we passed the Cognac back and forth between us.

"You ever thought about me having my own agency, Byron?"

I looked around in the darkness. "Unh, unh… I thought you were always happy working in this tall ass building and living in your high-rise on Park Avenue, sipping tea with all those literary types."

"Happy, yes, but not satisfied. It's not enough for me. I want my own agency, Byron. I don't always want to be the person beating the pavement looking for the next fuckin' bestseller."

Finally, Synthia was about to spill her guts to me. But I thought it was a good time to tell her about my new business venture since we were going there.

"Another one?"

"What do you mean, another one?

"Just what I said."

"Look, this one's a keeper," I told her.

Synthia tipped up the bottle again, then said, "And so was the last one, and the two before that. Byron, sweetheart, that's what I'm talking about here."

"About me?"

"Yes, you. You know I love you, and care about you a hell of a lot. Don't you know that?"

"That's what you say."

"Of course, I do. But you're not living up to your potential either and I think just maybe, how you're living is rubbing off on me."

At that point I just knew the Cognac had Synthia's tongue.

"Look, it's no secret that we all are a reflection of the company we keep. I'm trying to explain to you that I need to be more focused to accomplish the things I want to do with my life and right now; I think our friendship stunts my ability to do that."

"Wow, that really hurts, Synthia. Give me that damn bottle."

"I'm sure it does. But it's the truth. I didn't say this was going to be easy, Byron. Plus, you can handle it. You have your romantic interest, slash money-grubbing girlfriend to be friends with. No pun intended, darling, but just *spend* more time with her."

"Hey, that's not fair."

"But it's true."

"Look, I told you before. I give Karen money to help her out of tight situations."

"More like to get yourself into a tight situation." Synthia's voice reeked of sarcasm. "Which I highly doubt could ever be a reality."

I set Synthia straight when she said that. "She's not loose."

"Seems to be to me."

Synthia really began to irritate me. "Look, this isn't about her, and why the hell are we sitting in the dark, damn it?"

"You're right. It isn't." Synthia stood up. I watched her walk over to her blinds behind her desk. "Byron, come here a second." I walked over to her. "Ordinarily I keep these blinds open at all times." Synthia began to pull the blinds back. "But ever since it happened, I've been unable to look out my window. I haven't been able to look out this window, Byron, because of the site still down below." Synthia pulled the blinds back far enough so that we could see outside.

"Look down there, Byron. Look at the rubble from the terrorist attack. You know when it happened I was standing right here. I saw people down below being crushed and people from up above take their own lives in desperation to get out of those buildings. Right here in this spot, Byron, frozen absolutely still, unable to think or move, just frozen still."

I put my arm around Synthia. I remembered calling her when it was all going down. She answered the phone but wouldn't talk to me or get out of her building, which was just too damn close to what was going on.

"And as horrible as the day was, it did something to me, Byron. I saw life taken away right before my eyes and I've realized that we're here to do something worthwhile in our lives. We're not living to take up space. We are here to make a contribution to this thing called life and I have devoted the rest of my life to making a difference in what I do. I don't know how I can say this any clearer. I need to make a change in my life and only associate myself with people who are making a difference in life as well. So, I'm begging you to please. Please let me without making it harder than it already has been—to break off our friendship after all these years."

Clarke
Mom is buggin' out.

My therapist thinks I'm somewhat of an extremist. I'm not going to lie. When my mother made her decision to change her entire life into some life-saving conservative who only wanted to involve herself in things that mattered, I really didn't want to hear it. I thought it was nothing but a bunch of hot air she needed to get out of her system. If my doctor calls that extreme, then I guess I am. My mother's new life switch couldn't have come at a worse time in my life. The moment I'd been waiting for since I was in the seventh grade, and had my virginity taken by some thug named Thad who lived in Harlem, was finally here. Thad was the brother of a friend I'd taken ballet lessons with and one of the things he always would brag about was his senior year. The parties, being top dog on the yard and the mad fun he'd experienced—all that shit was appealing to me. It took five years to get to this point and all I wanted to do was finally enjoy my last year of high school, go to a few parties, enjoy my man, and choose the college I was going to attend.

This was my time.

When my mother burst into my room to let me in on her new attitude, I was splashing on some smell good and I was about to go out the door. My first thought was menopause finally had caught up to her. She had this quirky look on her face and was talking a mile a minute. I don't know why

I thought change of life. I'd seen the look on her face before. Mainly when she came in my room to talk to me, right before or after my father would go out on a date. And a few times when she herself came home from a date in the wee hours of the morning.

There hadn't been many of those times; I would say seven or eight since I was eleven. But when she did go out, she would sit on my bed with that look. I could tell when she came back home she was freshly fucked because her hair was always different than when she'd left. Each time she came into my room with her overcoat or fur still on, clutching onto it like she didn't want to take it off because she was afraid that I could see through her clothes and notice someone had been suckin' on her titties.

I have to admit, it was damn near unbearable to stand and listen to my mom when she started to get into all this gut-wrenching, heart-aching confessions about feeling as though she hadn't been there for me. Then she dropped the bomb and let me know that she'd told my father he had to move out of our condo. That's when I realized my mother was actually buggin' the fuck out!

Don't get it twisted. I really do love my mother. The World Trade attack scared the shit out of me, too. But shit, it's the life we live and I refuse to let those stupid ass people who don't give a damn about themselves, let alone me, force me to change the way I do things. They've been fucked up for a million years and it will probably be a million more before they wake up and realize their country is worth billions and can be used for good instead of so much evil.

Mom's timing with this shit was just all wrong. I had things to do, important things. For one, I had scheduled to take the SAT one last time and I really didn't need anything else on my mind. The last time I'd taken the test I was twenty points from a perfect score and I had planned to go in the test focused and ace that bitch before she'd decided to turn our household upside-down. For me, it was the worst decision she could have ever made. How could she tell my father to leave? Thomas was my rock. He'd always been. I love my mother to death, but my father is the one person in my life who I could open up and talk to without feeling as though I needed to watch what I said. Thomas always taught me to speak my mind with him without feeling guilty or in a box of submission. He was always there to help me with my most difficult decisions.

There was the one time, and I'm sure my mother still doesn't know about this because my father promised me he wouldn't tell her, that I thought I was pregnant and I didn't know who the father was. I was in the tenth grade and my hormones had taken over. It seemed like every single minute of the day I was thinking about sex. I hadn't even been sexually active for years after that first time because none of the guys at my school even came close to Thad. He knew things; at least enough to convince me to give it to him. But at the time of my hormone rage, my mind wasn't thinking about someone who could make me feel good inside my mind. I wanted to feel good between my legs and all over my body. I tried to do everything I knew not to think about sex, but it seemed that every place I went, especially at school, it was the topic of discussion. The guys were talking about sex and the girls. I even overheard two female teachers one day on the way to their cars saying how much they needed some dick. I couldn't handle the urge that kept making me jump and squirm every time I saw a cute guy, so I decided to act on my strong feelings twice in the same night, with two different guys— it was just that bad.

REGGIE WAS ABOUT SIX-ONE, light-skinned with brown wavy hair. We were in the same grade and had a lot of the same classes together. He played varsity basketball and had been getting letters from colleges since he was in the ninth grade telling him he was the best ball player in the city. Reggie had been talking shit to me every day at school. I mean he was talking so much that one day at lunch he had me literally soaking wet and if he would've tried to put his hands in my pants I would've just lain back and let him.

The other guy was Bill, but everyone calls him "Dollar." He was a real slick, dark-skinned quiet nigga who I'd met one day in Times Square. I was at the movies with my girls when I first laid eyes on Dollar. We were standing in line waiting to get in the theater. He didn't even pay me much attention, but when his boys started talking stuff to my girls, I got bold and asked him what his name was. He was acting all quiet and reserved like he didn't care if he knew who I was or not. For some reason, that shit turned me on.

My hormones made me scandalous. One day I decided not to go to school. I'd told Reggie about my plan the day before. I'd told him to come over to my house at exactly ten in the morning; that way I could make sure both my mother and father were at work. When he came over, we knew what the deal was, so I just took him by the hand and led him up to my bedroom. Being with Reggie was good, but I quickly found out that he talked shit better than he knew how to screw. But it was cool because he stayed with me until about twelve and after a quick shower and thirty minutes later, I had Dollar knocking on my door waiting to get his piece.

Now Dollar knew what he was doing. He didn't know that Reggie had just left but he acted like he did because he took time to get me back in the mood. Dollar touched all the right places with his tongue and was on top of me for about twenty minutes but made me explode three times. The next month I was scared that I was pregnant because I was three weeks late. I ran to Thomas and told him about it. My father didn't react negatively or make me feel like I was a little slut. More than anything, he was concerned about my future. He called a doctor friend of his at his job and he gave me a pregnancy test. Before my father told me the results, he'd made me promise I would be more careful, which blew my mind. He didn't make me promise not to have sex again; just to be careful. Luckily I was just late and I haven't had sex since, even with my boyfriend nor have I been so wild or reckless messing around with these knucklehead niggas. Thank God. I guess I was just going through a little phase.

MY FATHER WAS MY MOTIVATION. I never told my mother because I didn't want her to get jealous or upset that I went to him before her for things that I needed or wanted to talk about. And I never told my father because he just thought he was doing what good fathers do for their children. That's why I was pissed off when he grabbed his last bag and left letting me know that he actually agreed with my mother. Granted, I could see if my mother wanted him to leave because he was one of those men who hung around the house all day playing video games, like a couple of my girls' fathers. But my pops had it going on and was a fuckin' role model in every sense of the word. He had a really good job, knew lots of important people, and was well-liked all over the city. When Thomas shut the door and left the condo, I went into my room and refused to talk to my mother for the rest of the weekend.

It wasn't until Monday morning that I even laid eyes on her again, and she really had a lot of nerve trying to strike up a conversation with me.

"Hello, darlin'… will you be power-walking with me after school?" she'd asked.

I just hummed back my answer to her.

"That's all I get is, umm…hmm?"

"Ummm, hummm," I repeated.

"Did I miss something? Or should I prepare myself for this new language, baby girl?"

"Mom, really. You know I'm upset with you. So, please, just let me get through this, okay?"

"Still? After all this time?"

"It's only been three days."

"Well, if you need time, sweetheart, take all you want."

"I talked with Dad last night."

My words stopped Mom from pouring her morning coffee. "Wonderful. How's he doing?"

"Mom… he misses me."

"I'm sure he does. I would, too, sweetheart. To not see those pretty brown eyes every morning would be devastating to anyone. Don't you know every-one I show your picture to thinks you look like that actress, Lisa Raye?"

"Whatever. Mom, why'd you do it?"

"Do what?"

"You know what. Make him leave. That was so foul. I miss having Daddy around."

"Because, Clarke, that's what he was. Just around."

"That was a good thing."

"Yeah, maybe for you. But I'm still not too sure about that. Your father needed to be more than just around."

"I wasn't complaining and I thought that was the reason for him being here in the first place, to be here for me? Now I have to go way across town every time I want to see him."

"It was the reason, when you were younger, that we chose for him to stay here after our divorce because we both knew firsthand how difficult it is for a child in a one-parent home to excel."

"I know, I know, I've heard it so many times before."

"Well, it's true. Besides, Thomas can come over to visit anytime he wants. Your father knows that."

"Hell, if he does all that, he might as well move back in, don't you think?"

"Look, Clarke, your father being here was not working, okay? There was no way I could've continued living like that. It wasn't productive, nor setting a good example for you."

"It was fine, Mom. You never heard me complain about it. So, let's get things back the way they were around here so I can enjoy my senior year, okay?"

"No way, sweetheart. This is just the beginning."

I really hated how that sounded and decided my mother was really bugg'n the fuck out.

Synthia
Just couldn't pass it up.

The very same night I came home from my office after talking with Byron, I was shocked to see my boss, Barbara Scotch, sitting on my couch all alone with a glass of red wine in her left hand and flipping through my daughter's *Source Magazine*.

"Thought I was gonna have to spend the night." She smirked.

"Excuse me?"

"I didn't know if you were coming back or not. But I knew you had to come back eventually and I was prepared to stay as long as it took."

"Just had to get some fresh air, Barbara. Why are you still here?"

"Well, I heard what you said earlier, loud and clear, Synthia."

I plopped down in a chair across from her.

"And it makes sense."

"Really?" I was surprised she understood.

"Yes, it did. That's why I want to offer you a partnership in my agency. Right now, right this minute. What do you say?"

The smile on my face told her, "Hell, yes, I'll take it!"

IT FELT SO GOOD a couple of weeks later when Barbara said to me, "Now that all the partnership paperwork and contracts are in order we can get down to business, *partner*." I was thrilled to death and counting my blessings. When I made up my mind to go out into the world and establish my own company, it just so happens to fall in my lap. Barbara offered me a forty-nine percent stake in the company. I'd been working there for seventeen years. I'd helped build the agency and I would have been a damn fool to run off and start my own agency after the offer. The Barbara Scotch Agency already had name recognition; major books already under contract. The percentage in her agency would climb to eighty after she retired. The offer couldn't have come at a better time.

I was determined to make our partnership work. I knew there would be so many other agents of color watching my work. I'd gotten calls all day from well-wishers who'd heard about the partnership. News travels fast in the publishing industry and it seemed as though the agency solidified our legendary presence in the world of publishing, which was a very good thing indeed.

Barbara Scotch; Irish-American, sixty-three years old, chain-smoker, fierce competitor, always wore her hairstyle in a ponytail, lined her eyes perfectly with dark eyeliner; and her passionate ruby-red lipstick that hugged her lips was definitely her trademark. Over the years my partner had made a killing in the publishing industry. She'd started out as a very small boutique agency in 1964, having already worked in the industry for almost ten years. Barbara had seen it all and signed some of the greatest authors and books while making a huge amount of money doing so. It was in the late seventies when her agency took off for stardom and the big-boy agencies in town began to give her the respect she was due.

When I first began working with Barbara as an associate agent I remember being so humbled working for her. I'd heard she had a few slots opening up at her agency and I had just talked four publishers into signing four of my no-name writers who I thought were very talented for substantial advances. Word spread around town like fire and when I went in to see Barbara about her openings, she hired me on the spot. When I began working at the agency, we had exactly eight associate agents with Barbara running the show. I watched it grow to forty-three associate agents and the agency involves itself in every facet of entertainment. Barbara was a hard-working lady, but to tell the truth no one ever went to her office close to closing time. Everyone knew how long-winded she was and her enjoyment to drag anyone she could out to a trendy bar to talk business for hours and chain-smoke her cigarettes. I had endured many nights out with Barbara because I wanted to pick her brain. There were many nights that we just talked as girlfriends, getting to know one another, which turned into a very strong relationship where we both respected each other.

"BARBARA, I WANT TO THANK YOU once again for offering the partnership," I let her know while we were sitting in her office finishing up our paperwork for our new deal.

"Well, the writing's been on the wall for a while now anyway. The decision to offer the partnership was a no-brainer. When I first hired you, I promised you good things would follow if you worked hard and, now, here you are." Barbara was looking at me with proud eyes. I knew her partnership was truly heartfelt. "Now we can be the best Ebony and Ivory chicks on the scene," she said.

I felt a burst of energy and motivation. "So, what's on the agenda for our first official meeting?"

"I wanted to hand over the clients you'll be personally responsible for, along with the associate agents and what they have on the front burner."

I reached out to take the list from Barbara. Finally, the responsibility and leadership I had been striving for was about to touch my hand. I looked down at the list and realized it contained half of the agency's roster. Millions of dollars of revenue and movie deals for clients that needed to be brokered. Collaborations to be considered and requests for author appearances.

"There's loads of work to do, my darling," Barbara sang. I think Barbara saw the questioning expression on my face while I read the roster. She sat up a bit in her chair. "Is there a problem, Synthia?"

"All of my clients? They're all African-American or other people of color?"

"Umm-hmm, I thought I would let you handle all their accounts and I'll make sure everything else gets done."

"But?"

Barbara was quick to the punch; close to being rehearsed. "Don't worry about it, our agency needs a good swift kick in the ass in the urban and minority accounts and I know you're just the person to do it. Plus, I know as much as you do—some of our Black and Latino writers are becoming fuckin' fed up having to relay every little detail about the facets of their writing to our agents so that the agents can turn around and go back to the editors at the houses who don't know a damn thing about any culture outside of their own." Barbara eased a bit in her chair. "You know, I was thinking that with this move maybe some of the houses will take a look at how our agency is split down the middle in ownership, then turn around and give our writers, editors that can relate to their culture. Of course it means hiring more minority editors. See, your speech about doing something worthwhile in life at your party did something to me also, Synthia."

I could see Barbara's point so I smiled and said, "Oh, so we're going to become separate but equal? I'm feeling it—I think it could work."

"Sure it can. Look, let's flip the coin a bit. If there was a publishing house full of Black and Latino editors filled with a stable of our White writers, most of them would be calling here just the same about their clients asking us to get our authors to clarify the simplest things about culture as well. It works both ways. It's the way of life, culturally speaking. I thought it would be different but in my view, after all these years, cultures still don't know enough about each other. I'd be the first to admit to you, after work and on the weekends, I might not say one word to another person who isn't like me. I'm talking about my color, my background, and that goes for church, too. And it's not because I don't like anyone outside my culture. It's just the way we are. Tell me something? Do you have any white people that attend your church?" Barbara wanted to know.

I told her, "If we do, they joined right after the terrorist attack."

"My point exactly."

"I don't have a problem with it. Honestly, I don't. I was just looking forward to a little more rounded assortment of clients; that's all. But, like I've said, change is good."

Then Barbara really soothed my mind. "Of course, you'll keep all of your clients no matter what their backgrounds. Plus, the whole enchilada will come in time, Synthia, and sooner than you think. I have been getting the urge to travel, if nothing else, go to my condo in Naples, Florida and at least sit on the deck and enjoy the fruits of my labor. Most of my friends are already down there. Working out, playing cards, doing just about anything they want. Maybe I can even get my bed rest there after I have my plastic surgeon to remove the bags from my eyes. Have you ever been to Naples, Synthia?"

Before I could answer her, our secretary buzzed in and told me there was an important call for me; the mega female rapper named Lil' Shae.

Thomas Gage
Trust me, I'm okay with it.

Okay, I'll admit. Some of my coworkers call me Poster Boy. It all started a couple of years ago when the company I work for, Consolidated Edison of New York, sponsored The Ebony Male Fashion Show for a benefit. For some reason, everyone from my company began to express how well I blended in with the male models and, before I knew it, Con-Ed decided to plaster posters all over the city of me, particularly in Times Square promoting the company, as well as the first black male ever to run their public relations office.

It's not that I was bent out of shape about it. I think any man nearing fifty-three, who has been able to sustain middle-age midsection girth, keep bounce in his step, radiate confidence with his every movement without coming off overly arrogant or presumptuous, would somehow take the label all in stride. But seriously, *Poster Boy* had to take a little getting used to; especially when the guys busting your chops have known you for over twenty years. I don't know what would have happened if they'd found out that both Hennessy and Jaguar called to see if I would be interested in an advertising campaign as a model. My job was special though. It was definitely high-profile. It was a no-nonsense job and I took myself as a no-bullshit businessman who wanted to do the best job possible. Being responsible for reassuring that electricity and gas would continue to flow in

New York City is one huge task, and I was paid a very high six-figure salary to do so. I would say all in all, this small-town boy from North Carolina had done pretty well for himself.

I HAD JUST ABOUT COMPLETED GETTING MY OFFICE INSIDE MY CONDO INTO SHAPE, making it feel as comfortable as it was while living with my ex and my daughter Clarke. My Con-Ed *Man of the Year* award was centered perfectly behind my chair and my four *Best Dad Ever* plaques given to me by Clarke were directly on the wall in front of me. I never had been the type to bring much work home so my desk was nice and neat. Never more than my next two tasks would sit where I worked, along with my computer, phone, and a large calendar to help me keep track of appearances and meetings.

My new place was out on the East Side of the city on 63rd and York Street. It was very nice and upscale. I'd had my eye on the location for a while. I never knew how long Synthia and I were going to be able to keep up our "make friendly" relationship for Clarke. But I think we did a pretty good job for as long as we could, all things considered.

I could smell the aroma of something cooking really nice in my kitchen, which was located down the hall. Clarke had surprised me, come over with a grocery bag and told me not to disturb her until she called, but I just had to go see what she was doing.

"Something smells really good in here, pumpkin. Did I tell you how much I loved you today?"

Clarke smiled up at me. "No, you sure haven't."

I kissed her on the cheek and said, "Well, I do love you. Look at this. I can't believe I'm finally eating dinner in my own place."

Clarke placed her hand on her hip. A red and white apron covered her jeans and T-shirt. "That's right, Daddy, a home-cooked meal is what we both need. I can't continue to meet you for dinner at those restaurants. Have you forgotten this is my senior year? I have a figure to maintain and that mad cow disease scares the shit outta me."

What my daughter and I had going, I knew fathers envied, and probably some mothers as well. I don't know how to explain it, but it's truly a good feeling to know that your one and only child, your baby girl, thinks the world of you. The only thing that had gotten our relationship to that point was trust. I'd always wanted the best for Clarke and I did whatever I could for her to make her feel she was the most special person in my life. Time we spent together was not just about her homework or an after-school extracurricular activity. It was special.

Believe me; I didn't know the first thing about raising a daughter. Shit, who does? When the doctor told Synthia our baby was a girl, I was in shock. I never thought for one second that I'd have a daughter. I always knew I'd have a boy. It got to a point when she was a little baby that all I did was look at her without saying much because I didn't want to say the wrong thing. But as time went on I decided that I was going to be the opposite of most fathers, not be that played-out type of dad, and keep things as real as possible with her. Granted there had been times when Clarke's teachers would complain that her mouth never stopped running and they even called me on the job. But, instead of going to the school and snatching Clarke out the class and spanking her, I would take her to Mickey-D's, buy her all the fries she wanted, and let her talk to me. Yet, there have been problems that I'd like to really forget about. We have gotten past them, even though it was difficult for me to deal with. I tried my absolute best to handle it all without anger, spite, or judgment against by baby girl and it seemed to have worked out for the best in our relationship.

I moved in closer to see what Clarke had been doing in my kitchen. "Darling, you didn't have go through all this trouble for your father. I'm glad that you did, but I would've been happy with a sandwich or soup and crackers even."

"Daddy, soup and crackers? Maybe next time, but tonight something really good for you. Something that's going to keep those eyes, and deep dimples that my girlfriends love so much, into shape. You know you should be eating more home-cooked meals because you're moving toward old age. So all this good stuff is mandatory."

"I have you know that I'm not a day over thirty-five and in excellent shape. Did I tell you..."

Clarke cut me off in mid sentence and began nodding her head at the song that I'd been telling her for years. "Yes, that you ran over five miles this morning?"

"Exactly, five point three," I told her.

"So you say, big poppa. But I want you around for a long time. Eating properly when you're around me from now on is top priority. Plus, tonight we need to talk."

"Talk?"

"Yes, talk. Something we used to do quite often up until a few weeks ago."

"What about?"

"You, getting back together with Mom."

"Ha, I've heard it all."

I tried to brush Clarke off. Even though we had a stellar relationship she really had a problem putting her nose in my personal business. Her request made me go back to a point in my life and the reason she'd asked me the exact question the first time. The reason's name was Lisa, a New York Knicks cheerleader I'd met in '92 when Clarke was eight years old. I was at a party where the team was celebrating advancing to the second round of the playoffs. Our acquaintance led to a friendship, which led to an affair, which in turn became emotional. It lasted for well over six months before Synthia found out. Indeed Synthia was hurt behind the whole matter. But she somehow took the high road. After all, she had been with me at many parties and witnessed women hit on me right in front of her face. I'm not saying what I did was right, because I regret that it ever happened. I'd been strong enough to turn down many of the advances that had come my way. But not this chick Lisa, I couldn't do it.

She was twenty-four, had just graduated from NYU and had covered her expenses for college by being a personal trainer and aerobics instructor. Synthia inclined to dismiss the whole matter with an open mind and continued with our marriage because she understood that it was only sex and trusted that it wouldn't last much longer. But then I had to tell her that Lisa wanted more and felt she was in love with me. That's when Synthia became hurt and wanted a divorce. When Clarke found out about the divorce she became distant and cold toward both of us. Clarke completely shut down. Her attitude changed and I was depressed because I thought I had ruined a bright mind because she spent most of her time worrying about what was going to happen to our family. It was the reason Synthia and I decided to send Clarke to therapy to deal with our problems. Clarke took me from my remembrance of it all. When I came to, there was corn, broiled salmon and a nice green salad sitting before me.

Clarke said, "Hey, are you listening to me? I'm not finished yet."

"Clarke, Clarke, Clarke, Clarke, Clarke."

"Daddy, I hate when you do that."

"Do what?"

"You're stalling. Listen to me. I just want to find out what the chances are of you getting back together with Mom?

"You want odds, huh?"

"Yes, give me something. She's driving me crazy."

"Not a chance in hell. How's that for odds?"

Clarke said to me, "Not even a smidgen of hope?"

I shook my head no.

"Not the smallest ray of light?"

"Not an ass crack, no way, Clarke. You know your mother and I've been divorced since you were nine?"

"Being divorced didn't stop you two from living with one another."

"C'mon, you know we did that for you, sweetheart. We wanted to keep you in line. There was no way I could let Synthia go through raising you alone. But now, you're almost out of school. Hell, you're barely at home anymore. Soon you'll graduate from high school, and then it's off to college."

Clarke began to speak in her whiny voice that she knew irritated the hell out of me. "But Mom put you out in the streets like last week's garbage or something."

"Chill, Clarke. Does it look like I'm in the streets to you? Sweetheart, it was time for me to leave. I should've been gone sometime ago."

"But, what about me?"

"You?"

"Yes, me, your daughter. Your first and better be only child."

"We'll be closer than ever and that's the honest-to-God truth. This hasn't been so bad. Matter of fact, it's been kinda fun."

Clark sat on my countertop while I ate. "It's not the same anymore. I like having you home when I'm sleep. I like hearing you snore. Hell, I even miss you drinking all the orange juice all the time. Plus, Mom is going way overboard with all this *change*. Do you know she came to school yesterday?"

"For what?"

"I don't know. She was asking all types of stupid ass questions. It was so embarrassing."

"What type of questions?"

"About my homework, about upcoming events. Can you believe she wants to be involved in my life after all this time? Hello…I'm a damn senior now; pull back a little."

"I can believe it. Your mom's turned a new leaf."

"Well, I don't need her all up in my tree. These are supposed to be the best years of my life and now all I have to look forward to is seeing my mother peeking around the corners of the halls at school."

"I don't know what to say. I guess you're going to have to just deal with it."

"Is that all you can say?"

"I can't do anything about it, Clarke. Your mother makes her own decisions."

Clarke became quiet and she folded her arms.

"Daddy, can I be frank?"

"Aren't you always?"

"I think this new girl, Susan, isn't any good for you and I think you're letting your relationship with her cloud what's going on with me and my needs."

I was just about to enjoy my last piece of salmon. "Wait a minute now. You're about to spoil my meal here, Clarke."

"But she's not your style, Daddy. You need someone more like Mom."

Thomas
My girl.

The sexy woman sitting next to me on a park bench on 83rd and York looking out on the East River on the brisk but sunny day was named Susan Assata. I'd been seeing her close to a year.

"I'm a little chilly, Thomas, but all things considered, it's wonderful out today," Susan said.

I had anticipated she would need something warm to drink so I reached down into my leather Coach carrier and pulled out my silver Thermos. I opened it and the steam appeared widening both of our eyes. "Looky here, the best Minestrone you can find in Manhattan," I boasted.

Susan smiled and rubbed her hands together, then moved over as close as she could get to me. "So, how long do we have to enjoy each other for lunch?"

I took the top off the Thermos and began to pour the soup. "I sent my driver on an errand, so I say twenty, twenty-five minutes tops. I have a presentation to the board of directors of Madison Square Garden after we finish here."

"Sounds interesting."

"It's our yearly 'thank you for doing business with us' spiel and promise of…"

Susan cut me off with a smile. "Let me guess, high-quality service?"

"Oh, you know all about it, I see."

"More than you know, Mr. Man. What else is on the agenda?"

"Well, I have to sit in on a meeting with the chairman of the company who's going to explain the logistics of this year's power scheme for the New Year's Eve celebration. Besides that, it's pretty much an open day," I let her know.

Susan smiled after a spoonful of the soup. "You know, your job seems so interesting. It's as though you're all over spreading the good news about Con-Ed."

"Well, that's what I do. It's my job. So how is your job?"

Susan was hesitant. She took the spoon from me and then helped herself to another portion. "It's work, what can I say?"

"Well, I'm proud of you, too."

"Because I do what I do?"

"No, because you have the guts to do it," I explained.

"Wow, I don't know how I should take that."

"Take it as it's given. You're a survivor and I understand what you are doing is out of necessity at the moment."

"I know. But believe me I don't feel good about it. Sometimes I think I'm too smart for my own good. The jest of it all is, I'm just a twenty-seven-year-old, high school dropout, trying to make it the best way I know how; on my back pleasing men; who doesn't know the difference between Islam and Christianity, that you've become surprisingly interested in."

"We all have problems," I told her.

"Tell me something, Thomas? Do you feel odd sitting next to me in my veil?"

I shook my head no. "Why do you ask?"

"No specific reason. I just thought maybe you did."

"When I see you in your veil, Susan, it just reminds me of a young lady respecting her religion, that's all. You have to understand, in my line of work, I meet people from every imaginable background. This man here is well diverse and don't you forget it."

Susan smiled at me.

"But I do have a question and, believe me, I'm not being evil when I say this," I said.

"What is it?"

"How do you balance your work with your religion?"

Susan sighed. "I don't. I'm really struggling with it, Thomas. You know my father introduced my entire family to Islam when I first started school. He thought it would bring us more discipline. I saw my mother struggle, even resist Islam, until I turned nine; then she just submitted to the will of my father because she loved him so much. Of course, I wanted to be just like any other young girl at school, wearing the latest clothes, but I couldn't and I struggled with the lifestyle of being Muslim, period."

"Is that why you dropped out of school?"

"I guess it is. Don't get me wrong. I learned a lot under the Muslim faith growing up, but it was taking my childhood away from me. And now that I'm grown, it's like it's resurfacing—like I'm really missing something in my life. I'm telling you, Thomas. This is a hell of a fight."

"Well, I think you're fantastic."

She smiled. "Really?"

"Yes, really." We were silent for a while, then I blurted out, "Do you want to know what my daughter said to me last night?"

"So, what did Ms. Clarke have to say?"

Susan and Clarke had never met before. Clarke just knew that I was seeing a younger lady and Susan just knew how inquisitive Clarke was and how much she meant to me.

"She wanted to know the possibilities of me getting back together with her mom. It seems she's getting weary of embellishing all of her mother's new changes of life alone."

"New changes?"

"You know—her new lease on life I told you about. One of the reasons we now meet at my new place instead of yours all the time."

Susan lifted up her veil, then kissed me on the cheek. "And it sure is a lot of fun meeting there, that's for sure."

"Answer me this? Taking everything you know about me so far, what would you say is a problem that I have?"

Susan slightly kind of pushed her shoulders back into the park bench. "You? With a problem? The fine black man that walks around this city with all types of knowledge and connections? I don't see you with any problems."

"Well, I do have them," I clarified.

"Like what?"

"I think I let myself become too emotionally attached." Susan sat with a smile on her face. "I think I can become a threat to women emotionally, Susan. That's all I'm saying."

Susan said, "By being truthful and outspoken?"

"Yeah, see. You see it, too, don't you?"

"I understand what you're saying. But I don't see it between us."

I asked her, "Why not?"

"Because I enjoy your frankness and honesty. It makes me warm inside when I feel that from you, Thomas."

"That's what I'm talking about, Susan. My straightforward ways have been known to hurt people in the past and I don't want to do that to you."

"Don't worry. I wouldn't like you as much, Thomas, if you were any other way."

I had only seen Susan with her veil on about a dozen times in the ten months that we'd been dating. Like I told her, it didn't really bother me that she wore it because for one, it was her choice, her religion, plus I thought she was very sexy in it. When I'd first met Susan she wasn't wearing a veil but I knew there was something very special about her. We'd met at a small cafe in Lower Manhattan. I don't know, our eyes just kept meeting while we sat and I walked over and introduced myself. Of course, it was months after when she'd told me what she really did for a living. But after having dinner, going to the movies, sharing a few laughs and looking deeply into her wide brown eyes, what she did for a living really didn't affect me.

Not by any stretch was Susan ordinary. She was fine and she began to swirl emotions inside me that I hadn't felt since I was a young buck trying to talk Synthia into going out with me. Susan was young, eye-catching with her natural-style Afro, peanut butter skin and juicy lips. Fasting really helped her to maintain her body and devastating hips and curves that sat on her five-foot-ten-inch frame. At the time I was thinking about making what we were experiencing together a bit more intimate.

Byron
Look who's here.

When I made sure it was Synthia sitting in our favorite coffee shop, I actually felt as though I was stepping on eggshells as I approached her. It was our first time seeing one another since I'd left her office the night of her announcement half-drunk from the brandy we'd shared.

"Is anyone sitting here?" I asked her. It was genuinely good to see her though.

Her eyes were welcoming. "Hey, Byron."

I sat down as though we hadn't missed a beat, then we both waited for the other to say something. I took the high road. "I was wondering if I was ever going to see you in here again?"

"Well, you know me. I can't go too long without a cup of Marco's coffee. Plus, my schedule has been so busy, I rarely have time anymore."

"You sure that's the only reason you haven't been around?"

Synthia thought for a second. "I hesitate to tell you the truth, Byron," she told me.

"Why is that?"

"Because the last time we spoke truthfully, you didn't take it too well."

"Always the truth for me."

Synthia noticed I glanced behind her to the line of customers waiting to be seated. "Looking for someone?"

"Karen, she's here with me. Actually she's the one who pointed you out. Said she wanted to go powder her nose, to collect herself, you know, get her bearings."

Synthia picked up her coffee, then said, "Get her bearings? What's that all about?"

"Well, the night after your party, right after we spoke in your office, I had a few more drinks and ended up telling Karen what went down between us and telling her how you really feel about her."

Synthia kind of shook her head at me in disgust.

"Hey, it's the truth, isn't it?"

"Anyway," Synthia scolded. "Getting back to what we were talking about, Byron. I didn't want what just happened to happen. Us running into each other; that's why I haven't been around. That's the truth."

"So, you're still at it, huh?"

Synthia nodded her head. "Oh, you thought because I came here I'd forgotten about everything I said to you. No way, that's the old me. Saying and never doing." Synthia chuckled a bit. "The only battle I have lost so far is drinking Marco's coffee."

"I really want to understand this. You've thrown away our friendship because the Twin Towers are no more, Synthia? Shit, if you ask me, this is when we need our friendship. Besides, look back in history, these things happen."

"You don't get it, do you? The damn terrorist attack just solidified what I had been thinking all along. You know, like when you want to play that lotto number, pick four, or something. Your numbers call you, every day, and you don't play them, then one morning while you're drinking coffee and watching the news, your numbers flash across the screen and you feel like shit because your mind told you to do something and you sat down like a fool and didn't act. That's what this is all about, Byron. My mind has been telling me to do this for years."

I tried to understand Synthia but I stopped trying and blurted out, "Hey, by the way, congrats on making partner at the agency."

"You've heard?"

"Who hasn't? I'm really proud of you. Really proud."

At that point I began to feel our friendship diminishing on the spot. Ordinarily when anything good happened between us, we'd plan a party to celebrate on the town and I think Synthia felt it, too.

"Look, Byron," Synthia sounded apologetic.

"No, no, Synthia. You don't have to, I really understand," I told her.

"No, I need to say something. I didn't mean any harm and this whole thing for me has been more difficult than I imagined. But I truly needed and want to make a change in my life. Could I have continued to have Thomas living with me while he dates his little friends? Yes perhaps. Could I have put up with my job until I decided to retire? Maybe so. Could I have been there for you every time you had another problem with your friend? Yes, yes, I could've. But I felt it was time, so here I am, still at it."

"No explanation needed. None at all," I said.

"I just want you to know that you're not the only change I've made," Synthia clarified.

We both looked up at the sound of Karen's voice.

"Hey, lover, I'm back."

After about ten seconds I realized I was staring at Karen with a smile on my face. I remember thinking, *Look, Synthia, you're wrong about her. Look, she's so fine, she's good for me.* Karen was five-feet-seven and I would guess about one-hundred sixty pounds. Her tropical features were reminiscent of Barbados origin. Her cheeks lined perfectly down to her chin, bringing out her full lips and the slight dimple on the right side of her face. Her hair was permed, shoulder-length over both ears, with the left side covering her forehead. Before she smiled at me, she tucked her hair behind her ear on her right side and put her hand on her hip. Karen was wearing dark jeans that looked like they'd been airbrushed on her powerful hips all around to her ass. Her butt, by the looks of it, could have only been passed down from her mother who raised her in Queens.

I don't think Synthia liked Karen too much because she had some street about her. It was obvious Karen was the type of woman that would tell you what's on her mind without thinking twice about it. Mentally she was hard, but a loving soul inside out, if given a chance. Up under her full-length black leather coat, you could see Karen's tight T-shirt with the words "If you only knew" scrawled across her chest. One thing is for sure; I knew what was under her shirt. Karen had worn the shirt at my request because I loved how it snuggled her 36D's and on this particular day she'd left a message and told me she was wearing her shirt without her bra. Karen knew I had a fascination with her chest ever since I'd met her at the Essence Festival in New Orleans two years ago. Karen's breasts were equipped with the most sensual nipples I'd ever seen. They were about as long as a thumb, no matter if she was excited or not, and very sensitive. Being with Karen definitely made me a champion when it came to foreplay. Sometimes she would have to beg me to get to the last step when we had sex because I would be like a two-month-old infant in its mother's arm, sucking all night long.

I motioned to Synthia and said, "Karen you were right. It was Synthia."

Karen gave Synthia a quick glance, then said, "How are you, Synthia?"

Synthia said, "Fine, thanks." Then became rushed and began to gather her belongings. "Listen, I really should be going, Byron. It really was good seeing you two again. You two lovebirds take this table and enjoy yourselves."

I was kind of surprised but told Synthia to take care, then watched her walk away.

"Damn, I hope I have that type of lasting impression on you, Byron," Karen said to me.

"Aww, baby, c'mon, sit down, forget about it," I told Karen. "We've been best friends for years."

"I see she's still acting bitchy."

"So what'd you want to talk about, Karen?"

"Byron, I need some money. Is there anything you can do to help me out?"

Clarke
A sista needs to talk.

I should have known the annoying horn overtaking the madness on The Avenue of Americas was Leon, my therapist. I hollered for him to pull to the side of the curb and to be his ass quiet while I finished picking up magazines: *Seventeen*, *Source*, *Sister2Sister*, and a pack of gum. When I handed the newsstand attendant money for my things, I be damned if Leon didn't start honking his horn again.

"Can a sister get her shit first, Leon?" I asked him as soon as I opened the door to his dark blue Navigator, sitting on spinning rims.

"Sure you can, when you're on your own time. This is my time, *cousin*."

Leon finished elementary school at eight, high school at twelve, under-grad at sixteen and his doctorate at nineteen years of age and he was my cousin. My father and his father were stepbrothers.

"Anyway, cousin. I need this session like you wouldn't believe," I told him.

Leon looked in his rearview, entered traffic, then asked me, "Stressed out?"

"Like you wouldn't believe," I told him.

I don't know exactly what was playing in his CD-changer but it was sure enough bumpin' and Leon looked over at me and noticed that I was getting into the beat of the music.

"Babygirl, I just got these speakers put in about an hour ago. Some brothers put them in right on the street in Newark."

"They sound nice, Leon."

"One thing about niggas, yo—you give them the money and they will find a way to hook your shit up!" Leon smiled and turned up the volume another notch.

As long as I had known Leon, he'd always rocked long brown dreadlocks. Leon was cool but, at the same time, I thought sometimes he needed a shrink more than I did. He got off on the fact that he'd graduated from Princeton and he'd explained to me he'd become a psychologist because nothing could be more interesting than getting inside minds of human beings. Leon was very light-skinned. Almost an albino, if you ask me. He had thick eyebrows, a wild hairy chin, a wiry walk with a thin frame, and stood about six-three.

Leon made a quick adjustment to his stereo and said, "Okay, you're on the clock. What's so important?"

I couldn't wait to get it off my chest. "It's my mother, Leon."

He looked over at me. "Ms. Synthia, how is she these days?"

"Out her fuckin' mind."

"Really now?"

"She's completely hit bottom, Leon. And it's getting to me."

"That's odd. It doesn't sound like Synthia to me."

"How's this for drama? A couple of months ago, she decides she wasn't living up to her potential and distanced herself from her best friend, then made my father move out and is now driving me up a fuckin' wall." Leon didn't respond to me and I looked over at him. "Leon, did you hear a word I said?"

Like lightning, Leon blurted out, *"Problems are madness I can't stand madness/ I take it to my therapist/throw all my shit in his chest/hoping he'll tell me/what the fucks wrong with me..."* Then he looked over at me with a stern face. I was confused by the corny shit and the look on his face kind of froze me. "Just trying to get hyped for this; that's all." Leon explained. "I guess it's the hip-hop in me. Actually I'm working on those lyrics, thinking 'bout sending those shits to P. Diddy, Jay-Z, some damn body. I think he would come out of retirement for lyrics so tight."

"Leon...I'm a little concerned about you right about now," I told him. "Are you smoking crack?"

Without missing a beat Leon opened his ashtray, then said, "Uh, uh, weed." Then he pulls out half of a joint. "Push the lighter for me."

"Leon, you are so damn crazy."

"Haven't I always been?"

"But this weed isn't controlling you, is it?"

"Nope, just a little something to take the edge off. Yesterday, I sat with a mother who'd fucked her daughter's fourteen-year-old boyfriend last weekend because her own husband wouldn't do her. People are losing their minds and my smoke helps me to realize this is just a job. If I get too serious about it, I'll go crazy listening to all this shit. But I don't smoke nearly as much as I did in college and can stop blazin' whenever I want."

"Let's forget about everything else. I wanna discuss me. What should I do?"

"Okay, keep in mind that I'm a little high here, but I'm gonna go out on a limb. This has to do with getting your father back home, right?"

"I knew there was a reason Mom pays you all this money to talk to me."

"Yeah, I know you pretty well, huh, cuz?"

"I can't lie about that. See, I've been thinking about how I'm going to get things back to the way they were with my parents."

"Hold up now, Negro Barbra Streisand. You can't start undoing what I'm sure took your mother a hell of a lot of guts to do herself."

"Why not?"

"Because you can't. That's your mother's business. If she doesn't feel whole in her life for whatever reason, she has the right to make changes. Think about it. People make changes all the time."

I hated it when some of the shit Leon said to me made sense. "So what? I don't like it—it's no good for my father."

Leon put fire to his joint. "Thomas?"

"Now, suddenly he's spending all of his time with his girlfriend and I don't like it or her one damn bit."

Leon began to reflect with the joint dangling from his mouth. "Yeah, yeah, I remember meeting her. I bet he isn't complaining, as fine as she is." Leon noticed me cross my arms and give him the evil eye. "So what about it?"

"So? I've always thought as long as Dad was home with us, there was a chance for my parents to get back together because that's the way it should be."

I watched Leon expertly take a drag from his joint. Then he began to talk to me with the smoke still inside his system. I just shook my head watching this fool. "*Sorry, Clarke, but if they don't want it, there's nothing you can do about it.*"

"Well, maybe I need to make it happen because this is not what I had planned for my parents when I go off to college after next year."

Leon was trying desperately to hold his smoke inside. "*Make it happen? Shit, you sound like you're the one on crack.*" He finally exhaled and, without missing a beat, said, "Listen, Synthia and Thomas have been down that road before. Don't you think if they wanted to be together they'd be together?"

"Knowing how they both are? No."

I knew firsthand how stubborn my parents were when it came to telling each other how they felt. They were not going to admit they knew they should be together. I was trying to block out what Leon was telling me, because he hadn't lived with them like I had. Every once in a while I could see in their eyes; they still cared.

"Trust me, Clarke. I'm about to turn thirty. Looks are deceiving. I know these things."

"Not these looks, I'm telling you—I know my parents."

"Well, I must advise you to sit back and let life work its way, on its on, Clarke."

"Have I ever taken your advice before, Leon?"

"If you had, we probably wouldn't be sitting here now, would we?"

Leon stopped between two corners. All I knew, we were close to Lexington. "Here's where I have to drop you off," Leon said. "I have an investment banker meeting me here shortly. You shouldn't have a problem getting a cab back."

I started to gather my books and magazines. "Are you serious about making this your office, Leon?"

He told me that he already had. He liked to talk to his clients when he was driving the streets. He said that it opens them up more. I have to admit, it was kind of fun riding in the Navigator looking at everything going on in the city while telling him how I felt.

Synthia
Represent who?

I was sitting at my desk when Barbara tapped on my door. I could usually tell by her expression if her visit was business or water cooler convo. This time I couldn't. She came to see me because Harry Luongo, the publisher at Denison & Hall, a very good friend supposedly, discussed a deal I'd sealed with one of his editors for my writer Austin Brown.

Austin was a young fiction writer whose prose was very commercial but, at the same time, he had a knack for picking on social ills in a very unique way that I loved. He signed a two-book deal worth fifty-thousand dollars at twenty-five per, after being offered three-hundred thousand for a three-book deal with the publisher. When I told Austin about the big money offer he didn't want it. He told me if he didn't make back every bit of the advance he knew it would be difficult to get another deal with D&H and he wanted to have a long and luxurious writing career. I decided to side with him, but Barbara thought the deal was a bit soft. I understood his concerns and agreed to giving the deal a shot. I let Barbara in on my reasons why. After our discussion, Barbara wanted to talk Lil' Shae, the superstar rapper, who I had turned down a request from her agent to represent for a tell-all autobiography, then again after meeting with Lil' Shae.

LIL' SHAE HAD CALLED MY OFFICE the same day I'd signed as partner with the agency and had asked me to meet her at a club on the West Side. Even though I'd already said no to her agent, I felt I would at least give her the respect of a meeting. After all, she was the number one female rapper in the industry.

There is no telling how long it had been since I had been to a club that entertained hundreds of partygoers. I usually settled for intimate settings; especially to talk shop. I ordered Grand Marnier and waited for Lil' Shae to arrive. I always considered myself up-to-date; as far as music and what the kids were listening to. Clarke loved rap and it was the only thing we listened to when we worked out. I thought the music in the club was terrible though. Maybe because the speakers sounded like they were banging right across the side of my head. Supposedly I was in the VIP section located in the very back of the club.

A glass partition separated the VIP section from the dance floor and I use the word "dance" lightly. It looked more like a bunch of people dry fucking. I'm sure the real thing was going on inside, but I just didn't see it. Young girls with huge breasts hanging out of their shirts, various sizes of ass cheeks packed in tight pants and short shorts. Lots of glazed-over eyes staring at one another. The girls were confident-looking young women being pumped on from the rear by thuggish-dressed males, who may have been getting their pump on with one girl and their feel with another.

I sat back and took it all in and thanked my blessings that my daughter didn't club as much as she could. I didn't want to think of what she did while she danced. I noticed four young guys walk in VIP and look around as though they were casing the club. They all dispersed and sat alone in different sections of the room, which I thought was odd. Then the one sitting closest to me began speaking into his headset. Two minutes later, three more young men flanking Lil' Shae walked in and waited until she sat down with me before joining their friends. I guess Lil' Shae noticed the concern on my face.

She said, "Oh, don't worry about those guys. They're added protection. My record company thought it would be a good idea to have them travel with me since some of my good friends have either shot someone or been shot at." Lil' Shae smiled.

We had met before and even though I knew she had to be in her twenties, she looked like she was no older than sixteen. Her shirt was wide open, showing every inch of her small breasts. Her waist was small as could be on her five-foot-one frame. She couldn't have been more than a hundred and five pounds. No wonder they called her Lil' Shae. Her face was flawless— there wasn't a bump or blemish anywhere I could see and her smile was warming. After she found a comfortable position in her chair, she put her legs together as though she was about to chant a prayer or something. I asked her to explain our meeting.

"I'm interested in writing a book," she said. "I remember you approaching me a while back about a book, and I want to know if you and your agency can take care of it for me."

Lil' Shae knew that I passed on her book with her agent. I let her have her say just because I'd approached her almost a year ago about a deal when my head was on another level. I was not thinking of decency; just chasing money. She ran her mouth nonstop and it was difficult to get a word in; especially when she started talking about how her career started. I was surprised when she said her first shot at impressing a record industry mogul came while he was taking a leak in an uptown nightclub. Lil' Shae told me she'd burst inside the latrine and done a rap about how good her pussy was and he'd wanted to find out if her words were true and she'd showed him without hesitation and the rest was history; a star was born.

While she rambled about herself, I looked Lil' Shae over and noticed her platinum watch and bangles. Then I took a look into her eyes. Honestly, I tried to see if there was really a book inside this girl I could stomach; even though I thought there would have been months before. "What I was thinking?" spurted from my mouth. "But what would it be about?" I asked.

"About me? About my life, all the shit I've put up with in the industry to get where I am today. You know… about all these niggas out here—the haters who are jealous of me because of the things I have and the things they'll never see a day in their lives. About me, the book will be all about me." All of sudden I gathered the sound the DJ was playing was one of Shae's hit records: "That's my shit!" she hollered.

"May I call you Shae?" I asked.

She nodded while she popped her fingers overhead to the beat of the music.

"Well, honestly speaking, I don't know if the type of book you want to do is for me." Shae tensed a bit. "No disrespect to what you do and your music, Shae, but I've heard some of the lyrics in your songs and I personally find them degrading."

"Degrading?" Shae snapped.

I went on to tell Shae that I needed to be behind the book a hundred percent before I decided to share it with publishers. I let her know that I wouldn't feel comfortable going to a publisher and trying to get a deal for a young lady who talks about how good she sucks and how good her "stuff" is.

"Unless you've been living on another planet or some shit, then I could understand your reasoning, but otherwise, hell, no. I don't understand because sex sells. You, of all people, should understand that. Shit, it was you who even planted the seed in my head to do a book?"

"I was a different person then, Shae," I told her.

"Different? How so?"

"You wouldn't understand. Let's just say I was leaning on a change in my life and after the attack on the Twin Towers, it sealed the deal for me."

"Oh, so now you wanna blame that shit on what I do, too?"

"Shae, like I said, you wouldn't understand."

Shae began to ramble. She didn't want to be blamed for the problems of the world. She explained that her mother had given birth to her when she was fourteen and she even remembered sitting on the floor playing with her dolls while her mother lay in the bed with her boyfriend watching porno films for hours.

"It's probably the reason why I rap about suckin' dick so good." She chuckled.

During our conversation back at the office, I suggested to Barbara that if she wanted to do the book with Lil' Shae, she should take it. I wasn't interested. Barbara told me she would, but threw in a kicker: Lil' Shae only wanted to work with me, she let me know.

Thomas
Not a good day at all.

One of the drawbacks of having such a close relationship with Clarke is she tends to put her nose where it doesn't belong. On her way into my building to pay me a visit, she noticed Susan coming out and had the nerve to follow her in a cab. Then my daughter came back to my place claiming she had evidence Susan was cheating on me; even though she had no backup for making her claim.

When I get upset, I do one of two things—drink or shop. Since Clarke assured me she would never do such a thing again, I didn't really feel the need to go into my private stock of whiskey. It took everything I had not to though. But, I was in dire need of a new suit for an upcoming presentation, so I decided to go down to my favorite tailor and get fitted. My longtime friend Nick Scafidi, who was very close to eighty years old, owned the Italian men's shop on Irving. His specialties were silk, wool blends, and catchy ties shipped directly from Italy. That's exactly what I was in the mood for. I hadn't been in the shop more than a few minutes before I heard, "My, my, my. If it isn't Mr. Power and Lights himself."

"Well, well, well. If it isn't Byron. What're you doing in my favorite shop? Buying off the return racks?"

Byron had a sarcastic grin on his face. "It's my job to be here," he said.

"Oh… another job? Now somehow that's not surprising. What happened to your last one? You were working as a data entry operator, right?"

Byron's voice tightened low. "No, I was repairing credit," he clarified.

"Imagine that," I said. "So now you're selling clothes."

"And getting fifty-percent off my own wardrobe, I might add. You know, I don't think I've seen you since Synthia's new-lease-on-life party?"

"It's never long enough, is it," I said to him.

"So, are you interested in a suit?"

I looked around the shop. "Isn't there anyone else who can help me?"

Byron planted a cynical smile on his face. "Nope. Sorry."

"Where's Nick?"

"At lunch. Plus, he doesn't work the floor. Everyone knows that."

"He does for me. What about Dominic?"

"Vacation. He went to the Motherland to pay a visit to his family."

"Well, I guess you'll have to do. I need a nice suit. I like conservative, but sleek."

"Doesn't sound like you at all, but I'll see what I can do." Byron went through a couple of suits. "Here's one. A-charcoal-black-button-down-pin-stripe. It's one of the lightest wool blends available and one of our top-of-the-line suits. These are doing very well this year. Not too heavy and breathes like a soft woman in your ear. You want to try on the jacket to get a feel?"

I took a deep breath. "Yeah, why not?"

Scafidi's was a small shop. It was long in length and occupied the bottom floor of a business building. It only had four rows of garments, which seemed to run for days down the length of the shop. The platform sat in the middle and was carpeted with mirrors positioned so precisely you didn't have to turn around to check out your duds. I was looking in the mirrors as Bryon placed the jacket on me.

"You know, I heard some of the grumbling and whispers at Synthia's party. Some people were saying you were blaming me for her sudden change."

I had to make eye contact with Byron through the mirror. I looked in three different mirrors to make it happen. "You heard that?"

"Yes, I heard. You know that's bullshit, Thomas. If anyone had anything to do with Synthia not enjoying her life, it definitely was you."

"You're fuckin' unbelievable. You know that, Byron? Synthia and I were fine. Our living arrangements had been established and things couldn't have been better. I'll admit, it was a bit dysfunctional. Okay, more than a bit. I mean I had a feeling it was getting a little difficult for everyone with my dating. But if you want to throw blame around, maybe you should reflect on all the continuous drama you bombarded her with concerning your life with Karen when she was trying to concentrate on her job and raising Clarke."

"You don't have to admit it, Thomas, but you never were secure with our relationship."

"You mean after you tried to sleep with her when I was away on business? Is that what you're talking about?"

"How long ago was that? Hey, I admit that was my fault. I'd had a little bit too much to drink. That's all it was—plus that was damn near ten years ago," Byron said.

"And after all this time, you've never apologized for that shit. Now that's what I call a true friend of the family."

"Thomas, you know I've always been a friend."

I gave Bryon a hard look. He was right. At the beginning, when I'd first met Synthia, he'd been a good friend. It was almost like I had to have his blessing to even take her out. But Byron had always tried to play the big brother role with Synthia, and I hated that shit because I wasn't a fool. I knew if he had the chance he would try to do her as quick as lightning. As Synthia and I became closer, I thought that he was too involved in our matters. After we were married I kind of conceded to Byron's friendship with Synthia. But that was until about six years after Synthia and I were married. Reason being, she told me about the night that she and Byron were sitting around chatting and drinking and he wanted to know if he could sleep with her when she confided in him, that she didn't like how the company had begun to send me on so many business trips. I was running my hand down the length of the suit jacket. "Well, we don't have to worry about defining that friendship anymore, do we?"

Byron said, "Sure is a shame. I really enjoyed the times we all shared and that's no lie."

I really didn't want to hear any of Byron's bullshit. "Look, help me with this suit so I can get out of here, okay?"

Synthia
The path I've led.

My writing had been somewhat therapeutic since I had lost my father and I'd finally found a moment to jot down a few pages in my journal. I hoped one day when Clarke became a woman she would want to read about my life and my journey—especially womanhood. So much of my life had been placed in my journal. Much of it things I desperately wanted to forget and others that brought me sheer joy and wonderful memories. I only had a sentence or two to finish when I noticed Clarke scurrying through the condo placing items in her bag.

"Where are you going, sweetheart? I thought we'd spend some time today?"

Clarke said, "Can't, Mom. I need to get down to the library to check out some books. For some strange reason they aren't on the Internet and it's driving me nuts."

I walked toward Clarke. "Well, okay, maybe later." Clarke was almost out the door. "Clarke?" She stopped. "Are you going out dressed like that?"

"Like what?"

Clarke had on tight faded blue jeans that flared at the legs, and a tight body shirt that looked as though it had been dipped in three or four colors to give it a dreary bland look. "Don't you know, back in my day, some kids dressed like that and they all were called…"

"What, hippies?" she asked.

"No, outsiders, misfits or loners."

"I like this look, Mom. It's revolutionary, don't you think? Straight up Angela Davis."

"Since you asked my opinion, no, I don't think it's revolutionary at all. It's garb that doesn't say anything about who you are as a person. You know you can't dress like that when you go off to college, sweetheart."

"Oh yes, I can."

"I don't think the students at Brown dress like that, Clarke."

"Brown?"

"Yes, Brown. It's a very prestigious atmosphere and I don't want your growth stunted as a student by the type of clothes you wear on campus. You know what they say—perception is what gets you in the door."

"I'd like to know, who decided I'm going to Brown? I'm thinking Stanford or Cal. Irvine."

"Stanford is really turning into a party school, Clarke. I think Brown is best."

"I thought it was my decision what school I wanted to attend. What is this?"

"It is, Clarke. I just thought…"

"Well, let me make the decision then."

"You're right. You're right. I'm sorry."

I asked Clarke to bend down so I could kiss her on the forehead.

"By the way, I need your signature on my consent form to get a refill on my birth control pills for my appointment later this week," Clarke said. She read my eyes. "Now what, Mom?"

"Clarke, I don't think you should be on the pill."

"Huh?"

"I think I've made the wrong decision."

"Mom, what are you talking about?"

"I just think by allowing you to use birth control so early in your life it's given you the wrong impression about sex, me, and, most importantly, about how you feel about yourself."

"What? What ever happened to one pill a day and no regrets tomorrow?"

"I wasn't right in what I was saying, Clarke. I never gave your being on the pill any real thought. I mean, it was a really quick decision I made because I felt you were being pressured by the guy you were seeing. When you expressed your interest of getting on the pill, I just jumped at the opportunity. I didn't know what else to do, nor did I want you to get mad at me and go do something and get pregnant."

"Mom, you know what? Every time you write in that damn journal you walk away from it like you're on mountain high or something. Maybe you should go back to your journal and look in your entries of 1998 and 1999, when you were sleeping with that guy half your age."

"Clarke, that's not fair."

"It is fair. I want to take the pill and my doctor prefers parental consent until I'm eighteen."

"I can't. It would be like giving you a free pass to do what you want sexually and a girl your age shouldn't be doing anything at all."

"Who says I am?"

"Why do you need the pills then?"

"I've been on them for almost four years now."

"And you know what—it's time to correct it. I need to do right."

"I am so stumped here. Why are we even having this conversation," Clarke said.

"We're having it because I've put a lot of thought into this and I've decided it's the right thing to do."

"No doubt a subplot in your tired change of life scheme, I bet. I'm so freakin' tired of this."

"Sorry, but it's the right thing to do."

"Whatever," Clarke shot back before she shut the door and left.

Susan
What people do for money.

I wasn't exactly thrilled to be lying under my most demanding client, but hey, it was my job. I made anywhere from fifteen hundred to five thousand tax-free dollars a date—but I knew it would all have to come to an end because of Thomas. My insides were being driven into hard. Nonstop and it hurt. Most jobs do.

I'd known Matthew for a while. Actually he was my first date for hire. My friend Anita schooled me on how she used our job to meet johns during our breaks. And when he showed up one day looking for her—and she was nowhere to be found, I decided to give the business she raved about a try. I'd been working at the Food Emporium on 86th and Broadway. It was my place of employment for three years, seven days a week for minimum wage and no benefits. I was working there because it is the type of place that hires someone without a high school diploma. I learned a lot about people on that job. Always act like you care about any little problem they may have in the three to five minutes that it takes to ring up their items. Always smile, even when your feet hurt like hell and never forget to say thank you after they've finished with their transaction. So similar to the living I made lying on my back.

Matthew was in his forties, had salt and pepper hair that he kept cut like a Hollywood movie star, narrowing blue eyes and small, tight lips. He was owner of one of those money-making dot-coms along with major real estate in upstate New York. My client list was not a long one. It was very short because all of them were high-rolling men who didn't mind paying for quality time.

Matthew rolled off me and said, "I really wish you'd take me up on my offer."

"Which one is that, Matthew? There's been so many lately."

"The trip to the Poconos with my friends next week."

"You mean the orgy with all your friends?" I asked him. Matthew had offered me ten thousand dollars to go with him on the three-day trip, but I wasn't feeling it at all.

"It'll be good for you to get away, sweetheart," he said.

"I don't think so."

"Why do you always say that to me? Everything's always impossible. Nothing's impossible. Just pack a bag and come along."

It never was that easy. Never.

"You won't go because of all the interest I've been showing in you lately outside of our business dealings, right?"

As of late, he had been getting way too emotional for me. One of the things Anita had always told me was that when they start to become emotional take a break. Get away.

"Or is it that you don't date white boys in public?" Matthew pushed.

"Being white has nothing to do with it and you know it. I just wouldn't feel comfortable going away with you right now, that's all. I realize this has become emotional for you, but I don't feel the same way and it wouldn't be as much fun for me."

Matthew raised himself up on one arm to look down at me. "How can you say that? Haven't the times we've shared been fabulous?"

"It's been business, Matthew."

"Maybe we should look at this from another angle."

"Where is all this coming from?"

"I don't know. Maybe it's me getting older. I'll be forty-two next month and have nothing to show for it."

"What are you talking about? You're a millionaire."

"Money doesn't make a difference. When I come home with no one to share it with I might as well be a poor man."

WE ENDED UP DISCUSSING THE ORGY for a couple more hours. The more we talked the more I began to think about what I was doing with my life and how I'd been raised. Neither Allah nor God, no savior would have been pleased with me and what I was doing. Sleeping for dollars was really beginning to get to me because no matter how confused I was with religion at the time, I knew what I was doing was wrong.

Matthew tried to convince me his feelings were genuine. He said things like, "You make me feel like a new man and every minute of my life is consumed with thoughts of you being in my life." I was completely caught off guard and it made me uncomfortable because I never in a million years thought of him in the same way—ever. Our terms were strictly business— no feelings attached. Meet at five for dinner—most of the time, a glass of wine and spend a few hours, then collect my money.

During our last hour together Matthew continued to push me to go to the Poconos. When I refused, he decided he wanted to go another round and get his money's worth. He had never tried to have two orgasms with me in one night before and he struggled to get off again. He began to whisper things that I only wanted to hear from Thomas. "This is so right," he muttered. "I'll do anything for you." I blocked his voice out because I didn't want to hear it. I did what I needed to do and took control of the situation to make Matthew let go of whatever was left inside him into his condom. I turned over on my stomach, then onto my knees. I knew he couldn't handle it, he never could. I slapped my behind and his eyes lit up. I hated to give him this glance, but two minutes passed and he was done and I was out the door.

I DECIDED TO PUT A HALT TO MATTHEW'S SESSIONS. I felt it was best. He had fallen for me and I didn't like it. All of sudden, Matthew started to leave messages on my answering machine at home for dates, not sex. It startled me because I'd never given him my home phone number, always my pager. I spotted his car twice in the same week in places that there was no way he could have known I was going to be: once coming out of a bookstore after purchasing a pocket-sized Qur'an; then again right before I entered a bank on the East Side. I thought about calling to find out why he was following me, but I decided not to, hoping he would stop. Then the phone calls began. Every time I would pick up, someone would hang up after hearing my voice. Each time it happened I would call Thomas. Talking to him made me feel better. Twice Thomas came over to stay with me because he thought I sounded worried. One night we ended up talking the entire night.

We were sitting on the couch when Thomas asked me, "How does being with me feel?"

"What do you mean?"

"Me being here? Does it do anything for you?"

"It's awesome when you're here, Thomas. I just hate to drag you out here when I know you need to prepare for your job in the morning."

"No problem. I like feeling needed, you know. I felt needed when I lived with Synthia, but it was just because of Clarke. Nothing else, but being there for Clarke was enough for me at the time. I wanted her to know I loved her unconditionally; no matter what was going on between her mother and me."

"I think you really did the right thing, standing by and trying to do what was best for her. Synthia really should be grateful. That's the ultimate for a woman to know her child will always be taken care of. Clarke's going to turn out better because of it, you just wait and see."

"I've been thinking," Thomas said. "Maybe we should become more of an item?"

"As in you being my man?"

"Exactly."

I smiled and kind of blushed. Thomas wanted to know why.

"I've been thinking about the same thing, actually praying about it, but I didn't want to say anything because I thought I was already overstepping my boundaries. You know, because of my job. I didn't want you to think I was trying to take advantage of you."

"I would never think about you in that way. You know, Synthia asked me to leave because she felt she wasn't living up to her potential."

"Hell, I can understand that," I told Thomas.

"And I understand it, too. Since I've been living by myself, I've had a chance to look at things and put them down on paper. I must admit, on paper things look good. Good job, good money, bright future ahead. But the reality of the whole thing to me is really starting to stink."

"How so?"

"The way I feel inside. It took some doing for me to look inside myself instead of at myself," Thomas said. "You know what I've found out?"

I shook my head no.

"That I'm not really happy with me. I'm not happy with what I've turned into, which is a fast-talking, bullshitting, politician for a Fortune 500 company. My job is to keep a smile on my face and reassure the city the damn lights won't go out. That's what I am."

"Thomas, no you're not. You're a very respectful man. A really good person."

"That's what you see on the outside. Because on the inside, I don't know what I am anymore. I don't even know if I can love anymore. I've had relationship after relationship while living with my ex. How fucking unstable is that and now…"

"It's all right. Go ahead and say it," I told him. "You're sleeping with a younger woman who turns out to be a whore?"

"No, it's just that I've fallen for you and I want to find out if I can love again."

It was nice to know Thomas could open up that way to me. Not every man has been able to do that. In the past guys were afraid to talk honestly with me because of my looks. I don't care what anyone says, so-called attractive women don't get to see or hear life as it really is when it comes to men. Men are afraid of good-looking women. So afraid that most of the time, if they are lucky enough to get you in the bed, it's never worth the effort because it's over before things really get started.

For the next few weeks, I began to notice that the weird phone calls stopped and there were no more strange sightings of Matthew either. I felt good about the direction Thomas and I were moving in. We decided to date each other exclusively. Well, as exclusively as I possibly could with the job I had. I asked Thomas if he would still be okay with what I did as a profession and he told me that he didn't want to step in and make me stop what I was doing. He told me that knowing I'm with another man on some nights cut at his guts, but he believed it was a decision that I had to make alone.

Not long afterwards, I decided that he was just too good of a man to date exclusively and be a whore at the same time. So I stopped. Thomas had no idea that for the last two months I had gone back to work at the Food Emporium. The money was terrible and things were tight, but I felt good about my decision. I'd planned to tell Thomas as soon as I could, but I wanted it to be the right time—sort of a surprise.

Synthia
So they say.

It's so true what they say about keeping business separate from personal feelings. Personal feelings are an enigma to the bottom line. But that's what *they* say. The people who don't give a damn about how they are perceived or what or who their ultimate decisions affect, as long as they make that dollar.

I used to be the same way. That's why when Barbara first pulled that mentality on me concerning Shae, I came close to letting my mind side with her and pledge to the dollars like I had been doing my entire career. It was difficult, but I didn't. I didn't let her speech about never turning down a sure bet influence me. Point blank, I didn't like Lil' Shae's music; the way she lived her life, at least through the media because that's all I really knew about her; the way she looked at life and how the poor kids who look up to her were being hoodwinked by her nonproductive lyrics.

For a second time, Barbara told me she "thought" we should take Shae on at the agency. I still wasn't feeling it. Anyone else could have taken her on. I wouldn't have had a problem with that. We had forty-three associate agents, who probably would have loved to have their names attached. Then it wouldn't be me, contributing to the demise and proliferation of millions of young minds, I thought. But after another phone call from Shae and hearing that I flat out didn't want to do the project, Lil' Shae called Barbara and complained. She told Barbara she'd already made millions of dollars in endorsements and had heard that our agency was the best in town and she wanted to work with us—particularly *me*. I was working late when Barbara came into my office. I guess this was supposed to be her last stand. I could see it all over her face, as though I owed it to her to do this.

"Lil' Shae called me again," she said without any delay.

"Oh, really now? My answer's still the same, Barbara," I told her flatly.

Barbara was being diplomatic. "A book deal and a percentage of any movie deal based on it would be an enjoyable surprise for us, don't you think, Synthia?"

"This business is full of surprises, isn't it?"

Barbara's eyes tightened a bit. I could tell she wasn't angry with me, but stunned that I had taken my stand against representing Lil' Shae. "Synthia, I'm too old to be involved in a chase, so here goes. I think you really screwed up by not signing her, locating a writer and getting things under-way for an auction. Who knows, we probably would have a deal already."

My eyes tightened as well. "You're entitled to have your opinion, Barbara, but I don't want to work with that young lady. I think she's a disgrace to all women."

"Disgrace?" Barbara said, in a questioning tone. "Synthia, look. I know how you have put things in perspective after what happened on 9-11. Hell, we all have. But this is big. Don't let what happened on 9-11 stop you from earning or stop us from earning. If we do, it's like we are letting the terrorists win and we can't let them do that. Maybe you've even taken this whole bombing too seriously. Trust me, when you get my age you'll begin to put things in perspective. I've seen a lot of things happen in my lifetime that made me wonder if I was making a contribution or not. And the attacks on WTC were just one of them. It was the biggest, but we must move on. Trust me, it's not the end of the world, darling."

Of all things. Now I had Barbara thinking my decision to change my life was solely based on what happened on 9-11. First, Byron, now her? Evidently 9-11 was rolling around in their heads, too. I didn't even want to tell her that my change had been on my mind months before it ever happened.

She probably wouldn't have believed me anyway and it wasn't any of her business. It was mine, my personal business. I just tried to keep the conversation on Lil' Shae.

"Barbara, Lil' Shae doesn't stand for anything, but porno, filth and more porno."

About ten seconds passed before Barbara responded. "Synthia, do you know Lil' Shae well enough to make that accusation?"

"I know her well enough to know she has no respect for the little girls who listen to her music. The young girls who listen to Lil' Shae are not old enough to displace reality from fantasy. Tell me something. Have you ever heard her lyrics?"

Barbara shook her head slowly. "No, I haven't. But I've seen her face plastered in every teen, hip-hop, and entertainment magazine on the stands. This is about money, Synthia, not her lyrics. Let the critics and women's rights groups handle that."

I got a little heated with her comment. "Always the money, always the money. For once in your life can't you bypass money for righteousness? Especially for this abrasive *'I'll take it in the butt and suck his dick properly as long as he pays me, microphone slut?'*"

Barbara moved on the edge of her chair. "She says that?"

"You don't know the half of it."

Barbara paused, taking two drags from her smoke. She fought with herself about the whole situation. "I don't care," Barbara spit out with lightning speed. "I still want our agency to work with her. This is just too huge to let go. Not in a million years should we pass it up," she concluded.

I looked at my watch. It was time for me to call it a day. I was planning to tell Barbara she was making a huge mistake.

"Look, Synthia," she said. "This whole thing is not about right or wrong. You've known me too long for that. It's about profit. Profit so I can pay my staff and keep our business extremely solvent for years to come. For me, that's all this is about. Maybe over the years I've lost something. When I first started out I never dreamed I'd have a million-dollar company. But I do, *we* do, and it's our job to keep it that way, and, at the same time, take our personal beliefs out of huge deals that are thrown into our laps."

I was standing, briefcase in tow, when I said, "But I've already told her we weren't interested."

Barbara chuckled a bit. "And it pissed her off, too. Luckily this Lil' Shae is very competitive and doesn't like to take no for an answer. I believe it's the only reason she hasn't taken her business someplace else. Tomorrow, I'll turn on my charm. Woo her agent, kiss their ass, do whatever I have to, to get it done—then voila, have them sign on the dotted line." Barbara smiled. "Hey, it's my job. I'm an agent at a big-name agency who gets her rocks off on big-dollar deals," she boasted.

Susan
How could I forget?

I can't lie about the dilemma I found myself in after the demanding phone call I received reminding me that a bill that I'd somehow let slip my mind was flat-out due. I needed three-thousand dollars in twenty-four hours. To say the least, it placed me in a panic and the only thing I could do was go to Thomas. There was no way my job at the store would front me the money. When I arrived to see Thomas, I ran into Clarke in the hallway of his building.

"Look who's here." By the sound of her voice I knew she wasn't sincere.

I looked toward the door, hoping to hear her father's voice inside. "Hello, Clarke."

"So, what brings you over?" Clarke put her hand on her hip.

"I'm here to see your father. I need a favor. Why, isn't he here?"

Clarke told me that he was and then asked me what type of favor I needed, which threw me off a bit.

"We're seeing each other, Clarke, so I don't understand what you're asking me, nor do I think it's any of your business."

"I'm just wondering because I haven't been able to figure you out yet, Susan."

"What are you trying to figure out?"

"Answering a question with a question—nice. Let me make myself clearer,

Susan. I want to know what you really see in my father? Why is he such a prime catch?"

"A prime catch?"

Clarke looked at the apartment door, and then lowered her voice a bit. "You heard me, Susan. I've never gotten the chance to ask you what you see in my father. What's your angle?"

"I don't think that's any of your business, Clarke. Your father knows how I feel about him and that's all that matters."

"C'mon, it's not like there's some huge generation gap between us. You can tell me. Is he just the man you need for your career? Wait, I know. It's his money, right?"

I didn't like the conversation I was having with Clarke. It was difficult to even think she thought of me in such a manner. After Clarke walked away, she looked at me several times before she stepped onto the elevator. I stood still for a moment and began to think about how Clarke had enough gall to step to me about only wanting her father for his money. I was quite sure she had planted the same seed with Thomas and there was no way I could ask him for the money. As nice as Thomas had been to me, I felt like taking the chance. I really needed the money, but I didn't want to take the chance of losing him either. Maybe asking for the money would do just that.

I DIDN'T WANT TO, but I decided to call Matthew. This was going to be my very last job—*ever*. I hadn't seen Matthew in almost three months and I knew an entire night with him would get me five-thousand dollars. Matthew didn't hesitate. It was close to one-thirty when we met. I was sure that after I finished with him I would still have enough time to settle my bill with money to spare.

Matthew was on top of me like he had been without for years. We went two rounds within two hours and Matthew continuously tipped his bottle up during our session and during the short break we took. For some reason Matthew was a bit more physical than he had ever been. Our third round began with him in between my legs; licking, sucking and sticking his fingers inside of me. I faked at least six orgasms and it was like he was down there for at least an hour. Then he mounted me again and I was able to turn over and give it to him in a way he could never handle. But this time he did handle me for another forty-five minutes, then he lay on the bed next to me, trying to catch his breath.

"What is going on with you?" I asked him. "Did you take some Viagra or something?"

Matthew smiled, seemingly very pleased with his performance. "No Viagra for me. I'm running on pure stamina and a little bit of scotch, of course," he said. "One thing's for sure, I really didn't expect your call."

"Like I told you, Matthew, I really need the money," I said right after I looked at my watch. I had only been with him five hours and I had the rest of the night to go.

All of a sudden Matthew blurted out. "You didn't call me 'cause you missed me, Susan?"

"It's good to see you again," I told him.

"You know, it's really mind-boggling what people will do for money."

I didn't answer him. I was still as Matthew got up from the bed to blow out the candles on the nightstand. The room went completely dark. Matthew returned to the bed.

"I don't think I've ever told you," he said. "But I've done quite a few things myself for a dollar or two." He laughed a bit. "Yes indeed, I've begged and stole, literally, Susan." His laugh became deeper.

"Matthew, what are you talking about?"

Matthew lay on his back and placed his hands just above my private. Then he lightly began to touch her. And I hated every stroke.

"Well, it's a long story, Susan. One you'd probably not believe right off. Sometimes I can't even fathom it," he said.

"What do you mean?"

"Just what I said, I literally had to beg and steal to amass what I've obtained in my life."

"Sure…tell me anything," I told him.

"No, it's true. I mean how many people would believe you'd do what you do for cash?"

"Not many, that's for sure," I said.

"That's what I mean. None of my business associates know how I've come up through the ranks," Matthew said. "The question has never come up. All they see is my money."

"But you have a degree from Harvard. Your education speaks for itself," I reminded him.

"Yes, but my degree is just that. A freakin' piece of paper that verifies you've achieved. But in life, you need money, dinero," Matthew said. "A lot of those fuckin' guys I went to school with had long family money. School was just a passing of time for them. I didn't have family money, not a dime."

"How'd you make all your money then?" I asked.

I knew Matthew had lots of it. There was one month that I'd seen him three weekends in a row at my highest rate.

Matthew didn't hesitate to answer me. "I was a bum. I took my knowledge to the streets after graduation and lived in a box until I could seize an opportunity that only happens in America," Matthew said.

"Yeah right. You sure are full of it tonight."

I heard Matthew sigh as though I wasn't taking him serious. He grabbed my well-pronounced overlapping skin in between my legs and twisted it and I grabbed his hand. "I'm serious," he said.

"Hey, be careful. What's your problem?"

It was silent for a beat. "No problem," Matthew said. "Can I finish now?"

"Be my guest. Just watch how you touch me."

I sat and listened to Matthew. He seemed drunk. He continued to drink and every so often he would touch my thigh as to keep my attention. "I took a job with a law firm that promised me everything under the fuckin' sun and couldn't deliver a cold pepperoni pizza," he said. Matthew was stuck in a pity ante litigation unit in his firm. All the cases that some of the older lawyers botched and others no one wanted to touch but were still on file because the plaintiffs wanted the firm to represent them because of its reputation were his responsibility.

"One day while I was meeting with a client near 43rd and Broadway, a homeless man caught my attention. For some reason he became interesting to me," Matthew reflected. "He sat down with his hand out without a fuckin' care in the world with a sad ass look on his face. Without thinking twice people would fill his cup up with dollars all day long just because he looked like someone they hoped they would never become."

I could feel Matthew looking at me through the darkness. I didn't turn to look at him though. I was hoping the liquor would soon kick in and put him to sleep so I could go into the bathroom and call Thomas. So many things were going through my mind at that moment and hearing his story about a homeless man wasn't very interesting until I heard Matthew say the homeless man's life looked so interesting that he sold everything he had and moved to the streets. "I've always been a survivalist," Matthew continued. "I didn't mind trying my hand in the streets. Hell, like you say, I'm a graduate of Harvard. Fuck it, call it a case study." He chuckled.

That's when I turned to look at Matthew through the darkness. I couldn't see him much, but I did feel the uneasiness about him. It was like he had tensed a bit and if this were a joke he had gone on long enough without the punchline.

"There I was living on the streets close to five years and the fucking opportunity of a lifetime presents itself. Want to know what it was?" I didn't answer him. "The freakin' Rodney King verdict," Matthew pronounced with a chuckle. Something terrible wrong was going on with Matthew. I wasn't paying any attention to him and it didn't really matter to him. It was as though his story had taken him back to a place he loved. It took some time, but I slowly maneuvered my way from his hands and he didn't even seem to notice.

"So, when it went down," he said. "You know, the riots in L.A., I decided to rally the troops. Believe me when I tell you it was a spur of the moment happening. I saw a chance to make money, so I rallied somewhere around fifty people, mostly young black boys who looked like they would beat the shit out of you if you didn't do what they asked." Everyone in the streets apparently trusted Matthew. Mainly because he still had a bank account after all those years of living on the streets and could get cash if he really needed it. He had won their trust. "It was a brilliant plan. I talked everyone into getting off their dead asses and buying into my business venture. I had noticed that everyone in the city had gotten off work early that day. You know how it is with the media. After they saw the riots in L.A., they thought it would spread to New York City. So all of a sudden, there was a mad rush to get out of the city and I wanted to capitalize on the day's activities. I had the young black bucks stand with their hands out at the Holland and Lincoln Tunnels because traffic was at a standstill. It just so happened that the media wouldn't stop talking about the beating that truck driver took in L.A. and it scared a lot of people. It was like the drivers trying to get home to safety to Jersey went to the bank before they decided to get through the tunnels—as if they knew they would have to fork over money to my homies. I mean, there were commuters giving up fives, tens, twenties—whatever they had just so there wouldn't be any trouble. Isn't America great! I had those homeless bastards collect money, then bring it back to me so that I could give it all out evenly when the day was over and don't you know by dark, I had so much money that I decided to fuck them all and leave with it and I invested it all. Now that's the truth about how I came into my money."

Matthew was laughing so hard that he didn't notice that I was standing, looking for my clothes. Then he came back to reality.

"Hey, where are you going?"

"Matthew, I think it's time for me to leave."

"Leave?"

"Yes, I think I want to leave now."

"You can't. We have the rest of the night."

"I know, Matthew, but I need to get home. Look, don't worry about paying me, okay?" I managed to put on my panties and pants, then my shirt. But I couldn't find my purse, then I spotted it on the nightstand on Matthew's side of the bed. When he saw my eyes focus on it, he pulled for it and it opened up and spilled to the floor.

The first thing Matthew saw was my pocket-sized Qur'an. "What the hell is this?"

"It's my bible, Matthew." I walked over to the bed to gather my things and place them back in my bag.

"Wait a minute? You mean to tell me you're a Muslim?"

I kind of smiled at him. "Hell, I don't know, Matthew, I'm confused about religion right now."

"Well, why the hell would you be interested in this shit? Don't you know what these fools have been doing lately?"

"Yes, but I haven't been studying the religion of those types of Muslims. Look, I need to be going." I reached out my hand for the bible.

"Fuck that—a Muslim is a Muslim and I can't stand those bastards. For all I know you are a part of those rat bastards."

"Matthew, come on, you're being ridiculous."

"Ridiculous?" Matthew arose from the bed, then slapped me to the floor.

"Listen, I lost a lot of friends that day, good friends, and I tell you what—today we are going to make this right. Take off your fuck'n clothes, bitch! Take them off!"

Clarke
Daddy, where have you been?

I hadn't talked to my father since my run-in with his girlfriend. I kind of figured she was going to tell him and I didn't want to hear my father's mouth about it. I used my key to let myself inside his apartment. It wasn't like my father not to call me in four days; even if he was mad at me.

When I stepped into his place I could tell he was there. He always left the television on when he was at home. There was no sign of him in the kitchen looking for something to munch on and the couch sitting directly in front of the television set was unoccupied. I walked down the hallway and began to call his name, peeping into his office. I called out to him, then I saw him. He was sitting in his recliner turned toward a window. All I could see was the back of his head and it was tilted down. I asked him what he was doing, but he didn't answer. I walked around toward the chair. He looked like he was sleep. His mouth was wide open, he needed to shave, and the entire room reeked of alcohol. I looked down and saw a bottle under his desk.

"Daddy? Hey? Can you please explain to me why you're sitting in this chair looking like a bum off the streets or something when you're supposed to be at work?" He didn't move, so I shook the chair. "Daddy, get up." I opened up the window and lifted the blinds. When the cold air touched his face and sounds of a siren roaring down the street hit his ears, he sat up and opened his eyes. "Daddy, what the hell is wrong with you?"

"Clarke?" he asked while he tried to get his focus as the sunlight scorched his eyes.

"Yes, it's me, Daddy. You haven't called me, so I decided to come over to see you."

"What time is it?"

"Two-thirty in the afternoon."

"Aren't you supposed to be in school?"

"Damn school, something told me to come and check on you and I'm glad I did. What's going on?"

"It's Susan…"

I just knew she would—that bitch. "What about her? She dumped you, didn't she? I told you she wasn't any good for you. Look, she has you strung out and depressed like some homeless crackhead or something. If I ever see her again…"

"She's dead, so you don't have to worry about seeing her ever again."

"Dead? What are you talking about?"

"She's dead, Clarke." He handed me a newspaper from his lap and held it up. "It's all right here."

I snatched up the paper and while I began to read, my father opened up his desk drawer and pulled out another bottle.

Damn. She was dead. "Murdered?"

"Yep, she's gone, Clarke," he said, right before he opened the bottle and took a long, rough swig.

I tried to read the article as fast as I could. "Found dead in a parking lot in the back seat of a stored Mercedes on 44th on the East Side? Cause of death: strangulation? Daddy, what the fuck is going on?"

"Hell, don't ask me. I was supposed to meet with Susan, around the same time we'd last spoken. But she never came to see me. She told me that she needed a favor from me, but never showed."

I dropped the paper back into his lap and looked out the window. All of a sudden guilt dropped into my chest. "She did come by, I saw her."

My father tried to stand, but the liquor in his system pushed him back down into his chair. "What are you talking about?"

Damn it, I didn't want to tell him. Not now that she was dead. "Well, I spoke to her and I guess, you can say, we had words."

"Words?" My father was so drunk. "What kind of words, Clarke?"

"Just a conversation," I told him.

"Don't give me that bullshit. About what?"

My father never cursed me. "About how we felt. Put it this way—about how I felt about her trying to cozy up to you."

"Shit, Clarke. And?"

"And what?"

"What did you say to her?"

I looked down at the paper again and the headline just numbed me. "Daddy, I just told her I thought she was after you for your money and I didn't like it."

"You did what?"

I picked the newspaper up again. "I know I was…"

"Damn right, you were wrong."

I was stunned. "Look at this. They found a note taped to her body that said, 'High-priced Muslim Madam, she'll never be missed.' High-priced Muslim madam? Susan was a ho and a Muslim? Daddy, tell me it isn't so?"

"Wait a minute, Clarke, watch your mouth."

I couldn't believe it. "And you knew?" I asked him.

"Yes, I knew. Knew all about it and didn't care one damn bit. Susan was about to change her life; she didn't want to do it anymore. We were falling in love."

My father was hurting but it was hard to console him. A hooker, no way. "Daddy, how could you get involved with a hooker? That's all I want to know. That is so beneath you. I knew she wasn't any good for you. I knew it. How disgusting is this all?"

Byron
Remember when?

I was caught off guard when I noticed Thomas come in the shop, walk up to the first black suit that caught his eye, then pull it off the rack. He didn't look at the size, check the price, or even feel the material. I walked up behind him.

"Damn, I wish all my customers were like you, Thomas."

I didn't think I would startle Thomas, but he flinched at the sound of my voice and looked very uneasy. "Huh, what do you mean?" he asked.

"I mean, by the way you came in here and picked out that forty-five hundred dollar suit without a care in the world. Where the hell do you need to be?"

Thomas held the suit up and looked it over. "To a funeral," he said. "Forty-five hundred—for this?"

"A funeral?" Thomas nodded his head. "Whose? Everyone's okay, right? Tell me everyone's okay, Thomas?" Thomas walked away from me. "Hey, where are you going?"

"To put this piece of shit back," he said. "Forty-five hundred, my ass."

I took the suit from him. "Thomas, do you mind telling me whose funeral you have to attend?"

Thomas looked at me. His eyes were glazed. "Susan's," he mumbled.

"Susan's?"

"Are you hard of hearing, Byron?"

"I'm just surprised, Thomas. What happened?"

"She was murdered."

"How?"

"Strangled. It's been all over the news and in the paper."

"You mean the hooker found in the Mercedes?"

Thomas looked at me like he was upset that I'd heard about it. "That was Susan?" Thomas looked down and then nodded his head. "I didn't know she was a…"

"It was none of your business, that's why you didn't know," Thomas said.

"But when I met her at the party she seemed so nice." Her death was disappointing because when I met Susan she seemed to be a genuinely nice person. But just knowing Thomas wasn't as squeaky clean as I'd thought for so many years kind of recharged my intuition.

"She was nice. What the hell is wrong with you, Byron?"

"It's just a shock that she's one and the same as the victim," I said.

"Well it was her and I need a suit to wear to her funeral."

"You want to wear the one I fitted you for last week? I can have it ready for you in no time."

"No, give me something a little more subtle," Thomas said.

Thomas followed me over to a bunch of suits that we had on sale but were excellent purchases. While I fitted him for a single-breasted, three-button, charcoal black suit with pleated pants, I could see Thomas thinking about Susan while he looked into the mirror waiting for me to finish. I imagined it must have been very difficult to not be with the one you've shared so much time with. It made me think about Karen and all the times we had spent together, things we planned on doing together but never got around to it. Death sure has a way to put things into perspective. "Susan seemed like a really nice girl. I'd never imagine something like that happening," I said.

Thomas sort of came out of his daze. "Yeah, she was nice."

"But then again, I didn't know she was a hooker either." I wished like hell I hadn't said that after it came rumbling out.

"Just help me with the suit, okay?" Thomas said.

As I worked Thomas must have read my mind. He was looking directly at me through the mirror and it got my attention and I tried not to look at him.

"What, Byron, what the hell is it? I can tell you have something you want to say? You always do."

"Look, Thomas, I don't mean to pry, but shit. Did you know she was a hooker?"

"You're as bad as Clarke. What? Can't I know people who do things that some people think are deplorable? Yes, I knew, damn it. Anything else you wanna know?"

"Wow."

"Wow what?"

"You knew—wow."

"No, I don't know, 'wow'," Thomas pressed.

"You really are living the fast lane, aren't you?"

"No faster than anyone else. Look, man, Susan wasn't *really* a hooker."

"That's what I heard on the news."

"She wasn't, okay?"

"Yeah, sure, man. Anything you say," I told him. Thomas was getting upset and the last thing I wanted to do was get in a fight with a grieving man.

"She wasn't. She was a young lady who did what she had to do to stay afloat for money and not with a lot of men, mind you. I know a lot more women than her who have more sexual partners, okay?"

I eased a bit. "Okay, fine. If that's what you're goin' with—it's cool with me." I finished the last measurement on the suit and told Thomas I could have it for him by two o'clock.

"Fine, Byron. I'll come back and pick it up."

"Don't worry. I'll personally deliver it to you. I know you must have a million things running through your mind with all this shit going on. Just leave your address with Beverly at the front desk."

"Yeah, I do. Thanks."

IT HAD TO BE CLOSE TO ONE-THIRTY in the afternoon when the suit was finished. I made sure the suit Thomas had chosen a week earlier was completed as well, and covered them up, and took them over to him. When Thomas answered the door he was wearing boxers and had shaving cream on his face.

"C'mon in," he said.

I lifted up the finished suits, then handed them over to him. "Just like I promised."

Thomas looked over the suits with a quick glance. Then he hung them up on his coat rack, took the white towel from his shoulder, and wiped the shaving cream off the side of his face before putting one arm inside a white button-down shirt that laid on the back of a chair.

"Hey, man, in all seriousness…I'm really sorry about Susan," I told him. "Are you going to be okay?" Thomas looked at me; almost to see if I was sincere or not. "C'mon, Thomas. You should know me better than that? We've had our differences but something like this? Death? Shit, this is down-to-earth. Some real personal shit. Very, very deep. That's above how we've felt about each other over the years. My condolences are genuine and I mean that."

Thomas gave me one more interrogating look. "Thanks. Thanks a lot," he said.

I moved into his sitting area and looked around a bit. Thomas offered me a drink and I accepted. A glass of whiskey—neat.

"You know, Thomas, while I was waiting on your suit, I was thinking about what I'd do if something ever happened to Karen."

"Trust me, you don't want to know what this feels like; especially if you have feelings for her."

"The feelings are there, that's for sure. I'm still doing my best to keep her happy and, at the same time, trying to keep my fuckin' sanity; if that's even possible."

"If I've learned one thing over the years, it's that relationships are difficult and they never get easier." Thomas thought for a while. "You know, I was truthfully thinking about settling down with Susan. Of course, she was going through confusion with her religion and I could handle that because it was religion. If it would have been her faith, then we would have had a problem, but religion I could have dealt with. We'd finally worked out things and were beginning to talk to each oher and, shit, look what happens?"

"Forgive me for saying so, but I still can't believe she was a hooker."

"Get off that shit, Byron," Thomas said. "She wasn't, not in my eye. She was a lady who needed more money than she made on her job and really didn't have a choice with all the responsibilities she had in her life. Yes, she made money by spending time with men but it wasn't as farfetched as some might think. She was a good person. Did you know she was a high school dropout?"

"No, I didn't. I would have never thought."

"Yes, she was. But she was so bright. She reminded me so much of Synthia in her younger days. And it's funny because, in her young age, she wanted to make a change, too, and stop sleeping with men with money. She was close to stopping altogether but didn't make it." Thomas walked over and unzipped the suit bag. He was pleased with the fit of the pants.

"So, twenty years ago, when we'd run these streets until the early light, did you ever think our lives would turn out like this?" I wanted to know.

"Not in a million fuckin' years, Byron," Thomas said as he reminisced. I could see him going all the way back to when we would club hop, party, and have our customary Saturday-night card games of spades with Frankie Beverly & Maze or Marvin Gaye blaring in the background. "In some ways we're lucky though," he said. "But in others we should be crawling up the walls and terribly disappointed at the same time."

"I'd always thought I'd be a father by now," I told Thomas. I wanted three boys and one baby girl, who would never grow into a woman. Ball games on the weekends and homework at night. I even thought I would love every minute of being deprived of sleep because my kids would be happy and I would be in love with them.

"I wish I would have been there more for Clarke. Even though I was there with her I really could have done more. I think she knows I love her, but those times, family times we didn't have and I wish we would have. It wasn't until I moved into this place that I finally realized it; Clarke is damn near a grown woman and even though I was there with her to see her grow up, seems like I still missed it all."

"Well, at least we're here to see what's become of our lives."

There was silence between us. Thomas began putting on his suit and I took a few sips of my drink.

"Not much to it, huh?" I said.

"My feelings exactly," Thomas reinforced.

Clarke
Not my fault.

I was havingthe most difficult time trying to study with Susan's death and the look of despair on my father's face when I last left his place. It was so odd, looking at him in such a way. The first time I'd ever seen him with watered eyes was when I was a little girl. It was our first Christmas as a divorced family, still living together. He was so emotional. But I actually saw tears fall down his face when he talked about Susan and it really hurt me to see him that way. I called Leon and told him I needed to talk.

To say the least, Leon was being very *extra* with me.

"Clarke, if you'd come to see me like I'd asked before you went putting your nose in your father's business, maybe he would've seen her one more time before she was killed—maybe even prevented this shit. You're so hardheaded sometimes and I'm talkin' as family right now."

Leon was right. I shouldn't have said anything, but I didn't want to be blamed for her death. Death was so final. "Well, I didn't know, Leon." I even noticed the cry in my voice. "You can't blame this on me. How was I supposed to know she was going to get killed? I didn't know she was a damn ho."

"A ho?"

"You heard me. She sold her body and someone killed her. So since you have obtained all these fuckin' psychic powers from your topnotch colleges you've attended, nigga, tell me when all this crazy shit in my life is gonna stop happening?"

"Calm down."

"I am calm." But I was getting pissed because I was feeling guilty. I was looking out for my father because I didn't get a good vibe from Susan, even though my father had fallen for her.

"Look, Clarke, being a ho doesn't make her a bad person," Leon said.

"And?"

"And…things are going to begin to level off for you, Clarke," Leon told me in a much calmer voice.

"When?"

"In due time; that's when. Things are more complicated than before; that's all. It's the way of life. It's much too deep for you to even worry about at this point. How 'bout you just let grown folks handle their own business for a change? That means your mother and your father. You handle your schoolwork and your future. I seem to remember—when you did, things worked out better for you."

I tried to gather my thoughts because I remembered how hard it was for me to stay out of my mother's and father's affairs when we all were together. There were so many times I wanted to see my father kiss my mother. Even times when I asked him to kiss her while we were all in the kitchen getting ready for the day. When he kissed her on the cheek I felt good; even though it wasn't sincere. It made me feel good, but horrible that I had to ask him to do it.

Leon looked over at me and mentioned something about my arms being clutched tight, not listening to what he was saying. "You know, if this type of shit keeps happening with you, you meddling in business that doesn't concern you, our sessions are going to be longer and I'm moving you back to the couch because you're driving me out of my fuckin' mind," he said.

"Oh great, now I have a loony ass shrink."

"All I'm saying is that you need to start taking my advice. If you aren't what's the use talking to me in the first place? You've had this problem most of your life, Clarke. Always in your parents' affairs. I told you there would come a time when you'd wish you hadn't and guess what time it is?"

"Okay, Leon. Stop with the guilt, man. My father hasn't talked to me since the funeral. He hasn't said he blames me for what happened, but I know he's thought that she would still be with him if I would have just kept my damn mouth shut."

"And so have I, Clarke," Leon blasted back. "You see, there's something you don't know about adults yet and you won't until you become one."

"What is it?"

"It's plain and simple. Adults talk things out. Well, at least they should and if they don't, they should be riding with me so I can find out why they're not acting like adults."

"So, what's that have to do with me?"

"Everything, because I want you to let adults handle adult business. Stop putting your zing on every aspect of their lives. It doesn't concern you," Leon demanded. I finally agreed. Hell, what else was I going to do? It was my senior year and my father was grieving over his loss and my mother had gone crazy. Shit, I decided to just get through the school year and get the hell away from them both. Maybe next year when I returned for Christmas break or something, they'd realize how important I was to them and what fools they'd been.

Thomas
Boys again.

It had been exactly seven weeks since Susan's funeral. I'd already put things in perspective. The vibe around the city was already full of grief and despair because of the recent events so all the emotional articles, even radio shows, helped me to put what happened to her in its proper place. Byron and I had met for drinks at least once a week since the funeral. He really surprised me when he went to the funeral for emotional support and I was quite thankful he did. While we chugged down drinks we found out more about each other than we cared to ask while Synthia was in our lives. It was like our petty beefs were quickly disappearing.

"That's where Susan and I sat every single time we came here," I told Byron one afternoon at Central Park during lunch.

"Right over there, huh?" Byron responded, truly interested.

"Yup, that's it."

Byron pointed to a couple snuggling on the bench that held so many memories. "Looks like that poor unsuspecting soul has caught a bit of the love bug you two left behind."

"No question about it. That guy there has it bad," I told him. "Look how he's all over her."

"This might sound funny, but I wonder if he actually knows if his relationship has begun or not?" Byron realized the blank expression on my face. "I see you don't understand either?" I shook my head no. "You know…the re-la-tion-ship," he sang. "The relationship where they begin sharing together, planning together, and being *one*. That's what I want to know. I wonder are they at that stage yet."

Byron sounded a bit confused himself. I didn't know how to answer him. "Sounds like a topic for Oprah to me," I told him.

Byron took a bite of the sandwich that he'd brought along. "No, no, I think we could tackle it. I mean, we've both been in relationships. Hell, you've even been married."

"Doesn't mean shit though. If you didn't know while you were in a relationship, no way in hell now am I going to speculate and try to figure it out now. Relationships are too complicated, Byron, that's my opinion."

Byron was positive he could tackle the issue. "Okay, take Karen for example. We've been seeing each other for close to three years now and it doesn't seem like we've ever changed from 'just' the dating game," he ironed out.

"Dating game?"

"That's right. That get-what-you-can-now period because you never know how long he or she will be around. You know what I'm talking about, Thomas, help me out," he pleaded.

The length of time did surprise me a bit. "You've been doing that shit for three years?"

"That's right. Three years, and it doesn't look like it's going to change. I've tried to stay manly about the whole thing, You know, act like I don't give a damn one way or another. But damn, Thomas, who has time to waste anymore?"

"We certainly don't." Our conversation reminded me to update my insurance policy and will.

"Damn right, so lately I've tried to throw hints out to Karen," Byron explained.

"Hints. Like what?"

"You know, being a little bit more romantic. Cooking her dinner, candle-lights, running her bath water—the whole nine. All to make her notice things should be getting serious by now between us."

"Yeah? So how's it going?"

"It's not," Byron said bluntly. "Not working one damn bit."

"Have you told her, Byron? You know, expressed to her what you want. I remember I did that with Susan and she melted. Women like when you express your true feelings."

"I expressed it, as clearly as I could."

"And what did she say?"

"She flipped it and asked me for some money. I don't know, man—Karen turns everything into a money issue."

"Wow, money?" My mind took me back to Byron's unwillingness to see Susan's money issues and I was about to say something about it, but decided against it.

"I know what you're thinking, Thomas," Byron said. "And I get your point. It took me a while to realize it. Hell, Synthia even told me she was on the take, but I didn't want to hear what Synthia was talking about and didn't see it myself until recently."

"You really think she's trying to use you?"

Byron said, "I wouldn't go that far. At least my mind hasn't taken me there yet. But there's always something in her life that happens that she pesters me to help her out with. She has a million excuses, too. Over and over again," Byron revealed. "I know this may come as a shock, but it's gotten to a point where I might need to ask you for a loan."

Clarke
What's this all about?

My father called out of the blue and asked me to meet him on 70th and York on the East Side. He didn't say why, matter-of-fact, it was almost like a demand that I meet him. I hadn't heard the tone of voice he used with me since junior high school. Maybe he wanted to talk. Maybe he was still mad at me about Susan. All I know I was up in the air concerning what our meeting was all about.

I hadn't been standing on 70th for thirty seconds. "Byron?"

"Clarke?" he said back with wondering eyes.

"What're you doing here?" we said to one another.

"I was supposed to meet my father," I told him.

Byron poked himself in the chest. "So was I."

"Why?" I wanted to know.

"You tell me," he answered.

"I mean, why are you here? My father doesn't even..." I quickly remembered what Leon had told me. And I refused to say anymore.

Byron raised an eyebrow at me. "F.Y.I. we've sort of like patched things up, Clarke."

I looked down the street trying to locate his car. "So, where is he?"

Byron pointed toward a brownstone building to the right of where we were standing. "He's inside; at least that's where he told me he'd be."

I read the sign on the door. Saint Ignitis School for Girls. I looked at Byron.

"Don't ask me? Like I said, he asked me to join him, so here I am."

Suddenly the door to the school building swung open. "Hey, guys, I'm glad you're on time," my father said.

"Daddy, what's going on?"

"C'mon in and you'll find out."

There were only three steps that led into the building, which seemed to have about seven floors. It caught my attention instantly because there were paintings on the walls of schoolchildren. Not stick figures, but nicely done drawings by students who evidently had a lot of talent. There were pictures of balloons, houses with flowers in the yards; even a tribute to the fallen firemen killed in the terrorist attack. Daddy led us down a flight of steps, then down a hallway, which was plastered with posters and signs of high achievements on the yellow and blue painted walls. Then he opened a door and we were in a gym amongst about thirty students dressed out in their gym attire.

"Okay, we're here," Daddy said.

I looked at Byron, then said, "Here for what?"

That's when Daddy took me by the hand and Byron followed us. We sat in the bleachers. There were two instructors who evidently knew my father because they waved and called him by his first name. The gym was filled with girls dressed in white T-shirts and gray shorts; they looked to be eight or nine years old taking gymnastics instructions. "Daddy, what's goin' on?" I had become very impatient.

"Do me a favor and look and see if there's anyone out there that remotely reminds you of yourself when you were a little girl, Clarke," he said.

"What? Are you serious?"

"Clarke, just do it, please."

I noticed Byron squint his eyes and try to find a little girl first. He probably would find her quicker than I could since I didn't really remember how I looked and he was always over the house with us. Most of the girls were in a line waiting their turn to negotiate the springboard and horse that awaited them. I was not really enjoying looking at a bunch of yackety little girls who wouldn't stand still long enough for me to get a good look at them. I got tired of trying. "How am I supposed to get a good look? They won't keep still. What do they have? Ants in their training bras or something?"

Daddy was anxious for some strange reason so he said, "Here, I'll help you guys." Then he nodded his head forward. "Look at the seventh little girl in line. She has on the blue sneakers and her hair is in a ponytail." He pointed her out with pride.

I was going to mention his sudden joy, but I didn't. "Yeah, so?"

"She looks exactly like you, Clarke, when you were her age. What do you think, Byron?"

Byron smiled like he was looking at a little damn baby through a glass or something, then sang, "She sure does…imagine that?"

I looked at Byron and turned up my lip, then told them, "Well, I don't see it."

"Sure, look at her eyes and how she carries herself," Daddy said. "She is always smiling. I tell you, always smiling."

"Okay, if you say so," I concluded. "C'mon, let's go. You must be going through a mid-life crisis or something. First, Mom, now you. What'd you do? See her out on the playground or something?" Daddy smiled at me and shook his head while he watched her play with her friends. "Well, what's this all about then?" I asked.

"Clarke, she's Susan's daughter. Her name is Stacey."

Synthia
You do what you have to do.

I wasn't surprised when Barbara called to tell me Lil' Shae was all but signed, sealed and delivered to the agency. My partner was more focused than I'd seen her in quite a while after our last meeting; concerning signing the rapper. Barbara let me know that it was final and she was exhausted from negotiating the terms of the deal. She made sure I knew the only way the book deal would work was if Lil' Shae worked with me on her autobiography. What was I going to do? I was stuck; especially after Barbara announced the signing with all the industry publications via fax along with MTV. There was no way I could back down—it would have done major damage to the agency. I decided to just go with the flow.

I paused a few seconds before calling my new client. I decided I would make her book as painless as possible. I'd done celebrity books before and as I looked back on them all and through my experience, I really didn't have to spend a lot of time with Lil' Shae. The writers and I would iron out any wrinkles, if need be. So that was my game plan; assign a writer and be the facilitator of it all, then wash my hands of the entire situation.

During our conversation, Lil' Shae asked to meet with me at a place called the Hip Hop Café in Brooklyn. Before I could even check my schedule, she directed, "See you at two o'clock." Then the phone went silent. I was there on time; she wasn't. Thirty minutes later she arrived. She had on a white mink and loved every minute of the surprised gasps from fans.

Before she sat down with me, Lil' Shae slowly took off her leather gloves—finger by finger—keeping her eyes on me. I noticed two guys—bodyguards no doubt—sit a table away from us.

"I hope you don't mind meeting here in the open," she said. "But you know how it is—I have to *keep it real*."

If you must, young lady, I thought, as I watched this young, pint-sized girl posture for the entire café establishment.

"My manager thought it would be best if she handled all this preliminary foolishness, but I'm getting more into my own affairs these days. That's why I decided to take this meeting instead. Besides, being involved keeps everyone honest, so go ahead and start whenever you're ready. Has the waiter been over yet?"

I shook my head. I hadn't planned on breaking bread with Lil' Shae. I wanted to talk business and leave. "I thought we would discuss writers first," I told her. "I usually have three or four to choose from. But for convenience sake I'll just go with two writers who I know will do a wonderful job and pitch them the idea for your book so we can get the ball rolling. We'll make a decision on their ideas based on their proposals."

Lil' Shae signaled one minute to me. She reached into her Prada handbag, pulled out a piece of paper, then began to unfold it. She gave it to me. It turned out to be an article from a magazine. "That's the writer I want for my book," she said. "Her name is Shelly Givens. I want her, Synthia."

I looked at the article. It was two pages and came from an underground magazine I wasn't familiar with. "Is this writer a personal friend or something?" I asked her. Shae looked at me and shook her head. "Well, has she ever done a book before? Has she ever been published besides *this* article?"

Lil' Shae came at me with a hard attitude. "Who cares? The bitch made Oasis look good in this article. Had everyone in the city talking about what this bitch can do. How many rhymes she can spit per bar; even goes as far to say she has NBA players payin' her for her punany."

"I'm getting confused. Who's the bitch?"

"Both of them. It's a figure of speech," she said.

"In a good way though?" I wanted to know.

"I guess you can say, but in a *hard* way, you know, street. Are we going to do this or talk about slang?" Lil' Shae looked around. "Where is the fuckin' waiter?"

"Well, I don't know this Shelly Givens *bitch* as you describe her. And who the hell is Oasis?"

Lil' Shae shook her head and smiled at me. Then she looked over at the two guys she'd walked in with. Their voices were beginning to get a bit loud and she squinted her eyes at them. One was dark-skinned, looked like he had on two hats, a baggy jean outfit and construction boots. The other was slim, had a hood over his head, his hands in his pockets and was brown-skinned. Just ordinary youngsters. Shae looked back at me and said, "That's my boyfriend Outlaw and his thug ass friend J.B. I keep them around me. I'd wish they'd shut the hell up though," Lil' Shae said.

"Oh, I see."

Lil' Shae put her eyes back on me. "You're not going to give up, are you?"

"I don't know what you're talking about."

"Yes, you do. You're still not down with this, but it's okay. I can handle it."

"I'm never a hundred percent sure about anything." I looked down at the article, then back at Lil' Shae. "Now, if you really insist that Shelly be your writer, I'm going to have to locate her and make sure she can do it first."

"I'm sure she can do it. Just read the article and see how she pumped Oasis up. She talks about her record sales and all of her hits. Makes the bitch seem like she's sold millions of copies time and time again and nobody has done that in this business, but me. I'm at five million on both my albums and I want this type of juice in the streets about me—world-wide—in my book. Shit, by reading that fuckin' article, you'd think that bitch Oasis was me or some shit."

"Let me warn you, everyone can't write a book," I told her.

"She's who I want, Synthia," Lil' Shae said. All of a sudden she stood up and shouted. "Can we get a waiter or some shit over here?" The patrons in the cafe smiled at her aggressiveness. Everyone thought what she did was cute. Instantly a waiter appeared; obviously in over his head with customers.

"Sorry about that. All of a sudden it's gotten so busy around this place, it's crazy." He smiled as he looked around.

"I wonder why?" Shae said to him.

"I really couldn't tell you," the waiter said back.

"Because of me, fool. I'm the reason everyone stepped into this place. Don't you know who I am? This place is now packed because people want to get a glimpse of me. Shit, maybe I need to talk to your boss?" All of a sudden Lil' Shae shot me a look, then said, "Ask around because I will, sure as my name is Lil' Shae."

Outlaw
Have patience, brother.

A'ight, this is how it was going down. First of all, I was chillin' up in New York City 'cause my girl Shae wanted me to be there with her. At first I didn't even want to move to the motherfucker 'cause I was content chillin' at Mom's in North Carolina—drinkin' beer and smokin' blunts all day. How can I say it? Life was fabulous in North Kakalackey. Me and Ma done knew each other for a while though. Ma came to visit her relatives a couple of times in the summer when she was coming up and we just like bonded from day one. That was like back in the day when we was young, but we always kept in touch 'cause Ma enjoyed the way I hit the skins and banged her out. Always told me I was genuine with mine, not like the fake niggas she was used to dealing with in the city. So after we grew out of our puppy love, Ma kept in touch and told me she couldn't live without me. So I took the chance and moved in with her. I thought like this, *what the hell did I have to lose?* Shit…she was making big paper; I didn't have to work; it would just be the same thing for me in New York City like I was doing in North Carolina, but I would be going up in every nigga's fantasy woman on a constant basis. It goes without sayin' how quickly I came up in the streets when folk found out I was Shae's man. From day one, I had chickens hitting on me because they wanted to say I slept with Lil' Shae's man and there were more than enough people trying to get at me, so they could get next to Shae for a record deal themselves. That's one of the reasons I realized my boy J.B. befriended me and showed me so much love. But it was cool 'cause everybody's after something.

"Yo, why your girl keep looking over here at us?" J.B. asked me while we waited for Shae in the café.

"I could care less, you heard?"

"That's what I'm sayin', Outlaw."

"All I know is—she better hurry up with this business so we can go get in the studio and handle ours."

"True dat. So how long you think it's gonna be before she puts us on?" J.B. wanted to know.

"Trust. It won't be long. And that's my word." And I damn sure meant what I said.

Synthia
Well, what a surprise.

Lil' Shae's writer of choice, Shelly Givens, wasn't at all hard to find. I made two phone calls and by the end of the day I had all but talked to Ms. Givens. I called her and left a message. *"Ms. Givens, this is Synthia Gage at the Barbara Scotch Literary Agency. I would like to speak with you concerning a project at your earliest convenience. If you like, you're welcome to join me at Nat Shelby's book release party tonight at The Tavern on the Green at seven... If you are unable to attend, I will call again tomorrow."*

Somewhere around eight-fifteen, I was surprised to see, of all people, *Karen* standing in front of me with an overjoyed sarcastic smirk on her face.

"Hello, Synthia," she said.

"Karen?"

"Yes, I just wanted you to know that my pen name is Shelly Givens. You wanted to talk to me about something?"

Byron
Another level.

I wasn't the best cook, but I sure knew how to make four-layer lasagna, tossed salad and pick out the plushest fruitiest red wine any woman would love. I'd grown up watching my mother make lasagna for my two brothers and I had made it for Karen. To go along with our meal, I had spent an entire hour picking out a floral arrangement and another twenty minutes selecting the music for the night. Karen enjoyed jazz while she ate so I had Coltrane and Davis at the ready.

"Dang, baby, when you said dinner, I was thinking more in line with hamburgers or something," Karen said to me in much delight. I loved to hear her deep Brooklyn accent. She was younger than me, but when she talked and was happy, she made me feel even younger.

"Yeah, I ran into some money and thought I would treat you," I told her.

"Money?"

"Yeah, I gotta loan," I told her.

"Yeah right! From who, Damion the loan shark?"

"I would never mess with that fool," I told her.

"Whatever," she chimed.

"So you like what I've done here or what?"

"Yes, this is nice."

"I'm trying to impress you, sweetheart," I told her.

"So far, so good. What brought all this on?"

"I don't know. Maybe the conversations I've been having lately and understanding how important life is. I've been spending a lot of time with Thomas, you know?" Karen had almost finished her first glass of wine. I refilled her glass.

"I kinda noticed," she said. "But I wasn't going to say anything because I remember you telling me you two were kind of close years ago. I just wished for the best."

"Yeah, you know. Friendships fade in and out sometimes."

"So, Thomas and his suave self put you up to this?"

"No, this is something I wanted to do for us. Be a little romantic. You know, try to get this relationship to another level," I explained.

Karen put down her wineglass before she took another sip. "Another level?"

"You're surprised? Don't you think it's time?"

"For…"

"I don't know, maybe to start talking about what we're doing. What we plan to do with our lives, the future."

She smiled. "You sure are in a serious moment tonight, aren't you, Byron?"

WE ENJOYED THE DINNER. Karen had two helpings and then I had to listen to her complain about how fat her ass was going to get. I told her I liked her fat ass. I guess Coltrane and the wine made her feel at ease about my comment. We sat on the couch for a few minutes and the next thing I knew, Karen was naked and feeding me her breasts. She took some wine from the bottle and poured it on her nipples. It was my job to lick it all off. The sex was great and we sat watching *Law & Order* after we'd finished.

"The few times that you'd talked to Susan, did she ever tell you she had a daughter?" I asked Karen, right before I took the last swig of wine from the bottle.

"No, she sure didn't. No one ever talks much about personal business at those book chats. I'm still surprised Synthia was so cool with Thomas bringing a date, by the way she's been acting lately."

"Her name's Stacey and she's nine. Goes to one of those private schools over on the East Side," I told her.

"That must be expensive."

"Thomas figures Susan died because of it being so. Stacey told Thomas her mother was having a little trouble getting money to pay for the remainder of the school year. The officials at school even called the little girl in the office and told her if her mother didn't have the money at a certain date she wasn't going to be allowed in class and she was going to be forced to remove her things from the dorm."

"Now that's enough to scare the poor girl, isn't it?"

"It all stems from the voucher system, Thomas and I think. The government gives parents money for their kids to go to private schools," I told Karen.

"My cousin in Jersey was trying to do the same thing for her kids. She still had to pay thousands of dollars, even after the voucher, so she just gave up on the whole thing."

"Evidently, Susan received a voucher for two grand each semester. Then she found out that the school had raised the prices midstream and was forced to make up the difference."

"You think that's what she was trying to do when she was killed?"

"Can't say for sure but Thomas seems to think so because she'd come to see him for a favor, but Clarke upset her before she could mention the money."

"So, wait a minute. Their situation has brought this night out of you?"

"Not directly, but I've been thinking. Trying to put together what's been happening in my life in the last couple of months and I've been neglecting something."

"And what's that?"

"Just that nothing's promised. That's it—nothing's promised."

I wanted to tell her that Synthia's change of lifestyle and ability to keep her promise of renewing her values had kind of gotten to me; especially after talking to Thomas and finding out that Synthia's changes had been in the works for years. Karen didn't think too highly of Synthia after I'd told her how Synthia felt about her, so I kept all of my insight to myself. It's probably best that I did anyway. Karen kept cutting me off during my attempts to discuss commitment, engagement, and possibilities of marriage. She was oblivious to the notion. Here I was, for the first time in my life, as a man well past my prime, trying to get the point across that I was finally ready for commitment and she wasn't hearing me. Karen reminded me that she agreed to see me on an experimental basis and that's exactly where she still thought we stood; except I had "privileges," meaning I had access to her sex. After I'd digested her thoughts, I was ready for bed.

Clarke
Do wha'? With who?

It had been three weeks since I'd first laid eyes on Stacey. Sure it was stunning to see her. It was even more paralyzing to see the glow that shaped my father's face every time he looked at her. More than anything, I think he saw more of Susan in her than me. But hell, when you get in your fifties, I guess the shit you see is the shit you see. One thing's for sure, he was really stressing the fact that he wanted to somehow be involved in Stacey's life.

According to Daddy, she was placed in a foster home with a couple who already had six foster children and the change was a little too much for her. Luckily for Stacey, she only had to stay there on the weekends since she stayed at school during the week. The only thing that really stayed constant in her life was school. Daddy paid for the rest of the year and promised he would take care of the remaining schooling as well. He also went to meet her foster parents and told them if there was anything they needed for her to let him know. The Delaneys were a young couple in their thirties.

The time I went to see Stacey with Daddy, I got the feeling the wife couldn't have kids. The man—his name was Walter—seemed to be into all the kids more than she was. But even still, my talks with Leon were scheduled more often and, as he had promised, he moved me back into his office. I guess he thought my mindset was that serious.

"Can you freakin' believe it, Leon? Daddy wants me to take this little girl shopping and do lunch. He's insisting I get to know her. For what? Really, what can I do for her?" And I really didn't know. I couldn't even remember the last time I'd held a conversation with someone younger than me.

"I don't think it's a bad idea, Clarke." Leon was smoking another blunt behind his desk in his office.

I didn't want to hear that shit from him. "What? It has to be a bad idea. I'm no role model for this girl. Look at me!"

"Nope, it's a good idea because you're moving into the young adult phase of your life."

"Leon, spare me. I know lots of adults. Most of them don't do shit for anybody."

Leon chuckled a bit. "That's another topic. We're talking about you. What you need to understand is that your father feels for Stacey. Maybe he feels responsible for what happened to her mother. Or he could be just genuinely concerned about her welfare and, knowing my uncle, that's exactly what it is."

I wasn't going to get a reason from Leon good enough to tell my father I couldn't take Stacey out. "Whatever, Leon. Whatever." I sunk deeper into his couch.

"So you'll do it?" Leon asked.

I told him, "Anything to get my father off my back." I don't know why I hadn't noticed, but Leon had changed his office around. "Leon, care to tell about this seventies thing you have goin' on?"

Leon put his blunt out and stood up. "Sure, cousin. I'm in a new phase now with all my clients. Thought I'd bring them all into the seventies; at least the ones who aren't too far gone. And, by the way, this is where I live now. Why pay for an office and a place to rent when I can do one damn thing in one damn place? You dig?"

I shook my head and wondered what the hell kind of high Leon was on.

"So what am I supposed to talk to this little girl about?"

Leon picked up his blunt again, then a lighter. "How would I know? Most of my clients with kids ask me the same damn thing."

"So what do you tell them?"

"Tell them I don't know… 'Cause I don't."

THERE WAS NOTHING LEFT for me to do than be myself with Stacey. I took the ferry to Hoboken and the ride gave me a chance to think about what I was getting myself into for my father's sake. I attempted to read my literature assignment but Leon's lack of advice didn't sit well. A nine-year-old girl, what was I going to do?

Stacey was all smiles when she walked out the door of her house. We hopped in a cab to take us back to the ferry station and Stacey told me about the outfit she had on. It was the last thing her mother had purchased for her before her death. It was a blue jean outfit with a black turtleneck sweater that sat well under her oversized Tommy Boy jacket. I glanced at Stacey out the corner of my eye while we were waiting on the ferry and, both times, she caught me. I don't think my uneasiness bothered her because I think my father told her I wanted to be with her. Plus, I think she was just happy to be away from the Delaneys'. Daddy told me her mother talked to her all the time when they were together and the Delaneys only talked to her when they thought she may need something.

"So, are you gonna talk to me?" Stacey asked.

"Yes, of course," I told her. Then luckily the ferry began to move and it gave me a brief chance to think of something to say.

"So when?"

"When what?"

"When are you gonna talk?"

I took a deep breath and began to look at the city. All of a sudden Stacey grabbed my hand, bent her head, and seemed to be praying but I couldn't understand her. I listened to her for a couple of seconds, then took my hand from her.

"Hey, hey, what're you doing?"

She looked up at me. "Praying. Haven't you ever heard anyone pray?"

"Yes, many times, but not like that," I told her.

"It's Arabic. My mother taught me. When I remember, I pray at least five times a day. Sometimes two, but always once."

"Well, stop that, okay?"

"Why?" she shot back. "I can teach you, if you'd like?"

"No, that's quite all right. Just don't do that around me, okay?"

After that exchange, Stacey couldn't take her eyes off me. It must have been thirty minutes before she said another word.

"Thomas told me you might be a little shy," she said.

"Me? Shy… My father told you that?"

"Umm,hmm. He said you would be shy. Not that you were shy. Actually he said you sometimes have a problem of talking too much," the little girl mouthed. "But I didn't believe him because I thought he was just trying to be nice. Plus he smiled when he said it."

"Talk too much, huh?"

"That's what he said. So what were your plans today?" Stacey asked.

She confused me with her question. "To hang out with you," I told her.

"No, no. What were your plans before Thomas asked you to spend some time with me?"

"Nothing too major." Damn, I forgot that I was supposed to tell her that I wanted to take her out. Oh well.

"I knew this was all Thomas' idea. It's okay; at least I'm out the house," she said. "So you're a senior in high school?" I confirmed with a nod. "And you didn't have anything planned this weekend? Girl, you must have a boring life. Senior year is supposed to be full of events every weekend. I can't wait until it's my turn," she said. I did not want to be hearing this because I felt the same exact way about the situation. Stacey's smile was wide for a second, and then it began to fade. "I wish my mother would be able to be here. Did you ever meet her?"

I didn't know what to say. For some reason I didn't want to answer. "Hey, did you bring your gloves? It gets a little chilly out here, you know?"

FIRST IT WAS THE MOVIES. We watched a MTV-produced flick about four high school girls who were all madly in love with the same guy at the same time. The subject matter didn't seem to faze Stacey. I even overheard her chastising the characters on the screen. She thought the girls weren't showing "girl power" and solidarity to one another. I thought it was okay. Hell, if you like a man, you might as well try to get him. Shit, good men are hard to come by. I didn't even try to school her on the real though; she'd learn it in due time anyway. We all do. The movie even made me think of my boyfriend who was off in college. He was planning to come see me over the holiday break. After the movies we were off shopping.

Little Ms. Thang surprised me with her taste in clothes. She liked the baggy, but conservative look. However, she was definitely on the wild side when it came to hang-out clothes. She even picked out a hot NYU sweatshirt she thought "was to die for"—*go 'head, girl*—and they matched her new sneakers to a tee. We were both exhausted after shopping and sat down to eat a couple of slices of Sambaro pizza in the Square. I was only two bites into my first slice of pepperoni.

"So, you're not going to tell me, are you?" Stacey asked.

"Tell you what?"

"If you met my mother or not?"

"Yeah, sure, we met."

"I just wanted to know because I'd only met Thomas two days before she was killed. Thomas is the first man my mother ever introduced me to. She was protective like that. I guess that's why I stayed in school housing during the week so she wouldn't think I thought bad about her because of the type of work she did," Stacey said.

"You knew what your mother did?" I asked.

Stacey nodded her head. "Not proud of it, but I knew. But I was proud of my mother 'cause she wanted better for me."

Stacey's forwardness was almost too much to deal with. "I didn't know your mother too well, Stacey, but she was nice," I assured her.

Stacey gave me a look and it made me stop from taking another bite of my slice. "You didn't like her, did you?"

I paused for a second, then took a bite and with a full mouth said, "What makes you think that?"

"I 'dunno.' Just a feeling I have; that's all."

I CALLED DADDY as soon as my day with Stacey was over. He was so anxious to hear how the day went that he forgot to congratulate me on raising my SAT scores another fifteen points. I knew he knew about it because Mom told me she'd told him after she'd opened the letter to see how well I'd done. To say the least, I felt good about my score, but I felt even better that my day was over.

Daddy wanted blow-by-blow details. I wasn't so eager and told him that he had to settle for the plain and simple version. I sang it to him, too, just like I was talking to a girlfriend at school.

We had fun. No, I don't remember looking like that at her age. She had lots of questions. She wanted to know about high school. We went to the movies and shopping. Stacey got a little nosy and asked me about my boyfriend. The little girl asked me if I liked her mother. Didn't believe me when I told her I did.

Then I told my father to please never ask me to do a small favor for him again. That's when he sprung on me that he wanted to adopt Stacey. *Oh my goodness*, I thought. *This man had lost his freakin' mind.*

Byron
Things have changed.

Thomas and I agreed to meet for breakfast at a diner on 53rd and Broadway. I needed to talk to him about Karen. I was wearing two faces when we met. One of disbelief and the other of total surprise; especially since Karen had found out she'd be working with Synthia on a rapper's autobiography, of all things.

"It's almost too unbelievable," Thomas said as he sipped his coffee and picked up the *Daily*.

"A small world, it truly is. Karen says that Synthia looks good." Thomas looked from around his paper directly at my words. "Says Synthia seemed really relaxed and comfortable; even after her surprise of finding out that Karen is Shelly Givens."

Thomas placed his head back behind his paper, then read the rest of an article. "I had no clue Karen was a writer," he said.

"Join the club. She kept it from me, too. Makes me wonder what else I don't know about her."

"Don't sweat it. At least it looks like she's going to have at least a book deal to keep her employed for a while. She's going to take it, right?"

"I hope so. Hell, yes, she better take it. She didn't fill me in on the conversation with Synthia but it looks promising. And as broke as she claims to be all the time, she better not let this slip through her fingers."

The waitress brought us our food. I had scrambled eggs, toast, and orange juice. Thomas had some type of wheat cereal, a fruit bowl, orange juice, and more coffee.

"So how are things going with the adoption process of Stacey?" I wanted to know.

"Looking good. All the necessary recommendations have been forwarded. The Mayor even wrote a recommendation for me. I had three interviews last week, so the only thing left to do now is wait."

"You sure you're ready for this, Thomas?"

"Ready? Of course I am," he boasted. "How difficult could it be? Don't forget, I already have one daughter who's about to graduate from high school, with honors I might add, then off to college she goes. Stacey's going to be a breeze; no problems at all."

Thomas caught my smile right before I bit into my toast. "Why the wide ass smile?"

"Things have changed, Thomas," I told him.

"What's that supposed to mean? Things always change."

"That they do. But I'm talking about these kids. Kids nowadays are much smarter than when even Clarke was a little girl."

"It won't be a problem. I'm at the right age. She'll help to keep me on my toes. Plus, she needs direction, Byron. I firmly believe that. It's the least I could do. I mean, she lost her mother, man."

"You're not holding Susan's death over your head, are you? You know you're not responsible, right?"

Thomas sighed, then looked away from me out into the city streets. "At first I did; I really did. Then, as time began to move forward, I just took it all in stride. But sometimes I look back and wonder what would've been if she had just talked to me first. What would have happened? I was getting serious with Susan and getting serious with her meant being serious with Stacey, too. Susan had just introduced us, so that meant she wanted Stacey in my life. And now that she's gone, I want Stacey in my life. It's only right."

What could I say after that? Thomas had thought it through. "I hear you, man. Hey, I want you to know, if you need anything, I'm here for you. I'm here for you both.

Synthia
Just another change, that's all.

Shelly Givens. Anyway, Karen was sitting at my desk the next day looking through the standard contract our agency used for celebrity books. What it all came down to was she was responsible for writing Lil' Shae's life story. While she read over the contract I fought the demons trying to attack my mindset concerning our past disagreements and told myself that I would use this opportunity to work with Karen to better myself. I was prepared to take the high road and have a healthy *working* relationship. So far so good. Karen lifted her eyes from the contract and smiled at me.

"First of all, do you want me to call you Shelly or Karen? I want to make sure I don't offend you when it comes to your work," I asked.

"I understand," Karen said. "Shelly is just a name I thought I'd use because I'm not really secure with my writing skills yet. If the truth were told, I only used the name so that if I failed as a writer, no one would know it was really me. I hate people knowing when I've failed at something. It seems they always want to throw it back in my face."

Like the time you went out and got an apartment knowing full damn well you didn't make enough money to pay for it and it kept Byron in my face complaining about it for six months. Thank God, He gave us the ability to hold our mouths shut because the thought definitely was there. But I controlled it and stayed positive.

"As we discussed before, you'll receive a hundred-thousand dollars for the book. No more, no less, as your agreed-upon fee for working with Lil' Shae. I hope to go to auction as soon as you can get a proposal and brief outline into our hands," I told Karen as I read her expression. "You must be really excited." She was smiling from ear to ear. It only reminded me how much younger she was than Byron.

"This is happening all of a sudden," she said. "It hasn't even registered that Lil' Shae read my article in the first place."

"You'll learn that's how this business is, Karen. You never know what opportunities will come knocking. Hopefully from this book you'll be offered other jobs as well, so it's very important that you do your best work." I always tried to give my best advice to the writers I worked with. It fosters a relationship; plus they'll come back to you when the opportunity presents itself.

"So when do you need the proposal done?"

"As soon as possible. I'm going to give you Lil' Shae's number so you can begin discussing the book with her."

"You're going to give me her phone number?"

I nodded my head. "How else are you two going to discuss the book?"

"This is definitely out of this world," Karen said.

"It gets easier after the first couple of initial conversations. Just be yourself and ask questions that you would want to read about her. That's the best way to get over your jitters," I told her. "Have you ever written a proposal before?"

"No, not really. I've always thought they were a waste of time. Particularly because I do a lot of fiction and the one and only time I wrote a proposal I looked at the length of time it took me to complete it and I could have practically finished my book?"

"You sound like most writers," I told her.

"I've always thought of them to be a complete waste of time. But not this one because I see money signs at the end of the tunnel," Karen glowed.

"That's the way to look at it. Well, all you have to do now is sign the contract." I handed her the very last page where her signature was needed. "Do you have any questions?"

Karen hesitated. "You know, Byron really misses your friendship, Synthia," Karen spouted out and my eyes ventured toward the ceiling of my office.

"Karen, I was hoping that we could keep this on a business level," I told her. Karen twisted her lips a bit. "Honestly? How can we, Synthia?"

"Easy. By keeping our conversation related to Lil' Shae and the book you're writing about her."

"Excuse me for saying this, but just like you've changed your mind about not associating yourself with those who aren't living up to their *potential*," Karen shot at me, "I've decided not long ago myself to say whatever is on my mind, no matter what the situation or person. And to tell you the truth it has worked wonders with my stress."

We might as well get this over with. "Okay. It's a free country. What is it that you want to say to me?"

"Byron is right about you." I thought to myself, *Byron has the nerve to talk about me?* "We haven't really spent much time together; except for a few parties and functions that I've attended with Byron. So, I never did get to form a full opinion about you; even though I hear you've formed a pretty strong one of me. But anyway, I probably would've seen it with my own two eyes that you were a very controlling lady who always wants her way."

Phase her out. Move on. Do-not-let-this-girl-take-my-joy, and take me down this negative path. "Listen, Karen, I'm so sorry you had to hear that from Byron. But hopefully, through your association with me here at the Scotch Agency, I'm sure you'll be able to appreciate what I do and find out who I really am." I pointed at the contract. "Please sign on the dotted line."

Thomas
Finally.

It took almost a month after all the recommendations were read and interviews analyzed by three boards, but word finally came that my adoption of Stacey had been granted. I found out from a good friend that there was a bit of skepticism from some of the social workers that I may be too busy to handle the needs of a young girl who'd just lost her mother. So the adoption was granted on a trial basis, with the full rights to be given after a six-month review, which I gladly accepted. I knew I could handle taking care of Stacey. I really wanted to. There was also a hold-up because the authorities had to double-check that Stacey's birth certificate matched with the state's and that she had no other next of kin and no father listed.

I decided to have a small gathering welcoming Stacey. Stacey was as happy as could be and invited seven of her closest friends from school; five girls and two boys. The girls were huddled around the television doing the latest dances during some show called *MTV Raps*. The boys sat uninterested; eating up everything in sight. Clarke was there, as well as Byron and Karen. I gave Clarke a kiss on her cheek after I noticed her glancing at Stacey. Then Byron started in with the questions.

"So, Clarke. How's it feel to have a little sister?"

"I feel like I need to go see my therapist," Clarke said bluntly.

Byron and Karen both chuckled.

The last thing I wanted was my first-born to have a complex about having a new addition to our family. "C'mon, sweetheart. You're joking, right?" I asked her.

"Yeah, I'm joking, Dad. My life is a big joke," she said, then moved a step away from me.

"Good, because this is going to be great. Stacey will be able to see you grow into a beautiful woman and hopefully follow in your footsteps."

Stacey came bouncing into the kitchen. "Thomas?"

I just loved the way she said my name.

"Yes, sweetheart?"

Clarke moved another step away from me.

"The boys have eaten all the cookies. Can we have some more?" Then she turned to Clarke. "And they won't dance with us either. Clarke, can you make them get up and dance with us?"

Clarke uncrossed her arms, took Stacey by the hand, and walked in toward the boys. A few minutes later all of her friends were dancing.

While the party was going on, I asked Karen about her book deal. She seemed very happy about it and so did Byron. She told me that Synthia wasn't all that personable with her. She thought maybe it was the fact that she was Shelly Givens. I hadn't talked to Synthia since she'd called me to tell me about Clarke's grades on her SAT. It was kind of odd talking to her on the phone about our daughter. But we both struggled through it. I could tell Synthia tried her best not to say anything about Susan and I'm really glad she didn't. Synthia had met Susan on numerous occasions and every time they'd seen each other they'd both just smiled and moved on. Susan thought Synthia was so beautiful. One time she'd told me that I was a fool and she was even a bigger one for being on my arm in the presence of my daughter and Synthia. But Susan quickly understood our living arrangements and after a while, as far as I could tell, had become as comfortable as she could with seeing Synthia from time to time.

Byron
This is about respect.

After the party Karen hopped in a cab with me and went back to my apartment. I was relieved Thomas' building had cabs parked out front at the ready because I didn't feel like playing that game where I had to use Karen to hail the cab and then jump out the bushes and jump in with her to get a ride. I hated that with a passion and I didn't care who knew about it. New York seemed to be getting back to its normal self as much as it could after the terrorist attack and I was really enjoying the traffic and the sounds of the horns that moved the city through the night.

"Stacey's a pretty little girl, isn't she?" I asked Karen.

She smiled. "I'm glad Thomas was able to adopt her." Then she burst into a ball of energy. "Oh look, I want to show you something." Karen went inside her purse, pulled out a white eight-and-a-half-by eleven envelope that had been folded over, and took out its contents. "Look, my advance for the book came. I got it right before I met you at the gathering. Sixty thousand dollars! Look at this check, Byron," she squealed. "I've never held this much money in my hand and, damn, it feels so good!"

"Whew! That is a lot of money. I'm so proud of you, Karen." And I was. It was more than I had made in the previous two years.

Karen finally stopped bouncing in the back of the cab. "And the good thing about it—I get forty more when the book is finally published. Things are definitely looking up," she said.

"Yes, they are."

"I can't wait to call my mother and let her know that I won't be asking for any more money. She's not going to believe this."

"So, what're you going to do with it all?"

"First, I'm going to put most of it in some type of savings," Karen said. "Then I'm going to find myself an apartment, pay the rent for at least the next year, and put a little furniture inside. Nothing too dazzling; just something to sit my ass down on."

"Wait a minute. You're moving out?"

Karen smiled at me and gave me one of those fake ass kisses on the cheek that I hate. "Yes? Don't you think it's time I gave you your space back?"

"No. I mean, I wasn't having a problem with you sharing my space, Karen. I've told you time and time again, I like spending time with you."

"But it's not fair to you," she sang.

"Why would you say that? It's what I want. I'm trying to build something here."

Karen took a deep breath. "Byron, you know I only moved in with you because I didn't have anywhere else to go. I didn't have options. Now I have options."

I tried to get a better focus on Karen as the city lights glared inside the cab. "You only moved in with me because your ass was out in the streets?" Karen nodded her head. I kind of felt a sharp bolt go through my body and a temper that I hadn't had to deal with rushed out of my mouth. "You're fucking unbelievable," I told her.

Karen snapped back. "What? What'd you think?"

What did she mean, what did I think? "You knew my intentions. I spelled them out to you on more than one occasion. I thought we were moving in the next direction of our lives and beginning to see if things could work out between us. If you haven't noticed I'm no longer the age where I have time to move in and out of people's lives for the sake of a place to stay or a good fuck every now and then."

"A more permanent relationship?"

"Yes, something stable."

"Okay, Byron, I've been hearing what you've been saying to me."

"But?"

"But I just wasn't feeling it. And now things have finally started to work in my life and I just can't let it all go now; not for the sake of a relationship. Plus, I'm going to need lots of space to write. Most of my writing has been done in the library. But now I'm going to need to spread out more and not only that, write at very odd hours of the day. Writing is difficult."

I looked away from Karen and tried to collect myself. It was like things were slipping away fast. "At least there won't be a problem asking you for all the money I've given you back, since you have it to give," I poured out.

Karen turned her entire body toward me. "Excuse me?"

Since she took that attitude with me, I continued, "All the money I've given you over the last couple of years, I'm going to need it back," I told her.

"You must be out of your mind, Byron."

"No, I'm quite serious. If you haven't noticed, I work at a men's clothing store for close to nothing; along with commission. Now all of a sudden, with much help from you, my once comfortable account that I'd been saving for nearly thirty years is almost completely depleted. My rent is two weeks' late and since I've loaned you money on several occasions that stretches into thousands of dollars, the least you could do is pay it back."

"Thousands of dollars? How do you know it's been thousands?"

"Because I've been keeping track; every last dollar. The big loans and the small ones; every time you'd ask for a hundred here, two hundred there."

"You never said they were loans."

I shook my head at her. She was already letting the money go to her head. "But you did. You've always asked me to *loan* you money."

"How can you loan someone money who was barely making any money at all?"

"I had faith in your writing skills," I told her.

"You never knew I was..."

"So when do you think you can get some money to me?" Just then the cab stopped and the driver turned around.

"That'll be thirteen dollars," he said.

Karen gathered up her things and looked at me. I opened up the cab door and told the driver she was paying.

"Wait... Wait a minute, Byron. All I have is this check!" Karen yelled. The cab driver's eyes widened, then I walked away.

"I don't care," I told her. "Work it out."

Thomas
It's the least I could do.

I'd been so busy with Stacey that I realized I hadn't spoken with Byron in more than two weeks. I'd called him twice and the lines were busy. I thought maybe the phone company was having some fallout from 9-11. After all this time, things still weren't all working. I decided to drop in at the shop.

As soon as I walked through the door I noticed how hard Byron was working. He was helping four different customers at one time. One with a suit, another with an overcoat, the third man with shoes to match a suit, and the fourth with a tie to match his suit and shoes. I looked around until he was finished. By then he'd already spotted me.

"This place is certainly not employee-friendly today," he said with an exhausting smile.

"How's it going? Haven't heard from you so I stopped by before my meeting with the Mayor and his people."

"I'm doin' okay. So you have a meeting with the man himself?"

I told Byron that it wasn't anything really special. As long as I'd been in my job, the Mayor, whomever it may be at the time, always got especially nervous when New Year's Eve rolled around. We had three meetings in a month. All I had to do was smile and tell him a couple of hundred times that there would be no problem on my company's end with the power. The world will once again be proud of his office; even though they didn't have a thing to do with it.

"So, how's Stacey?" Byron asked.

"She's great. Keeps me on my toes just like I expected. Just the other day she asked me to take her over to Rockefeller Center to ice skate." Byron's face was full of surprise. "And I bust my ass more times than I care to remember. But it was fun; it was what she wanted to do." Byron sighed when two more customers strolled in the door. He told them he would be right with them. "You look like you've been working yourself ragged. What gives?"

"Oh, you know me. I need the money. Oh yeah, if you're here about the money I borrowed from you, I have to tell you I haven't been able to save a dime of it yet."

"Don't sweat it. So how's Karen?"

Byron hesitated, but he told me what had happened with her after they'd left Stacey's party. I was surprised that she'd decided to move out and get her own place but, even more, I was blindsided when he told me that he'd been evicted from his place and had been living in the back office of the shop for the last two days.

LATER THAT NIGHT, I WAS ATTEMPTING TO HELP STACEY with her homework. I didn't even remember doing such complex work with Clarke. Since we'd been together I had helped her write a seven-page paper for literature complete with bibliography, start on a science project on the car industry, and we were now in the middle of doing her math.

"Wait a second. This is algebra, isn't it?" I realized as I checked over her work.

Stacey giggled. "Yup. You just now figuring that out, Thomas?"

"But you're only in the fourth grade?"

"Weren't you doing these in the fourth grade, Thomas?"

"No, never. Not until the ninth or tenth," I told her.

"Wow, education back then was scary," she mentioned. Stacey slid over a sheet of paper full of numbers and formulas to me. I looked at them and tried to hide my nervous smile. It had been way too long for me. I didn't even like math in school. Luckily the doorbell rang to save me for the moment. "Oops, someone's at the door," I said so relieved. I put down her work, brushed off my hands, and gladly went to open it. It was Byron.

"Hi, Uncle Byron," Stacey said from the couch.

Byron stood outside the door. He had as much stuff as he could carry on his own. Under his arm was a small tote bag and, sitting behind him, a nice contemporary duffel bag.

"Thomas. Stacey." Byron's voice was lower than usual. His eyes looked around inside. "How's everyone doing?" he said.

Stacey jumped off the couch. "We're fine."

"What are you going to do? Stand out there all night? C'mon in," I told him. I sideswiped Byron to bring in his duffel bag. I noticed Byron hesitate before stepping inside. "Welcome. Make yourself at home. You already know where everything is, so have at it," I let him know.

"Look, I don't know how to thank you, Thomas."

I cut him off. "Don't worry about it. These things happen sometimes. We have more than enough room here. You can have the bedroom down the hall. It has its own bath and everything. You don't have to worry about anything; end of story."

I was happy that I could make the offer to Byron. The plain and simple truth of the matter was I'd never realized how hard it would be to take care of Stacey alone. At the shop I reminded Byron of the time when he'd told me things had changed with kids today. And he was right. It was more difficult than I'd imagined. I was having problems adjusting to a more stringent schedule. Following it to the tee. Having Stacey quickly reminded me why Synthia and I had decided to live together while raising Clarke. In the few weeks that Stacey had been with me, my thoughts had definitely gone out to all the single mothers because it was not easy.

Byron eased a bit. "You two won't even know I'm here. I'll be as quiet as a mouse."

Stacey looked up at him. "Why, Uncle Byron?"

"Just a figure of speech," I told her.

"Uncle Byron?" Stacey's voice squeaked.

"Yes?"

"Do you know anything about algebra because Thomas doesn't and I need to get an 'A' on my homework?"

I said to Stacey, "Hey, I was doing fine." I was lying.

"You were doing fine looking at my handwriting. But I need someone to check it. Go over my problems with me. Get down and dirty," she said.

"Oh, excuse me," I said, right before I patted Byron on his shoulder.

"Sure," Byron said. "I think I can help you out, Stacey. You know back in the day when I was growing up, all the kids would ask me to help them with their algebra. I was what they called the algebra king."

"That's funny, Uncle Byron. But like you say, that was back in the day and today is a new day, so let's go see if you still got it. Because this is new math." Stacey walked over to her workstation.

Byron looked at me and whispered, "New math?"

"Yeah, the new math," I whispered back.

"What's new math, Thomas?"

"I don't know. But I tell you one thing, I couldn't make it out."

Byron blew on his hands, rubbed them together, and walked over to Stacey highly motivated. "Let's see what you got here."

I began to take Byron's bag to his room.

Stacey gave Byron her worksheet and began telling him all about it. Byron was ready to get to work and Stacey interrupted. "Uh, oh...wait a second," she said. "I want to sing my song first."

"Your song?"

"Yeah, it's a song I made up that I sing when I wish my mommy was here with me. I sing it every time I start to miss her."

"You wrote a song, sweetheart?"

Stacey nodded her head and smiled. I stopped when I heard her mention the song in the hallway, dropped Byron's bags, and made my way back out. "Will you sing it with me, Uncle Byron?"

"But I don't know the words," he said.

Stacey went into her folder and pulled out a sheet of paper for him. "Here. These are the words. I've already memorized them."

Potentially Yours

I didn't want to spoil the moment so I stood still; plus I didn't know what else to do. Stacey told Byron to just follow her lead. In her lovely, high-pitched voice that I adored, she began to sing:

When everything seems so bad
When everything makes you sad

When all your favorite clouds are low
When you miss the one you love so

When you can't feel their touch
Just remember the times that were

And when you begin to feel
Cloudy and blue with tears

Remember the one you love
And all the goodness you shared

It's okay, to feel this way
It's okay, to feel this way
It's okay, to feel this way
It's okay—It's okay

Byron began to sing the chorus with Stacey. I liked the song so much I joined them, too, and we sang her song until Stacey was complete.

Synthia
Signed, sealed and delivered.

Sometimes when celebrity books hit the auction block there is a possibility of getting a really big taker. In Lil' Shae's case this was the time. Cloughten & Close, a major publisher who has been in the business for over fifty years, made a preemptive million and a half-dollar offer for Lil' Shae's book just from the press release Barbara sent out on our agency signing her to do the book. There was no need for Karen to hammer out a proposal since we weren't going to auction. All she needed to do was decide what she was going to do with the extra fifty thousand that went to the writer as stated in the contract if Lil' Shae's book deal went over a million. But, I still wanted to see an outline to see which direction she was headed.

Karen and I scheduled a meeting at Justin's, the restaurant owned by Puff Daddy or P. Diddy as some call him; Sean as I knew him. Karen was really big-eyed about the meeting; especially after Sean came over and said hello and congratulated me on making partner at the agency.

"Wow, this is nice," Karen said. She was really amazed at the energy inside.

"Yes it is, and what thrills me about this place, it's owned by such a young brother," I pointed out.

"He's really doing his thing."

We both had a few drinks and dinner. We didn't talk about much. I tried to give Karen some pointers on what made a good celebrity book and ran down some of the other books; especially by rappers who had failed miserably and why. She seemed to soak up my knowledge about the industry and was very eager to do a good job.

"I have to admit, Karen, you really captured just about every avenue of Lil' Shae's life in the outline. But the publisher thinks, and I have to agree with them, that one thing is missing," I let her know.

Karen nodded her head in agreement as she sipped on a Long Island Iced Tea. "Her childhood?"

"Exactly."

"It's exactly what I've tried to tell Lil' Shae. Matter of fact, I wanted to start off in her childhood, but she didn't want to talk about it."

I was interested in this because how could readers really understand her if they don't know how she arrived with the values of life, so I asked Karen to tell me all about their conversation.

"Well, I actually had to start my working outline and work ass backward with Shae. She's so hyped about her new album coming out; it's all she talked about for our first three meetings and it kind of got me in a jam. She babbled off about everything from her clothes or advertising deals with the cosmetic companies and clothing lines to the cover of her new album to why she came up with the new title of it."

"What's it called?"

"*Pussy To Die For*," Karen answered, then chuckled a bit.

"I should've known," I said.

"Well anyway, for days she rambled on and on about every cut on her CD and she's really adamant about making sure everyone knows what's behind her songs' meanings—this time out. I mean she is really hyped about this book and the album being released on the same day, but she's not giving me the background I need."

"I don't really think this has been done before and, if it has, it wasn't done right because no one remembers that I've talked to," I told her.

"Well, after she finished telling me about the last song on the CD, about how she had to sleep with three rappers in a group four different times because they promised to introduce her to their record company, but never made the introduction, she completely shut down."

"Completely?"

"Basically. Especially about anything prior to her becoming a rapper. It's like she only wants to discuss the time period between how she got her record deal to the present. Nothing about her adolescence whatsoever. Another thing, she seems really ready to talk it up when we're alone, but when this guy, I guess he's her boyfriend or whatever, walks in, she just shuts down. I don't know why, but he doesn't say anything. He just sits down, listens, and, one or two times, he has been with a friend or two."

I described the guys to Karen that were with Shae when we met at the café and as far as I could tell, they were the same ones. "Have you mentioned how important her upbringing is to the scheme of the book?" Karen nodded her head. "You're going to have to get next to her then," I suggested. Karen's eyes were questioning. "I'm going to set it up where you get to spend even more time with Shae. Maybe it's something there that she's hiding and doesn't want people to know or something. But the thing about it, everyone will respect her honesty if she just lets it all out and stops hiding so much. Another reason I'm doing this, Clouhten & Close will not want to hear that she doesn't want to discuss her childhood. The money has been delivered and they want her entire life story. Let's try not to make a big deal out of it just yet. Let's try to get her to talk while you're spending time with her."

"She's pretty guarded, but I'll see what I can do," Karen said.

DURING THE NIGHT everyone in the business seemed to patronize Justin's. The atmosphere was stunning and this time, when Karen brought up personal matters, I thought I'd try to stomach them. I realized there was no possible way we could not, but I was determined to still keep her at a distance.

"Did Clarke tell you that I met her for the second time a couple weeks back at her father's?" Karen asked. I nodded my head and took another sip of my margarita, then smiled at a few friends at a table over. Clarke had told me every detail. If Clarke were younger, I would have sworn she was jealous that her father had adopted this child. All she did was talk about her. Thomas seemed to be so happy with her. I tried to explain to Clarke what happens to men when they reach their fifties, but Clarke didn't want to hear what I had to say. She told me my interpretation of the situation was completely wrong. She told me that Thomas really loved this child.

"What a sparkling little girl Stacey is. Have you met her?" Karen wanted to know. I told her no. "She's cute as a button and too smart for her own good. Talking with her is like talking to a full-fledged adult. I think Thomas is exactly what she needs, now that she no longer has her mother."

I wanted Karen to be quiet. I really didn't want to talk about it. Maybe I was as jealous, too, that Thomas had finally decided to *take care* of someone. I tried to "flip the script" as my daughter would say, and I asked Karen, "So, how's Byron?"

She was kind of surprised that I'd asked. "He's okay, I guess." I didn't want to ask, but the margaritas allowed Karen to read my face. "We're not together anymore," she said. Then she read my face again. Damn drinks. "No, I had to tune things down a notch. Concentrate on my writing. Plus, he was getting a little too involved for me. He was becoming a bit too dependent on me," she went on to explain.

Since she was all in my business, I had to let her know my feelings. "Dependent on you? That doesn't sound like Byron. Byron always wanted to give you all that he had; at least that's what he told me." Even though Byron wasn't in my life anymore, I wasn't going to let Karen drag his name in the dirt; even though he'd done it to me with her.

Karen said, "I don't know if you knew this or not but Byron has serious money issues, Synthia."

It was hard for me to tell Karen what I really knew. My conscience was pressing me, but I listened to it without releasing my thoughts. *I'm sure he does have money issues with you hanging on his arm for the last couple of years.* I looked down at my drink. "Yeah, money problems are a big issue nowadays, Karen. The economy is all screwed."

"No, I mean really bad, Synthia. Don't you know he lost his apartment and even had the nerve to ask me for a loan?"

I see he finally asked you for the money he spent on you all these years. My conscience shot out.

"A loan? How could he?" I asked Karen. I think she spotted my sarcasm.

"But there's no way I would ever give him a dime of my money. No way," she said.

I told Karen, "That's understandable; it really is." *My, aren't you selfish.* "So how was your dinner? Good, no?"

Clarke
Christmas just ain't Christmas.

When I walked into the kitchen and noticed my mother in her robe drinking coffee and glaring over another manuscript, it dawned on me that Christmas was two weeks away and the only decoration we had in our place was a lame fruit basket sent to us from the guy who'd redecorated our place named Apolis. I asked her if we were going to decorate and she told me that she planned to make good on her promise to help serve food to the homeless at the missionary on 42nd Street. She even had the nerve to ask me if I wanted to come along.

"No, thanks. I'm spending Christmas with Dad." His place was festive and he'd asked me over to help decorate the tree with Stacey and Byron.

I don't know why she asked me, "And you're going?" She seemed surprised that I was. "I thought you said Stacey was a pest and she gets under your skin?"

"She just takes a little time to get used to. Leon told me it was natural for me to have little patience with her. He says age differences in siblings have that sort of problem." She was kind of stunned when I called her my sibling. "Well she is. She's my father's adopted daughter, right?"

My mother had never told me if she'd wanted more children or not. I do know that she didn't want to have a girl. I know because I overheard her telling my father once when I was seven years old that she wished I would have been a boy. Then she wouldn't have to handle someone who was so much like her. It kind of hurt, but when I asked my father about it, he'd smooth it over like he'd done so many things and told me that my mother just wasn't used to seeing someone so much like herself.

Mom and I talked a few more minutes. I must have given her at least ten reasons why I didn't want to go down to the missionary and feed the homeless. They were basically the same reasons I'd heard her give to the director over the past three or four holidays. *Those people will only think I'm there for the day and won't respect me. I don't feel like fielding any questions about knowing what it's like to be homeless.* But we did agree on one thing. We agreed that we would keep our traditional mother and daughter day-after-Christmas shopping spree date, which suited us both just fine.

"One more thing, Clarke. When will I be getting your decision on what college you'll be attending?"

"New Year's Day," I told her. "I already know where I'm going but just in case I somehow change my mind, I want to give myself a couple more weeks to be sure."

She seemed to be fine with that. I'm glad she was because she probably would have hit the ceiling if I had told her I was going off to Stanford.

I wanted to go to Stanford because Roland, my boyfriend, went to school there and he'd been sending me so many fabulous letters about the freedom he had and all the time we'd be able to spend together. Plus, I wanted to live out West for a while. After growing up in New York City, I thought I might need a change of scenery; especially now that it was evident my parents' split was permanent. I just wanted to move on with *my* life.

I went to the closet to grab my coat.

"So, where are you off to?"

"Mom, I have to find something to wear for the holidays. Just a couple of pieces though. Didn't I tell you Roland was coming home next week?"

"No, it must have slipped your mind," she said. It didn't; I just didn't want to talk to her about him. Even though she liked him more than my father, I didn't want to get all into my personal business about him and hear her sermon about having more than one male friend at my age. "Clarke?"

"Yes?"

"We never did finish talking about the pill issue?"

See, I knew it was coming. I had already taken care of it. "No need to worry about it, Mom. Dad already signed the paperwork for me."

"He did what?"

"He signed for me. I already have a new prescription and everything. Thanks anyway though."

That's when she finally put down her manuscript and came walking toward the door. "Clarke, you shouldn't have done that. Going behind my back wasn't a responsible thing to do. It was our decision together to get you on the pill. Your father had nothing to do with it."

"You know what, Mom? You're absolutely right. But it is my decision if I want to protect myself; not yours. I'll see you later, okay?"

ON CHRISTMAS MORNING I WAS SOUND ASLEEP at my father's when I felt someone crawl into the bed with me. I looked over at the clock and it was exactly five-thirty in the morning.

"Hey, Clarke? Clarke? You sleep? Clarke?"

"Stacey, what are you doin' up so early?"

"Have you forgotten? It's Christmas."

"Oh, yeah, wake me up in another two or three hours, so I can see what Santa brought you."

She began to laugh. "Hey, Clarke? Clarke?"

"What is it, Stacey?"

"You still believe in Santa?"

"Yeah… Don't you?"

"Girl, no. Ain't no Santa Claus. Now get up so we can see what Thomas bought us. He and Byron are already up. I heard them sneaking out presents. They're waiting on us to get up."

I dug into the covers a bit more. "Good, let them wait about two or three more hours. C'mon, you can sleep in here with me." I laid my head back into my pillow and Stacey lay down also. I couldn't fall asleep because I could feel Stacey staring at me. "You're excited, aren't you?"

She whispered. "Yeah, sort of. Aren't you?"

"Yeah, I guess," I said. "C'mon."

IT TOOK US ABOUT TWENTY-FIVE MINUTES to get washed up, then it was out to open the gifts. Daddy was all smiles when he saw me walk into the living room holding Stacey's hand; so was Bryon. I found out that he was excited because while they were waiting on us, my father had invited Byron to a big New Year's Eve bash with a bunch of dignitaries and the greatest fighter ever to step into the ring. Muhammad Ali was scheduled to make an appearance and Byron was a huge fight fan. Stacey told everyone it was my idea to get up so early, which I thought was so funny. Stacey had so many gifts under the tree that it made my head spin. But I understood and thought my father was wonderful doing what he did. He wanted to take her mind off her mother. The only gift I had under the tree was my shopping spree money and it was fine with me. After Stacey opened her gifts she began to sing a song. I didn't know it. But Byron and Daddy sure knew all the words and, after a few times listening to them, I did also.

I WAS BACK HOME BY SIX that evening and barely an hour before Roland would be knocking on my door. As soon as I opened the door in a rush to get ready, Mom came out to greet me.

"Hey, sweetheart," she said. "Did you enjoy yourself at your father's?"

"Yes, it was fine."

"I know it must have been really difficult for you. This being our first Christmas without both of us being there for you."

"Don't worry about it. Life's full of adjustments, right?"

"I guess you're right. So where are you and Roland going tonight?"

I tried to be as direct as possible. I didn't want her to bring up the pill issue again because I was way past it. "Are you sure Roland isn't too old for you, Clarke?"

"C'mon, Mom. Please don't start. Besides, you've known Roland since he was a sophomore in high school."

She eased. "Okay, I guess you're right. Tell me something. What are you doing New Year's Eve?"

"Hanging out with Roland, of course."

"Well, how'd you two like tickets to see Lil' Shae perform live in Times Square on MTV?"

"Lil' Shae? Please, who wouldn't want to?" I asked. That's when my mother brought from her back tickets to the show.

"Here you go, two tickets, VIP section. Merry Christmas, sweetheart," she said.

"How'd you do this?" I gave her a hug before she could answer.

She smiled. "Got them from a writer who signed with the agency to do a book on Lil' Shae. You remember Karen, don't you?"

"Byron's Karen?"

"One and only. You'll be sharing a limo to and from the function with Karen and Lil' Shae herself. I hope you like."

Thomas
Do you want to party?

We arrived at the New Year's Eve bash close to nine-thirty and, as expected, the party was all ready at full throttle. There was a live band as well as a D.J., including what seemed like a wet bar every ten to fifteen steps inside the very top loft of the Marriott Marquis.

As soon as Byron hit the door he was off. He wanted to see the night's festivities up close and personal. He had made up his mind that the New Year was his; and Karen was history. We started the night with a bottle of champagne at the apartment, just after the parents of Stacey's classmate came to pick her up for a sleepover. It looked to be close to seven hundred in attendance; most of them high-level city officials and their guests. We were sitting down at our reserved table taking it all in.

"Now this is what I call a night out," Byron said right before he toasted his glass to me. "And meeting Muhammad just takes the cake!" Byron was right; it didn't get much better.

"Hey, I barely noticed your tux. Look at you, man. You look like a million dollars," I said to Byron.

"Now if I can only get one of these fine women to think that's how much I'm worth because Monday this puppy is going back on the rack at the shop," Byron promised.

"Well, there are plenty to choose from tonight and I'm happy to say that I practically know just about every single lady in attendance."

Byron turned from me and had a delicious smirk on his face. "Well, if that's the case, why don't you tell me who she is?"

I turned to look. It was Debra Payton, daughter of the late Senator Randolf Payton. She had on a black sequinned dress, was caramel brown all over, and had curves in all the right places with delicious brown eyes.

"Wow. Now that's a lady," Byron said.

"She's just back from Africa where she took part in the placement of prestigious historical black colleges and universities in the Motherland."

"My, my. She sure has a way with that dress, doesn't she?" Byron admitted.

"I could introduce you if you like?" I told him.

Byron hesitated before answering me. "That's okay. What am I going to tell her when she asks about my employment? Tell her I sell suits? Women like that want to know how a brother is making ends meet. But she sure is nice to look at."

Somehow it became the perfect time for me. "Byron, I've been meaning to ask you. How do you like your job?"

Byron was still eyeing Ms. Payton. "It's not bad. Wish it paid a little more, but I can sell most people two left shoes."

"You always could. Listen, I was trying to make things happen before Christmas to lift your spirits but things got a little delayed. But, hell, it's the beginning of the New Year, so I guess this is as good a time as any."

"To do what?"

"To offer you a job in one of the departments under me—selling power to some of the largest consumers and businesses that New York City has to offer Con-Ed."

Byron finally took his eyes off Debra when he realized what I'd said. "Are you serious?"

"Of course I am."

"I don't know a thing about selling power, Thomas."

"Don't sweat it. There's a sixteen-week program you'll have to complete. But hey, you get paid for learning a great job."

"Are you serious?" Byron asked again.

"Stop asking me that. Yes. It pays eighty-five grand a year."

"What'd you say?" Byron took a gulp of his drink.

"Eighty-five."

He took the last gulp of his drink and as a barmaid walked past us with a tray of champagne he took the bottle. "That's what I thought you said. Don't I need a degree or something?"

"I say you don't. Now what do you say?"

Byron straightened out his tux and tie. "I say, take me to Ms. Africa and introduce me."

On the way over to the introduction, Byron tapped me on the shoulder twice and asked me the title of his job. I had a feeling he was about to run it into the ground, but it was all good.

Clarke
Rolling with the big dogs.

I was holding Roland's hand in the VIP section of the MTV live broadcast. It was just so hyped. I had my cell phone with me and was calling all my friends every single time a star walked past. Roland took the phone from me after a while because he said I was trippin'. I wasn't though; I was having fun. Plus, after he took the phone from me, guess what he started doing? Calling his boys telling them where he was. We were having such a good time. At first I didn't know how much fun we were going to have. Instead of the limo picking me up at my place, I had it pick me up at Roland's. His mother and father had left earlier in the morning for Connecticut for a party with friends, so it gave us a little time to be together alone. After all, I hadn't seen him since he'd left for school in August.

To be expected, we were all over each other. First it was the hug, then the kiss and, in no time, he had my clothes off and I had his off. We were kissing and panting, but when it came down to actually having sex, I got off his bed and put my clothes on. It really seemed to piss Roland off. It wasn't like I wasn't ready because I was. I was extremely moist and he knew it. But while he was on top of me, I began thinking about what my mother had been so adamant about. While he was lying on top of me, it was like what she was saying to me was true. Roland was upset and I really didn't blame him. He eventually cooled down. I could see how he had matured since being away at college. He didn't argue; maybe he thought later in the night would be the best time to try again. Not trying to force me made me feel special. It was like the three years that we'd claimed each other was kind of worth it. He respected me.

Roland was from a good family. That's one of the reasons my mother and father didn't trip too much about me seeing him. Plus he had gone away to school so it worked out better for them my senior year. They knew I was committed to him, but they didn't like the possibility of me ending up at the same school with him after graduation. We looked good together. Roland was thin, close to five-ten, and he loved to rock blue jean outfits of all colors with Lugz boots. I loved how his ears stuck out just right on his long light-brown face that was covered with stubble over his lips and trimmed perfectly on his chin. I had to set him straight after Destiny's Child walked past us after their performance. He was just smiling and cheesin' at them like I wasn't standing there on his arm. "You betta' watch yourself, boy!" I told him, pushing him in his ribs with my elbow.

"Aww, baby. They were great. You know those are my girls," he said.

"I thought I was your girl?"

"You know you are. I just can't believe your mother came through with the tickets, babe. I have to thank her for sure. Riding in the limo with Lil' Shae was a treat in itself, wasn't it?"

"Sure was. I couldn't have had fun with you not being here, Roland. And don't act like you didn't see Lil' Shae staring at you. I think she thinks you're cute!"

"You think so?"

I moved over to Roland. "Yes, I do," I told him. I was just about to kiss him when Karen walked over to us.

"Hey, guys. Just make yourselves at home and enjoy the show. I'm going back and forth to Shae's dressing room as she gets prepared to take the stage." Karen disappeared into the madness. There were all types of things happening around us. It was like a madhouse. Assistants of every act were making sure their artists and their guests had everything they needed. We moved to a couch next to a monitor that was being fed the show. We could see the stage from our seats.

"Only one thing would make this moment complete," Roland said, then he put his arm around me.

"And what would that be?"

He moved closer to me and in no time we were in a long, loving kiss. After a while we began to hear cheering and I opened one eye and saw us on the monitor. Our kiss was being televised to millions—it was even on the huge screen perched outside of Times Square.

"Ah, New Year's Eve at its best," the host of the MTV special announced.

"I can't believe they did that," I told Roland.

"I'm a star, baby," he said. Then Roland told me he had to go to the little boys room. In a matter of minutes, the guy riding in the limo with us, who was sitting close to Lil' Shae, was sitting next to me. He was wearing an oversized St. Louis Rams football jersey with a white turtleneck sweater underneath, light-brown boots, and a knit cap on his head.

"Whas' up wit ya?" he wanted to know.

I moved away from him a bit. He was all up in my space. "Hi." Then I turned my head to the monitor.

"My name is Outlaw." He smelled like weed.

"Nice to meet you."

"You rode with us over here, right?" I nodded my head at him. "Shae's my girl. I come to this type of shit all the time. Shit don't even faze me anymore," he said. "Matter of fact, I hang out with these niggas anytime I want." Outlaw seemed to be waiting for me to give him a loud reaction or something, but I didn't. I kept my eyes on the monitor and looking—hoping Roland would hurry back. "So you think I could get one of those New Year's Eve kisses you laid on that cat a few minutes ago?"

I couldn't believe this thug had the nerve to ask me for a kiss. "I don't think so. He's my boyfriend," I told him.

He looked at me like I was crazy. "So?"

"So, no," I told him.

Outlaw stood up and looked down at me. "Stupid bitch!" Then he walked away.

Thomas
So far so good.

It had been well over an hour since I'd introduced Byron to Debra and by the look of things Byron had thrown out his bait and Debra was biting. They were conversing, dancing and drinking. Byron seemed to be energized by the news of the offer and I was glad to see he was on the prowl and ready to forget about Karen. I saw Debra step away from Byron for a minute and I thought I would rib him. "You don't waste any time, do you?" I asked him.

"With a woman like that? There's no time to waste. All I need now is to get two full glasses of champagne. I plan on bringing the New Year in with a bang," Byron boasted.

"So it's like that?"

"She asked me what was I doing afterwards."

"Oh, really now?"

"And said something about being relieved to be back home. She said all those months in Africa were full of pressure and she needed to let it all go." Byron smiled.

"Let it go?"

"Let-it-flow." Byron chuckled. "So how's it going for you? I know you're not just looking around. Who will you be holding onto once midnight strikes, my brother?"

I had my hands in my pocket and nodded my head. "There she is. Two o'clock."

"Is that Pam Grier?"

"Could be her twin sister, couldn't she? That's Congresswoman Miea Allen. We've known each other for many years." Congresswoman Allen's ears must have been burning because she looked right at me. I winked at her and she returned my gesture with a smile.

Byron nudged me on the arm. "They don't call you the Cognac Ebony model for nothing, do they?"

Synthia
She calls that music?

I was on the couch enjoying a log in my fireplace, and a glass of wine with Karen's manuscript on my lap. I had been invited to several parties including the one Thomas and Byron were attending, but I had decided to go at it alone. I was comfortable. It dawned on me that I could see Shae's performance on television since it was scheduled for midnight. Maybe I'd get to see my baby girl, too. As soon as I found the channel I heard the announcer say, "Don't touch that dial. Lil' Shae's up next."

When the show returned there was Lil' Shae appearing slowly from under a cloud of white smoke, standing in a black cat suit, breasts hanging out, high-heels, a thong on the outside of her suit and wild glasses that looked like Elton John wore in the eighties. *Poor little baby.* The music was blaring and suddenly Shae was all over the stage strutting her stuff for all to see.

"You hadn't gotten enough of seein' me?...
Guess not—that's why ya bitch got the call from MTV...
That's right, take it all off for me, nigga
when I get done you won't believe how much you finish sin'in'
Take a sip—open wide—let my juice flow
from side to side/head back
tongue out

go' head and lick it yo
this is New Year's Eve
and I came to party tonight
take yo time
ain't no rush cause Lil' Shae goin' to keep you licking til she cum, damn right."

It's not what you think—er'body needs some
It's not what you think—I got to get my freak on
It's not what you think—er'body needs some
It's not what you think—I got to get my cum on

I was left speechless.

Synthia
Not my baby!

I became frantic when I received Roland's phone call minutes after Shae's performance. He called to tell me Clarke was unconscious and he didn't know what was wrong with her. The only thing Roland could tell me was EMS was working on her. He seemed to be in shock. Karen wasn't much better. She was able to tell me that the technicians seemed to think something was in Clarke's system and then she let me know they'd asked her if Clarke was a drug user; of all things. Karen relayed that Clarke's temperature was rising and would not stabilize and the medical workers decided to do as much as they could where they were. They feared the traffic in Times Square wouldn't allow them to get her to a hospital in time. I stayed on the phone with Karen and used my cell to call Thomas since he wasn't far away. I could feel his mouth fall open when I told him the news and he assured me he was on his way to our daughter. When he and Byron arrived, Thomas couldn't believe Clarke's condition. He said she almost didn't look like his baby girl and I could tell that he was in tears. I wanted to be with my daughter. Thomas said her temperature was still sky high and she was having problems breathing. He instructed the emergency squad to transport her to the hospital where our doctors would be awaiting them. I had a neighbor drive me to the hospital. Karen was the first person I saw when I ran into the emergency room.

"Do you mind telling me what the hell is going on with my daughter?"

"Synthia, I don't know what happened," Karen said in a very frantic tone. "Clarke was doing just fine the last time I saw her. Then all of a sudden I came out of Lil' Shae's dressing room, after I heard some commotion, and that's when I found her lying on the floor unable to respond to anything."

Everything was happening much too quickly and I didn't know how frantically my hands were shaking until I couldn't grab onto Karen's hand. Then I saw Thomas. "Where's Clarke, Thomas?"

"Still with the doctors. I haven't heard anything yet and Byron is standing right next to the door trying to find out everything he can."

After thirty minutes, Dr. Lucas appeared from the emergency room and explained to us that Clarke's bloodstream was flowing with an extremely lethal level of the drug ecstasy. He told us that Clarke had not gained consciousness and her temperature was so high that it was threatening her central nervous system. Dr. Lucas was really in a rush to get back to Clarke but I didn't understand how any of this could've happened and wanted to know what could happen to my baby.

"Synthia, I've seen this time and time again. Lately, more times than I care to; especially with this drug coming from Florida in such a rapid pace. This drug called ecstasy is very lethal," the doctor let us know.

"Ecstasy?"

"Your daughter's temperature is one hundred-six degrees and we're doing everything possible to keep it from reaching any higher. In most cases it means fatality." Thomas grabbed my hand when he heard the doctor mention death. "I had a case, not even a month ago, where a young man's temperature rose to one hundred-five degrees and he succumbed to 'burn out' nearly seven hours after we'd achieved getting his temperature down. This is a very serious situation. Right now your daughter is not only fighting for her life, but she's fighting to keep her mental capacity as well; if she succeeds in beating this temperature."

"Can we see her?"

"They're going to move her into ICU soon. I suspect you'll be able to see her then, but only for a short time," he explained.

As soon as the doctor walked away, Thomas said, "Where the hell did Clarke get ecstasy?"

"I don't know, Thomas. Clarke isn't a druggie," I told him. "Drugs are just not her style. You know how she feels about her body."

Thomas walked away from me and right over to Roland who was sitting in a row of chairs with his face buried into his hands. I saw him lift up when Thomas reached him, then I walked over to hear what he had to say.

"Is she going to be okay?" Roland wanted to know. Thomas shrugged his shoulders. "Well, what's wrong with her?"

Thomas said, "Ecstasy. That's what."

"Ecstasy? Clarke doesn't do any X."

"Well, how did it get into her system?"

"I don't know. She was doing fine until just after midnight and I was with her basically the whole night."

"So, Clarke wasn't doing drugs? Did you give it to her, Roland?"

"What? No way. Clarke wouldn't take that shit and I would never give it to her. Are they sure that's what it was?"

When Thomas nodded his head, I could tell Roland was going back to the time Thomas had sat him down in our living room and told him if anything ever happened to Clarke while she was with him, he would literally take his head off. Thomas gave Roland an awful look and it lasted a while. I thought I might have to restrain him. Roland must have felt his fury as well because his eyes were overcome with fear and he stood up and walked away. Byron walked over to me and hesitated before he put his arm around me.

"Clarke's going to be all right, Synthia," he said. "You just watch." Then he attempted to smile.

"You think so?"

"Of course. She's always been a fighter." I thought about his words. "You remember the time she got lost in the city without a dime to her name when she started junior high school?" He chuckled.

"How could I forget. I was beside myself."

"We all were. And we all went separate ways looking for her and when she finally decided to call from 125th Street in Harlem, at damn near eleven o'clock at night, we all knew that girl had courage. Back in those days no one stood by themselves on 125th Street. Hell, they still don't."

"Yeah, she's a survivor," I said. Byron pulled me closer to him. "Damn, you still can make me feel good, Byron. Thanks," I told him.

"Sign of a true friend, don't you think?"

I was kind of embarrassed and kissed him on the cheek.

THE BLUR OF THE night had my head spinning at an incredibly rapid pace. I was sitting in the waiting area next to Byron, peering out at Thomas who was standing next to the window right beside the busy revolving door that seemed to never stop moving as he blew on a steaming cup of coffee. While my mind couldn't stop thinking about my daughter, I remember glancing at Karen a few times as she sat on the couch with her legs crossed and turned to her right closest to Roland who was talking to another lady who I'd never met before.

The inside of the emergency room was packed and I remember I kept asking myself were they doing everything they could for my daughter. There were people sitting around waiting to be seen; some of them in my estimation needed help right away. "Mama, it hurts," a young black boy said. He looked to be about fifteen years old and his face looked as though he'd been beaten to a pulp. His mother told him to shut up and he wouldn't be feeling so bad if he'd stop hanging around with his thuggish friends. She was hopeful that his beating would finally turn him around. I heard Roland tell the lady he was sitting next to that he felt so bad for Clarke. Then Karen reached across for his hand and told him that Clarke would be okay. As soon as Karen asked the lady sitting next to Roland her name I felt Byron clinch my hand, then he dropped his head.

"My name is Debra Payton," the lady said. I began to wonder where I had met her before.

Karen asked her, "Have we met before? You look so familiar."

Debra shot a look over at Byron. "I'm the late Senator Randolf Payton's daughter."

"That must be it," Karen acknowledged. "Do you know Clarke?"

"No, I sure don't, but I'm sure she's a lovely young lady. I spent a beautiful night with Byron at the Marriott Marquis and not knowing how serious she was, I came down here with him when I saw how shaken he was."

I think I looked at Byron the same time Karen and Debra did. Byron smiled at us all, dropped my hand, and took Debra by the hand and walked away.

BY NEW YEAR'S DAY Clarke's temperature had improved somewhat, but she had yet to become coherent. She wasn't responding and her condition had left the doctors feeling as though maybe her temperature had forced her into a "burn out" condition, which practically would have left her that way; maybe for the rest of her life.

Thomas and I went in to have a meeting with Dr. Lucas about Clarke's condition. Dr. Lucas really didn't know what to say to us. He told us that it was just too early to tell. Thomas wanted to bring in a specialist. That's how Thomas had always been. He never liked to feel that there was nothing he could do about a situation. Dr. Lucas told him that no doctor anywhere could tell him what condition Clarke would end up in. I started to cry and asked him what to do. He told me to wait and pray.

Byron
Time couldn't move fast enough.

Two very long dreary weeks had passed since Clarke was admitted into the hospital. Due to the circumstances, I took it upon myself to help out with Stacey because there was no way Thomas could handle everything going on. At times it was hard for me to see Thomas sit at the hospital all day long next to Clarke, then come home without her condition changing. I still had another week until I began my training on my new job and, for some reason, it didn't seem to move me like it did the night Thomas had told me about it. I was just like everyone else; depressed and hoping Clarke would soon be better. I didn't know how long I was going to be required to pick Stacey up from school nor how long it would take me to get to Brooklyn where the training would take place. So I began to take practice runs every morning to Brooklyn and in the afternoon from Brooklyn to the East Side of Manhattan to pick up Stacey.

All the years I'd lived in the city, I'd never enjoyed riding the subways. Cabs were my mode of transportation, but it really pissed me off how over the years cabbies seemed to disregard my business and leave me standing on the street. There was a bright spot in my life though. Debra and I had kept in touch and, at the moment, she was really good for me. We had spent the night together twice and what she'd promised me on New Year's night was terrific. Because of our hectic schedules we found time to meet in a coffee shop quite regularly close to her office.

"Wow, life really changes quickly sometimes," Debra mentioned to me after I was rambling about everything happening in my life at the time.

"You're right about that. Who would have believed this time last year that in about forty-five minutes I'd be on my way to meet a nine-year-old girl to take her home to study for her math test," I said.

"That's so honorable, Byron. You're taking ownership."

"I have to. Stacey means everything to Thomas and he is a good friend. I mean we've had our ups and downs but overall he's the best and so is she."

"You seem to be enjoying this time. Your smile tells me so when you mention Stacey's name."

"Come to think of it, I really am," I told her. And I was. I didn't have any kids of my own after all these years and if I had a daughter, I would have wanted her to be just like Stacey. For some reason I was given a chance to experience what I might never have. Plus, Stacey was scared. She loved Clarke and was really getting to know her. First, her mother being killed and now Clarke in the hospital unconscious; it was one of the reasons Thomas and I thought it was best if she not go see Clarke until she regained consciousness.

"Does Stacey talk much about Clarke and her mother?" Debra wanted to know.

"With her eyes, she's a wanderer. Always in a deep thought about things. I try not to pressure her when I notice she's in a zone, but I always let her know there's nothing to worry about. Maybe she's worried how she fits into the scheme of things now."

"I'd planned on having kids when I was younger," Debra told me.

"Younger? You still have time." I pushed and she seemed to think my statement was funny.

"If that's the case I better get started right now. You say I have time, but how much time is the question."

"What are you now, thirty-two?"

"Thirty-six in two months," she replied.

"The window is still open," I told her. "We're living longer these days."

We exchanged smiles. I thought about how nice it would be if she asked me to get her pregnant and right away. Then I laughed my thought off. *Ain't no damn way that was happening, brother.*

Karen
Breaking ground.

I don't know what I expected, maybe forty-ounce beer bottles and hordes of groupies hanging out at Shae's condo. But I was totally surprised at the layout of her place. It was nice. So nice that it was hard to picture her in it. There were fresh flowers and classy vases everywhere and sprawled all throughout her condo were matching furnishings to each vase. I couldn't tell how many bedrooms she had. But it was at least four because she told me she liked company and one of the rooms was filled with a big screen and those games guys her age loved to spend their time on. She said that room was her man's, Outlaw's, and he hated for anyone to go in there at any time.

Shae and I had spent the entire night working on the manuscript and Shae had invited me to stay. I realized Shae wasn't planning on returning to the couch so we could continue working and I didn't blame her. I was tired also. When Shae disappeared, it was close to three in the afternoon and for hours I flipped through the endless magazine covers she had graced. Shae was a media darling and knew it. The magazines were in full view for any-one to see; all sprawled out on a studded oval-shaped glass table.

"I didn't come out here to talk," Shae said in a very groggy tone. "I just need a glass of water. How come you still up? I thought you were sleepy?"

I told her that I hadn't been to sleep yet and I was looking through her material.

"Fair warning, I don't get up until close to two; maybe three. Then after my workout we can get back to it." I had to take a double-take at Shae. She walked past me and stepped into the hallway wearing a pajama suit with elephant footies. I didn't say anything; just took a mental note. Shae stopped before she disappeared again. "Find anything interesting?"

"Plenty."

"How much of it do you believe?"

"All of it. You wouldn't lie to your fans, would you?"

"For money, fame and fortune? Hell yea. Who wouldn't?"

I heard Shae's slippers begin to move down the hallway on her hardwood floors.

"I wouldn't," I blurted out to her, just loud enough for her to hear me.

I heard her stop, then she sighed and the next thing I knew she was standing in the hallway holding up the wall. "Well, everything isn't a lie, but some of it… Yes, most definitely."

"Like what?"

"For the book?" she asked.

"No, for me. I'd like to know."

"Let's see. I lied like hell about living in the streets for five years. But that was legit because I had to do it—to gain my street credibility. I mean, if you really look at it, it's not that far of a stretch because I did leave home from time to time for two or three days at a clip."

"What else? What else is not totally the truth?"

"Without question the sex. I mean, don't get me wrong. I've done my share of niggas and had my clock properly cleaned; probably more than the next bitch. But not the way I tell it. Not even close."

"So your image is pure sexual fictional imagery?"

"Look, sex sells and I'm a hell of a saleswoman. Those magazine covers in your lap can attest to that."

"Stop me if I get too personal; since this conversation will never end up in the book," I told Shae.

"Don't worry. I have final approval anyway."

I looked down at the magazine cover that was giving me the toughest time all night. It was Shae in a doggy-style position clad in a thong with two shirtless men standing in front of her as though they were waiting their turn to ride. I lifted up the cover. "How much of Shae is really you?"

Shae giggled a bit, then sipped on her bottled water. "You're lucky I like you, Karen. Really lucky. I would have to say thirty-percent of Lil' Shae is me. And that's only because I like to rap. I like being on stage. But the rest of this shit? The working out every day. All these bullshit designer clothes that get sent to me on a daily basis for me to wear. These fuckin' endorsements and movie offers. The damn near pornographic pictures plastered on every bill in the city. That shit is for the birds. But guess what?"

"What's that?" I asked.

"I'm not complaining. Besides, what else am I going to do?"

Before I could answer, Outlaw came into the condo and I could smell the weed and alcohol before he entered the room. He stumbled in and looked at me, then at Shae.

"What the fuck is this?" he asked. "A damn clit rub or something?" He walked up to Shae, took off his jacket, let it fall to the floor, and staggered back into the hallway.

Shae was somewhat apologetic. "Don't mind him, he's..."

"Shae, get your ass back here and give me some pussy," Outlaw demanded. And she disappeared.

Thomas
If anything happens.

When I awoke from my sleep, Synthia was still in her chair next to Clarke's bed in the hospital. The doctors had taken Clarke off forced oxygen, but she still hadn't regained consciousness. It had been weeks and I was beginning to struggle with my faith she would be back with us full strength.

After Dr. Lucas continued with his diagnosis I called in a specialist from California who ran tests on Clarke and told us her recovery was fifty-fifty. Synthia and I hadn't talked much. I don't know; maybe we were somehow blaming each other for Clarke's situation. Clarke had told me about their spat about the birth control pills, but I didn't think that would force her to try drugs. I'd even talked to Leon. He told me that even though Clarke was upset about me leaving the house and my relationship with Susan, then the adoption of Stacey, he would bet everything he owned that she would not take the drug, which really soothed my heart.

Synthia and I basically sat in her room. Silent. Looking at our daughter and her condition. I knew things were wearing on Synthia. She looked like any day she would just fall out from exhaustion. I looked at my watch and it was close to ten in the morning. I'd forgotten to call Stacey and wish her a good day. I decided I would make sure I was home when she got back from school to tell her I loved her and everything would be okay. Synthia's eyes were glued to Clarke's face. There hadn't been a day that she didn't make sure Clarke was looking as normal as possible. She'd brush Clarke's hair in a ponytail, wash her face, and keep her up as much as she could. I walked over to Synthia, tapped her on the shoulder, and asked her to have a cup of tea with me in the cafeteria. Synthia didn't want to leave Clarke's side, so I went down, bought the teas, and came back to the room.

"Sugar?" Synthia asked.

"I wouldn't dare," I told her.

"You still remember."

"Some things you never forget."

"Funny you should say that because out of all the times I've watched Clarke sleep, I never thought I'd be watching her from a hospital bed wondering if she's going to wake up or not."

"She will. Let's keep faith," I said. My words did wonders with my doubts as well.

"But what if she doesn't get any better, Thomas? Have you thought about that?" I didn't want to answer. "What are we going to do, Thomas, if she doesn't? It's been three weeks and we can't continue to live our lives like this. I haven't been home but twice to fill my suitcase with clothes. I've completely put everything on hold at my job without knowing where anything stands and, at the same time, I keep putting off looking into arrangements if I have to take Clarke home with me in her present condition. There are thousands of things that need to be done but I can't get the strength nor the courage to do them all."

I'd always been good at finding the right words to say. It was my job. But this instance I couldn't find one. I took Synthia by the hand and clutched it tight.

"How long before we concede, Thomas? How long?"

"My baby girl isn't a quitter, Synthia. I instilled that in her when she was a little girl. She knows how to fight and I know deep down inside that's what she's doing right now. But you're right. We need to plan; we need to be proactive. Let me handle finding out what steps need to be taken if we decide to take her home or not. Will you let me handle that?"

"But she comes home with me, Thomas. I need to have my baby home with me."

I told Synthia that I wouldn't have it any other way, then convinced her to go out and get some fresh air with me. She was hesitant, but finally she did.

Karen
Let's get down to it.

Shae wasn't lying either. She woke up around two-thirty in the after-noon; by three she was downstairs working out in the gym they had in her building and by four, we were sitting on a stoop in Queens.

"This is where I grew up," Shae let me know. "It wasn't this wild though. When I used to sit out here, there weren't niggas just blatantly sittin' out slingin' dope. When I was coming up, you had to go to the back and cop or go over the main man's house. But now look at it. Seems like everybody selling the shit. I don't see how niggas making money. I saw it coming though when I was younger. I knew it was going to turn out like this. I was sitting right here when the first drug dealer stood right across the street and began selling that shit to anybody who would try it. Muthafuka even tried to get me to smoke that shit when I was eleven years old. When I wouldn't do it, he waited until I was thirteen, then tried to shoot game at me and fuck me." I looked down at my tape recorder. I wanted to make sure I had enough tape for this session because it seemed as though Shae was going to open up a bit more for me. "But I wasn't having that either," Shae said. "He even started buying me shit. But my mother taught me early on about niggas in the street. Taught me their game and how they like to treat women, then fuck over them. I never found out how she knew so much. Especially about these niggas walking around in Queens, being that she grew up in tiny ass Dayton, Ohio. But I guess a nigga is a nigga, huh?"

"So you and your mother were tight?"

"Yes. My mother was the shit around here. I didn't have a father so most of the men, married or not, wanted to fuck my mother and that was every day. One fool would bring groceries one day; the other would come over to fix this or that. Another came over to clean whatever she couldn't reach and she never fucked any of them. She really practiced what she preached." Shae spoke a bit louder over the continuous blast of police cars racing down the street.

"What do you mean she practiced what she preached, Shae?"

"She taught me to have a man for everything; one to fulfill my every need."

"So you started out that way, when you were a teenager?"

"Nope. I was stupid and fell in love. My stupid ass fell in love when I was fourteen with a grown ass man and he turned me the fuck out, point blank."

I realized that I kind of snickered at Shae. I don't know; maybe it was her facial expression or something. I could feel her beginning to trust me. "You mean to tell me you fell in love with a married man at fourteen?"

"His ass was twenty-nine, had two kids, a dog, and was doing his high school sweetheart right along with me and his wife."

"Did you know about all of this when you first started seeing him?"

"No. You know how niggas are. He tricked me. I knew he was too old to be trying to talk to me, but that bastard was persistent. Every time I walked to school he was there. Anytime I went to the store down the block, he was there. He got me used to seeing his ass and the next thing you know, I'm driving around in the car with him and missing school at the same time."

"And you didn't know he was married?" I asked.

"Unh...unh? A young bitch my age? I wasn't checkin' for no stupid shit like that."

"Why not? You didn't think about it or you didn't care?"

"Why should I worry about it? I didn't know anything about no damn marriage. My mother wasn't married so I really didn't have a perception of what that shit meant anyway; except for the stupid shit that was on television and those muthafuckas are always arguing anyway. Look, I've never seen my own father. I couldn't even tell you his name. None of my girlfriends lived with their fathers either."

"So how did you find out about his wife?"

"I found out about his wife and girlfriend in the same damn week. He wanted me to ditch school with him and it was the first time I'd gone over his house. He'd usually just fuck me in his car. Have me sit on him or something like that. It was really fucked because the nigga lived right around the corner and I never knew it until then. I walked into his house about ten in the morning and when I started to look around there were all kinds of kids' toys and shit lying around. I saw a baby crib, a got damn Hot Wheels track, all that shit," Shae remembered.

"So that's when you asked him?"

"Yeah, I asked if he was married or not. And the nigga said he didn't know whose toys they were."

"He didn't know?"

"That's what he said and before I could ask about it again, he grabbed my hand, took me upstairs, and introduced me to my first sex toy and you know the rest."

I told Shae, "No, no I don't."

Shae looked down at my tape recorder. "I don't know if I want all my business out there like that, Karen."

I reached down and turned off the recorder. I wanted to hear what Shae had to say; maybe she would tell me something to make me understand her even more. "So what's holding you back now?"

"Shit's just so personal and does it really matter what happened?" I nodded my head at Shae. "Why?"

"Because, on your records, your lyrics, you always seem to tell people what you've done or had done to you while in the bed. It's you, Shae. It's what you do, right?"

"Yeah, but I never told anyone any of this shit before. When people ask me about my lyrics I tell them they have to decide what's true or not. Sometimes I wish the shit would have never happened because the nigga wasn't about shit anyway."

"I know, like most of them," I shot back.

"You got man problems, girl?"

"Never mind. Shae, you have a real opportunity here; whether you know it or not."

"Opportunity? Opportunity to do what?"

"Help other young girls who are about to go through the same thing you did. You know, they are going to be the main ones reading your book."

"You think so?" Shae's eyes brightened.

"Yes, I do."

Shae looked down at my recorder, then back at me, and then turned the recorder back on. "So what you want to know?"

SHAE TALKED SO LONG that my tape ran out. So I had to revert to my dictation skills. When I asked her why she wanted to do the book, Shae told me that it was because of an article that had appeared on her in *Accent* magazine that had literally ripped her to shreds. It was a letter written to Shae about how bad she was for black women. She felt she was being crucified at the hands of a reporter trying to make herself look good. I had read the article. I must admit it was a bit rough in the way it was done. But the article did hit home on a few points that I thought were valid; particularly since I myself had interviewed Shae. But I could see her point when it came to the magazine using her photo on the cover to attract and sell millions. Shae told me it was character assassination and she hasn't done an interview since, but she would have the last word with her book.

"Are you sure you're getting all this?" Shae wanted to know.

It seemed like the longer she talked the more relieved she became. I have to admit, hearing about the sexual escapades of her married lover even made me realize why she didn't want to talk about growing up.

"Girl, don't worry about it. I'm glad I took shorthand in college. Keep going. I'm right with you," I ensured her.

"Like I was saying, the sex between us was really new for me and the things I did with this man, now that I look back on it, I can truly say it was wild and I was nasty. But I was brainwashed to think that what I was doing all girlfriends did for their man. I'm telling you right now, if I ever have a daughter. I'm going to make sure she stays away from any man who steps to her who isn't her age. I might as well tell this, too. This man was actually the very first guy to go down on me." I was scribbling so fast that I didn't even respond. "One day he was on top of me and then like lightning speed, he was down in-between my legs with his tongue all over my cat like he was eatin' his last fuck'n meal or something."

"What'd you do? How'd you feel?" I asked trying to keep up.

"I was trying to understand what he was doin'. I started to cry after a while because he wouldn't talk to me. He just held my legs open and licked me. When he saw me crying he started to laugh. I told him that I didn't like what he was doing, then he got all mad and shit."

"Mad at you?"

"Yup, said I was nothing but a little ass young girl and I was supposed to be enjoying getting my pussy eaten."

"So he played with your head then?"

"So much that he told me, since I didn't like him eatin' my pussy, get on my knees and suck his dick, and my stupid ass did it, too, for what seemed like hours."

"He treated you as bad as Outlaw did last night, huh?"

Shae looked at me hard. "What do you mean by that?"

"Just the way he talked to you and demanded that you come in his bed and satisfy him."

"Outlaw ain't shit. If you must know, the nigga fell asleep before he could even take my pajamas off. He hates those pajamas and that's why I wore them 'cause I knew how his ass was going to act when he came home." Shae smiled. "But that's my nigga though. For real."

I felt sorry for Shae. I was realizing that she had been a victim and was still being one. "You think having your mother around more would've stopped you from getting involved with this man?"

Shae chuckled a bit. "I don't know because he was so persistent and I had a hard head. When I wanted to do something I just did it and it's a shame; that's about the only thing that hasn't changed about me over the years."

"So would you say the reason for your lyrics being laced with so much sex and promiscuity is because of the relationship with this older man?"

"Maybe. I don't know. Could be a part of it. I think where I grew up and the things that I saw with my own eyes as a little girl helped to develop me more than what that fool was teaching me."

"Tell me about the type of things you saw."

"Some of the things I saw happened right here on this block. You know, I would notice early on how the women would dress to get men to look at them. I used to sit back and watch the girls who weren't dressed so nice and then look at the girls who were. And I'd always notice the nice-looking girls dressed in clothes that made them look like they'd fuck a nigga on a whim. They would always have the guys chasing them."

"And you liked that?"

"Let's just say I noticed. I didn't know what I liked yet. But when I would go over my aunt's house in Brooklyn, which was like twice, sometimes three times a week, because my mother worked late, I'll never forget there was a pack of girls, maybe in high school, college even, who really when I look back at it, made me start thinking about how to treat guys and what to say to them to get what I wanted."

"What part of Brooklyn was this?" I asked.

"Prospect Park. They called themselves the 'The Get Paper Crew.' They always, no matter what time of the day it was, looked fly. Everyone wondered how they got all of the things they had. And one time one of the girls in the crew noticed me eyeballing what they were doing and walked over to me and said, 'Girl, don't let anyone tell you any different; all these niggas want is some pussy or to think they're getting some and you can stay paid for the rest of your life.'"

I was taken back by the words. "She said that to you?"

"Sure did, plain as day," Shae confirmed.

"How old were you?"

"I was around twelve or so, but I remember it like it was just yesterday."

"I can't believe she said something like that."

"Hey, such is life," Shae said. "Speaking of life, how's Synthia's daughter doing?"

Thomas
Just a little talk.

    After being out in the crisp air for a couple of hours and getting a chance to renew her spirit as much as she possibly could under the circumstances, Synthia got an urge for soup and a hot shower before she went back to Clarke's bedside. I suggested we go to my place, since it wasn't far away, and we could pick up soup from my favorite deli on the corner. Then Synthia could shower and make it back to Clarke within the hour. Synthia didn't think twice about the offer. She was feeling upbeat and I have to admit, so was I. We finally *talked* about Clarke's situation and the years we'd spent together with Clarke. We talked as friends, comfortable with the choices we had made thus far in our new lives without each other as a family unit. We were just finishing up the soup.

    "Upbeat question?" I informed Synthia.

    "Sure. Why not?"

    "I'd been meaning to call you weeks before Clarke was hospitalized. But how's your new plan for life working out?"

    "You mean my new direction?" I smiled and nodded my head. "Call it what it is now," Synthia poked.

    "Yeah, that potential thing you were dealing with?"

    "It's fine. I had a good handle on keeping everything that wasn't positive in my life away. And I even had some ideas at work I was trying to incorporate that didn't fly because of the mighty dollar. But I have to say, since my baby has been lying up in that hospital, my outlook on life has been challenging, very challenging. I even think what I was going through may be the reason Clarke is in the hospital."

"No. No way."

"I don't know, Thomas. Clarke was really bummed out about my sudden change of life."

"I know. Believe me, I know. But still."

"She thought my decision to ask you to leave was a little rough, then I decided not to sign for her birth control pills, trying to be the mother that I never was for her and it put tension between us. And, of course, I was really anxious to hear what school she was deciding on. I gave her the tickets to Lil' Shae's show to ease some of the tension. Maybe I put too much pressure on her and it pushed her into taking that crap."

"I refuse to believe Clarke took anything. I believe what the doctor told us. I believe someone slipped her something. Roland said the only thing he saw her drink was a cola. That's it and that's what the test showed was in her system."

"Who would want to do that to her?"

"I can't even begin to wonder. All I know is I want her to get better and she will."

Synthia stood up. "Okay, where's the shower?"

WHILE SYNTHIA SHOWERED I snatched the last potpie out of the freezer and plopped it in the oven for Stacey. For some reason she loved pot pies. I don't know if she didn't like my cooking or not, but every time I asked her what she wanted for dinner her answer was the same. Tonight was supposed to be our night. Byron told me she'd been very sad about Clarke and the whole incident made her think of her mother. He was running out of things to say to her that would convince her things would be okay. I'd just finished setting the table and placing ice cubes in Stacey's cup when I heard Synthia scream from in the shower. The next thing I knew she was standing in the hallway with a towel around her body.

"My eyes feel like they are on fire, Thomas! I have soap in my eyes," she cried. I didn't know what to do other than stand beside her while the soap ran its course.

"Did you rinse your eyes?" I wanted to know.

"No, it only makes it worse," she snapped. "It'll be okay. I just need for it to subside; that's all. Damn it!"

As my hands were afraid to touch Synthia in any way I heard a deep clearing of the throat and turned around. It was Byron who was standing holding Stacey's hand, with a bit of a quirky look on his face as though he'd interrupted something.

"Oh, hi, guys," I said, trying to cover Synthia as best as I could.

"Who is it?" she wanted to know.

"It's Byron and Stacey. Synthia, it's okay."

"Oh my goodness," she mumbled.

"Hey…Synthia," Byron acknowledged while Stacey stood with a smile on her face. They both stood looking at what was going on.

"Byron, can you take Stacey in the kitchen to check on her potpie, please?"

Stacey moved toward me instead and looked up at Synthia. "Hello, my name is Stacey. Are you okay?"

Synthia took the towel off her head and as her hair dropped down to her back she began to use the towel to wipe her eyes. "Yes, I'll be fine. Thank you very much." Synthia was attempting to get her focus back and look at Stacey. "My…don't you look like every bit of my Clarke when she was your age?"

"Thank you. I hear it all the time from Thomas." Stacey blushed.

AFTER SYNTHIA LAID eyes on Stacey there was no way I could tell either of them that Stacey still couldn't go and visit Clarke. It was Stacey's idea after she and Synthia shared a visit. They bonded quickly. I suspect Synthia was amazed at the resemblance to Clarke, and Stacey was so happy to have a woman she could talk to because I was sure she missed her mother. Stacey smiled so huge every time Synthia wrapped her arm around her waist and hugged her. It was therapeutic for them both. After they left to go visit Clarke, I thought I should explain to Byron what he'd walked in on. We weren't long into our conversation when the phone rang. Surprisingly it was Karen and she wanted to speak with Byron. He was quite hesitant before taking her call and the next thing I knew he was getting dressed to meet Karen for dinner.

Synthia
Just couldn't believe my eyes.

I went into the bathroom and cried my eyes out after first seeing Stacey. I could never dream of seeing a little girl who looked so much like Clarke. Seeing Stacey and realizing my daughter was in the hospital unconscious was a bit much, I must say. When I saw Stacey, immediately I knew what Thomas saw in her. I know what kind of man Thomas is; the type of man who likes to fix things. There was no way he was going to let Stacey stray without attempting to find a loving home for her.

Stacey had so much to say on the way back to the hospital. We were riding in a cab and her ability to hold a conversation somewhat stunned me. I kept having to tell myself that I was in the back seat of a cab with a nine-year-old. Before we went into the hospital we sat down on a bench right outside the hospital doors.

"Okay, sweetness, I want you to understand that Clarke's in a deep sleep right now and she won't be able to talk to you."

"I understand." Her voice was so innocent.

"So you'll be okay with it?"

"Yes." Stacey looked at me with glowing eyes. "Maybe I can wake her up?"

"I don't think so, sweetheart. Clarke's not doing so well."

"My mother always told me that when she wasn't feeling well and I held her hand it would always make her feel better," Stacey recalled. "She said I was very special that way. I even wish I could've had the chance to hold her hand before she died. She would still be here with me," she said.

I took Stacey's hand. "I'm sure you did make her feel good, but Clarke's unconscious right now, darling, and the doctors are doing everything they can to get her back to us."

Stacey thought for a second as she took my words in. "C'mon, let's go," she said.

CLARKE'S ROOM SEEMED MUCH DARKER TO ME. I thought it was probably because of the sunlight outside. The break away from Clarke's beside seemed to work out for me, but as I took off my coat and noticed the look on Stacey's face, my motivation sank down a few decibels.

"She just looks like she's sleeping, that's all," Stacey said while she removed her coat.

"It's exactly what she's doing, Stacey." I could feel my voice trail off. "Just sleeping."

"How long will she be sleep?" Stacey asked.

"I don't know. Nobody does."

Stacey walked over to the bed. She was just tall enough to see Clarke and stood for a while thinking as I looked on. "Can I hold her hand?"

"Sure, baby."

Stacey took Clarke by the hand. I could tell she thought it was odd that Clarke's hand felt lifeless. Stacey looked over at me, then back down at Clarke, and said, "I know you told me to never do this again in front of you, Clarke, but it's the only thing I know to do."

Karen
Every single dime.

I was beginning to believe Byron wouldn't show. He was already thirty minutes late. Byron always called if he was going to be late. But then again we weren't together anymore. What a wonderful way to show me that he didn't care about me leaving him; by letting me sit in the diner alone. Payback is always a bitch. I couldn't blame him if he didn't show up. I was direct and matter of fact with him when I'd made my decision to go in another direction, and if he wanted to let me know by having me sit alone, so be it. I was planning on giving him twenty more minutes, then I was on my way to work on my manuscript. There were five more minutes left on my watch when Byron showed.

"Sorry I'm late," he said. His eyes were wandering and he took off his overcoat and asked the waiter for a cup of coffee.

I kind of smiled. I think it was embarrassment for being such an ass. "No problem. Thanks for joining me," I said back.

Byron sighed as though he was very agitated.

"Problem?"

"You know, these damn cabbies are out of control," he said. "Why do you think I can never hail down a fuckin' cab?"

I told him I didn't know.

"You think it's bad luck? Of course that's what it is, because every fuckin' driver in the city couldn't be afraid to pick up a black man. I mean, really, what is the problem?"

"Don't feel bad. Danny Glover had the same problem, remember?"

"I ride in more cabs than freakin' Danny Glover. I've been riding for so long I even remember the faces of these cabbies. Look at me. I'm not wearing any baggy clothes; I'm not fitting any description whatsoever." Byron lifted up his hand, then looked down at them. "Oh hell, what am I talking about? I'm black, reason enough." He smiled a bit when his coffee came. "So how'd you get out here?" he wanted to know.

"Lil' Shae's driver," I answered.

"Oh, lucky you." Byron began pouring cream in his cup. "What? What are you smiling at?"

I didn't tell him. But I was remembering how he always got upset when cabs wouldn't stop for him. We were still for a moment.

"So, what'd you want to see me about?"

I wanted to come straight out with it. "I've been thinking and I owe you an apology."

"About?"

"It just wasn't right, the way I ended our relationship."

"Don't worry about it, Karen. Hey, it's just one of those things that didn't work out; that's all."

"Well, I need to do this for myself, Byron." I didn't know what else to say so I opened up my purse and took out an envelope and slid it over to Byron while he sipped his drink.

He looked down at it. "What's that?"

"All the money you've *loaned* me over the years, with interest." Byron's eyes were skeptical and narrowing as he looked over at me. "This weekend I really learned something about myself, Byron."

"Yeah, what's that?"

"I've learned that how we've been all our lives and where we're from doesn't make it necessarily correct how we treat people that come into our lives." Byron didn't understand anything I was trying to say to him. "Hear me out, okay?"

"I'm listening."

"I spent this weekend with Lil' Shae. And a lot of things that I believed in and have done in the past have done nothing but trickle down to the younger generation without me really paying any attention to what I was doing when I was doing it."

"Okay…" Byron was still confused.

"Meaning, I'm partly responsible for the foul lyrics that erupt out of this girl's mouth. I helped to lay the foundation for what she spits out her mouth."

Byron looked even more perplexed. "Karen, what're you talking about? How can you take that responsibility?"

"Easy. I can take it without any second thoughts because I found out that when this girl was younger, she learned a lot of her doctrine about men from a group of girls."

"I'm following you."

"A group that *I* hung out with in Brooklyn. We were called the 'Get Paper Crew' and we didn't care anything about anybody; especially men who we used to get anything material we needed by any means it took us to get it." I felt so embarrassed; telling Byron about my past. I'd always told him I was a square and didn't hang out much.

"So, you're telling me that you used to sell your body?"

"Now that I look back at it, that's exactly what it was. But I had like *sponsors*, a select group of men that would do things for me. I mean, I wasn't walking around like a ho selling it to men driving in cars or anything. I did have a bit more sense than that but…" I don't know if Byron was looking at me differently all of a sudden, but I sure as hell felt like it. "Yeah, now that I'm older I sold my body for clothes, and anything else I could get. But when I was young I called them sponsors. Hell, everyone around me was doing it."

"Hey, I'm not judging you, Karen. Where is all this coming from?"

"I just wanted to tell you why I'm giving you the money you loaned me, Byron."

Byron picked up the envelope and looked at it before he opened it. "So Lil' Shae's from Brooklyn?"

"She had family there. On the same block that I lived on and when she brought up my old crew, I just knew she was talking about things she more than likely saw me do when I was growing up, but she just doesn't recognize my face."

"And you think her lyrics come from what she saw?"

"Came straight out of her mouth. She adored us, Byron. We were like silent mentors. She watched how we used to walk the block using our bodies as power. Unknowingly, we taught that girl that what was between our legs could get us anything we wanted for money."

"I'm trying to take all this in, Karen, and I still don't know what this has to do with me?"

"I just realized over the years I hadn't let go of it. Hadn't let go of my past and carried a lot of things I learned growing up into my relationship with you. So I'm giving you back the money you loaned me and I hope that you can forgive me for being so foolish, selfish and rude to you."

The envelope was nothing but cash. "Wow. This is really surprising, Karen," Byron said after he'd opened the envelope. "I don't know what to say."

"You don't have to say or do anything. It's what I needed to do. When I think about what Lil' Shae learned from just watching us, it just shows me that I was part of the society that raised her. I'm basically somewhat responsible for her views. Just like I taught Shae, she's teaching millions of little girls the same thing and her ideas are spreading like the plague. Have you seen these girls out here lately?"

While Byron finished his coffee I told him that spending time with Shae had me see the light of sorts. Writing the book had been incredible and had shown me how powerful a tool my medium could be. I really understood Shae. I understood why she said and did the things she did. But I didn't have to like them. Nor agree with them. Shae, in my opinion, was sending out only one message to young girls and that was promiscuity. Byron told me he was impressed with my insight. But I wanted to do more than just speak about it. I wanted Shae to realize what she was doing was wrong and get her to understand how her behavior and lyrics trickle downhill. I just didn't want Shae to look at herself when she's my age and realize the same thing that I had.

"So what're you saying, you want to re-create Lil' Shae?" Byron asked.

"No. I want her to live up to her potential and show how much good she can do," I told him. "Someone needs to do that for her."

"There's that word again," Byron said.

"What's that?"

"Potential. It's the same word Synthia used months ago."

"Imagine that. Scary, huh?"

Synthia
Funny how things seem to work out.

I took Stacey back home at close to nine o'clock in the evening. The entire time we were in Clarke's room I noticed she didn't let go of Clarke's hand. Even when she began to fall asleep, her hand stayed clutched to Clarke. It was so evident that she missed Clarke and I didn't know if she fully realized the condition she was in, but I didn't want to go into any more detail because there was such a calm pleasure on her face.

I asked Thomas if I could help put Stacey to bed. That simple gesture brought back so many wonderful memories. Thomas and I sat around long enough to drink a cup of tea. I told him I wanted to make arrangements to get Clarke back home. The hospital was getting to be a bit too much. I never could stand the smell and the horrendous feeling I'd always get when I ventured down the hallways to and from Clarke's room. I thought maybe if we could get Clarke home she would somehow identify with her surroundings and wake up. Thomas was concerned that having Clarke home would be too much work for me. I told him that being with Stacey for those very few hours taught me a very valuable lesson. If she could move on with her life in such a positive direction after losing her mother, I thought I could at least be just as strong with Clarke back home. I could tell Thomas was getting a little depressed about the whole situation. I hadn't seen him cry since the day Clarke was born. But tears dropped down his face after he told me he was so terrified for Clarke and had never been so frightened in his life. I tried to be strong for him and when he finished talking about how much he missed his baby girl I tried to lighten the load for him and change subjects. I was surprised to find out Byron and Karen had met for dinner. Thomas thought it was interesting also.

THE NEXT MORNING I walked into Clarke's room and bent over and kissed her on the forehead. I felt bad for letting Clarke sleep alone for the first time since she was admitted. I had planned to go home, pick up some fresh clothes, then go back to the hospital, but I sat down for one second next to Stacey and when I awoke it was seven in the morning. I wanted to make it up to Clarke and I told her so. I turned on the television set, raised Clarke's bed up and began to brush her hair while I talked to her about Regis and Kelly. Karen faxed me some pages that she thought I would be interested in reading so I sat next to Clarke, put on my reading glasses and began to read. Close to twelve, Clarke's doctors came in and we talked about all that was needed to take Clarke home. They recommended a nurse and I agreed. All I had to do was talk it over with Thomas to find out what would be the best day to take her home.

I was impressed with the pages Karen had faxed over. Lil' Shae had finally opened up and the information about her formative years was all very informing and entertaining. While I was reading about Lil' Shae's views on living without a father I suddenly stopped and looked into Clarke's bed. *Did Clarke's foot just move?* I quickly dismissed my thoughts because I had made the same mistake at least four other times. I'd even gone so far as to call for the nurse and when she wouldn't tell me what I wanted to hear, I had her bring in the doctor. A few minutes later, again I thought I noticed Clarke's foot move. I set my work down and took off my reading glasses and sat on the edge of my chair. I focused my eyes on Clarke's bed. I swear, I almost went into shock when I saw Clarke's toes move under the cover. I jumped out of my chair holding on to my heart, then clutched Clarke's right hand with both of mine. I said to her, "Clarke? Clarke, sweetheart, can you hear me?" I was very rushed. "Clarke, if you can hear me, baby, squeeze my hand, baby girl. It's all right. Just let Mommy know that you're okay. C'mon now, squeeze my hand, Clarke." It didn't happen as quickly as I would have liked and I started to look over Clarke's body to see any more movements. Suddenly tears began to roll down my face because my daughter had applied pressure to my hand, not once but twice, and I knew right then she was going to be okay.

Clarke
What's all the fuss about, really I'm fine...

After six weeks of nothing but rest and relaxation, I was certain I was ready to get out of my P.J.'s and house shoes and get back to life. I didn't know how many more of Mom and Dad's tests they had planned for me to take to ensure I was ready to resume living my life, but putting on my clothes and taking a cab down to Times Square alone, then making it back after two hours with *only* one hour of shopping time, was quite ridiculous because the spring fashions were already in the windows and looking fabulous.

Actually I couldn't blame them. They were both so happy for me and worried about me at the same time that I don't think they realized how simple they were acting. My entire time away seemed like nothing more than a nap to me. When I awoke Mom had frightened me like she wouldn't believe because she was standing over me with so many tears flowing from her eyes. Then I realized I was in the hospital and I wanted to know what had happened. The first thing that came to mind was that I had been hurt in a terrorist attack because I did remember being at Lil' Shae's performance but I didn't remember her ever finishing. When I found out what had happened to me I didn't want to believe it. When I assured my mother there was no way that I would ever take X, I was so happy to see her glare of possibility turn into a complete and loving smile.

My only saving grace from going completely crazy from all the pampering and doctor visits had been spending time with Stacey and being allowed to do my homework so that I could stay on track for graduation. Stacey would come over to visit and stay hours at a time filling me in on everything that I'd missed and talking to my boyfriend Roland on the phone. She was hysterical. One day after she came over from school we had a chance to talk. Stacey told me she thought I should know that even though I asked her to never take my hand and pray ever again in Arabic, she did anyway, but it was in complete silence. She smiled when I kissed her on the cheek and told her thank you. It was the least I could do. I felt bad when she reminded me of asking her never to pray in Arabic in my presence. I just didn't understand the words she was saying and instead of being the bigger person and trying to find out, I had made her feel isolated and I promised her that I would never do that again. Matter of fact, I told her to pray for me anytime she wanted.

Leon thought it was imperative that he see me before Mom and Dad released me from captivity and let me go back to school. At that point I was just about ready to do anything to get along with my life. We really didn't talk about much. I could tell by the way he was observing me that he was trying to see if all my motor skills and my thought processes were all together. I told him there was no need for the look-over because I was fine and I was back to my normal self. I told him I didn't remember anything past falling out at the show and waking up with Mom crying in my face. That's when Leon began to switch his whole visit from me and began to talk about himself. He shared that he'd made a wager with God as soon as he'd found out I was in the hospital. His wager was that he would stop smoking weed if I recovered and he hadn't had a joint since.

Synthia
Getting back to normal.

I didn't know how much I missed the office until I sat behind my desk underneath a slush pile of queries from writers looking for representation and projects for some of my clients that desperately needed my attention. I was eager to get back to work and very thankful that my daughter had totally recovered. Barbara made me feel special when she peeked in through my office door and welcomed me back for the second time. We sat down and talked about Clarke's whole ordeal for a couple of minutes, then she wanted to make sure Lil' Shae's book was still on track. I ensured her it was.

Barbara mentioned that it seemed as though my desire to do the book on Shae had softened a bit and I admitted it had. Karen was doing a great job, much better than I'd expected, and the best news of all, my daughter was healthy, which put things in a different perspective all together. I must have been motivated because by eleven-thirty, I had already given my secretary the queries I was interested in and had made phone calls to every client who had projects that had been sitting on my desk, which was great because I was due to have a meeting with Karen.

The very first thing Karen did when she sat down in my office was apologize for not being a better chaperone on New Year's Eve for Clarke. I told her not to worry herself because Clarke was okay and I didn't know if she could have stopped what happened anyway. I wanted to talk business; I wanted to know how the book was coming and if there was anything I could do to help move it along.

I was taken aback when Karen said, "I'm a part of Lil' Shae's story, Synthia."

"I don't understand?"

"It's true. Some of the things she says in her music, some of her ideas, have come directly from me," she sputtered.

Karen told me what she meant. I thought her perspective was interesting but needed to know whether or not she felt that what Shae had told her was going to keep her from doing the best possible job.

"No." She was stern. "It makes me want to do my very best and bring out her past so that people can understand how she was molded. There was an article in *Accent* magazine I read. It was so critical of Lil' Shae and she hasn't really been open to the media. She wants her book to help people understand her more in spite of the article that made her out to be nothing but filth. The least I can do is paint the clearest picture for her so her readers will understand her point of view."

After Karen went into detail about the article, I found the writer of the *Accent* article to be quite on point with my views of Shae. I made myself a mental note to pull the article before Karen asked me to keep her past and how she feels it affected Shae between us.

"Listening to Shae these past few weeks has made me realize that she has a lot of potential," Karen admitted. "She's just like any other young woman. She wants love, family and a man to share her life with, but she's misunderstood and through this misunderstanding she's trapped herself in this maze of foul lyrics that I don't really think are her at all."

It was wonderful that Karen was getting so involved in the book. For most of the celebrity books I'd done in the past, the writer almost always couldn't stand the celebrity and felt as though they had to kiss too much ass to get decent information, which made the books dull. But I could see Karen was focused and quite concerned that her actions could have somehow influenced Shae.

Potentially Yours

I was really surprised when she told me she'd given Byron back all the money he'd loaned her over the years. Her information kind of broke the ice between us and we began to talk about things I would only say to Karen with my eyes when I would see her with Byron. We discussed why I'd felt the way I had about her and, to my surprise, she understood and admitted she realized she had used Byron. She didn't really mean to hurt Byron, but it was the doctrine she'd grown up on. *Get as much as you can get from a man and give as little as possible while you're doing it.* Karen realized it was part of her warped street philosophy and she told me that I was a good friend to Byron for trying to make him see right through her.

Lil' Shae
Oh no you didn't?

I was at Club Kitty and about to perform. *Hyped* is the only word to describe how I felt. The club was jam-packed with my fans; my adrenaline had me bouncing off walls until it was my turn to take the stage. I'd been backstage in my dressing room for entirely too long. Outlaw was there with me and mad as hell because I wouldn't give him any. He always did that to me before a show. I don't know if it was the thong and stiletto heels I was going to take the stage in or because he knew all the niggas and most of the girls also were going to be trying to sneak a peek of my nana while I was on stage performing.

I stood just offstage and watched UK, the group I'd brought back to the states with me after hearing them in Europe. They were rocking the crowd just like I expected them to and the performance they were giving enticed me to give a hell of a show. After all, we were performing for true hip-hop heads. The audience loved to be hit with tight lyrics and dope ass beats and I wanted to give them every penny they'd spent to come see us so I rushed back to my dressing room to make some last-minute adjustments after my stage manager told me I had about fifteen minutes before I took the stage. When I got back to my dressing room I could hear Outlaw on the phone.

"Yeah, Ma, I'm backstage right now. Shit is off the chain as usual. Where you at anyway? Gettin' your nails done? Fuck that. Tell them to hurry the fuck up and get your ass here as quick as you can. I didn't give your ass those backstage passes so you could come up in here late. Get here, you heard?" Outlaw closed the cell phone I was paying for, then mumbled to himself. "Bitch, so I can slip some X in your drink, then take you back to Harlem and fuck you 'til I don't want to see your skank ass anymore."

Of course, I was pissed. "What'd you say?"

He looked at me with a crooked smile, wishing he could erase his words. "Shae? You ready for the show, baby?"

"Unh, unh. Don't give me that shit, Outlaw. I want to know what you just said."

"What?"

He knew what I was referring to. He tried to use his voice and cop an attitude.

"About lacing somebody's drink with ecstasy? That's what."

"Oh, that shit? That bitch? I'm just planning to get her a little high; that's all. It's not like you don't know I get high wit' these bitches, Shae. I already told you that."

"But I heard you say, you were going to give her X and fuck her all night long, nigga."

"Naww, naww. I ain't say that shit, Shae. You mistaken, love."

I know what I heard and I had an idea Outlaw was messing around anyway. I knew because a few times when he'd asked me for head it was like my mind was telling me he'd been fuckin' around; especially when it took him forever to come. I wasn't proud of having a man that I knew wasn't being faithful to me. But Outlaw had been with me way before I'd made it in the rap game and I thought it was best to stay with him and take his shit because any of the other niggas that would step to me would more than likely want me for what I do on stage and what I had in my bank account anyway.

"So you're not fuckin' around and putting X on people?" I asked Outlaw.

Outlaw turned his back on me, thought for a second, then walked up to me and got in my face. "Yeah, I'm fuckin' these bitches. So what? What'd you think? You knew anyway, so don't act like you didn't. What the hell am I supposed to do around here while you get on stage and shit? I'm fucking, so what? Now what? Just like your lyrics say. *'When I'm getting' mine/ Got to feel fine/love to be high/ roll it up/ den hit it from behind.'* And that's what-the-fuck-I-do."

"You are a stupid bitch, Outlaw."

"What?" he challenged.

"Don't take this shit so literally." Then it dawned on me. "Hold up? You're the one who slipped that girl a hit of that shit on New Year's Eve?"

"Naww', that shit wasn't me," he tried to say.

"You a damn lie. Don't try to bullshit me, Outlaw. You did it. Didn't you?"

Outlaw looked as though he was caged in. "So what? The bitch was acting all stuck up and shit. So I hit her up. I didn't know the bitch wasn't going to be able to handle the shit."

"Don't you know you almost killed her," I told him.

Outlaw snickered. "I didn't do it. The X did."

"You must really be out your mind. How many girls have you drugged, nigga?"

"I don't know. Fifteen, twenty. I lost count."

I didn't know what to do or say to Outlaw. I know that I didn't like him drugging people to sleep with them. I wanted to punish Outlaw like I was his mother or something. "Give me my cell phone, nigga." I held out my hand.

"What?"

"You heard me. You don't pay the bill on that bitch. Give it to me."

"Shae, you're trippin'."

My hand was still waiting. "No, you are. Shit you're doing is wrong."

Just then my stage manager and Karen walked in.

"Hey, girl. You ready for the show?" Karen asked.

AFTER THE SHOW I didn't want to be bothered with anyone. I was drained. It took so much out of me to smile and give the audience a good show when I had bullshit on my mind. I even missed a couple of steps with my dancers because my mind wasn't clear. I told my bodyguard to stand by the door and not to let anyone in. When I heard him outside the door talking to Karen, I went to the door and let her in. That's when I told her about

Outlaw and his ecstasy. I even told her that he was the one who'd slipped the drug into Synthia's daughter's drink. She wanted to know if I was sure of it. I told her yes, and that Outlaw acted like it meant nothing to him. I couldn't tell if Karen believed me or not because she said it was some heavy shit to blame someone for. I told her I wished I wasn't sure, but I knew what I'd heard my man say.

Synthia
A child will lead them.

"Thank you for taking me shopping, Ms. Synthia," Stacey said, right after we got into a cab for our ride back home.

"You're welcome, sweetheart. It's been such a wonderful day," I told Stacey and it had been. I'd wanted Clarke to join us, but she'd decided to stay home. I suspected she had choosing what college she was going to attend on her mind.

"You think everyone will like my dress for Clarke's party?" Stacey asked.

"Of course, they will. It looks fabulous on you."

"I like to see you smile, Ms. Synthia."

"This isn't the first time you've seen me smile, sweetheart. But, thanks anyway."

"Yes, it is the first time." Stacey pushed. "All the other times your smile was covered with a cloud because Clarke was in the hospital. But now, it's full of sunshine."

I grabbed hold of Stacey's cheeks with my fingers. "You know what?"

"What?"

"It feels good to smile, darling. For a while there I didn't know if I was ever going to be able to smile again."

"Did you lose faith, Ms. Synthia?"

I thought for a second. "Well, I don't know, sweetheart. I think I was becoming very doubtful for Clarke. Things weren't looking too good for her." I took Stacey by the hand. "Listen, you remember the day we went to the hospital and you sat beside Clarke's bed and held her hand?"

"Umm-hmm. I remember."

"Well, that day, I wanted Clarke to awaken with all my heart because of what you told me on the ride over about your mommy always telling you that you made her feel better when you held her hand. While you were holding Clarke's hand, I just sat and watched and hoped she would awaken. But she didn't, so I was a little sad about that. I guess it was my last hope of sorts." Our cab stopped at a red light and the car was silent for a block or two. I looked over at Stacey and she had a wondering smile on her face. "What is it, sweetheart?"

"Remember I told you my mother taught me things to never forget?"

"Yes, I remember."

"Well, one of them was this. She said that God may not always come when you call him, but you best believe He will always be there right on time. And He was for you and Clarke."

The child's wisdom brought a tear to my eye and I took Stacey's hand and placed it in my lap, holding it tight. "You're so right, sweetheart. You're so right."

Synthia
A long time coming.

Valentine's Day was Clarke's day to tell us what college she planned to attend. We'd missed her New Year's Day announcement but I wanted the moment that we had been waiting for all our lives to embellish the love we had for her, so Valentine's Day could not have worked out better.

I took a day off from work and decorated the entire condo with red and white streamers, red hearts and candy along with a huge poster of "Congratulations, Clarke! We Love You!" hanging on the wall. There were at least thirty-five people in attendance and we had an abundance of food and drink. I made sure Clarke's favorite New York style cheesecake was just the way she liked it.

For the first time since I'd told Byron I was moving in another direction with my life, he was at my place and it felt a bit odd as I stood with him and Karen. Karen and I were discussing Lil' Shae's book when Byron walked over to say hello.

"It's really good to see Clarke back on her feet again," Karen mentioned as we all stood in a semi-circle glancing over at Clarke who had just been surprised at the door by her boyfriend Roland.

"It sure is," Byron said before he placed his fork inside the thick cheese-cake on his plate. He didn't even get a chance to put the cake in his mouth before Karen asked him how things were going.

"Pretty good. I started my new job this week and it's really interesting," he told her.

"New job?"

Byron looked at me as though he thought I would have told Karen about the position Thomas had lined up for him since we had been spending so much time together. "I'm with Con-Ed now. In the sales division. Working in one of the departments Thomas is responsible for; among the many other things he does."

Karen looked at me as though I should have told her about Byron's appointment. "I didn't know that," she said, still off guard. "Congratulations."

"Thank you," Byron said back. A few seconds passed and Debra, Byron's date, walked in the door. "If you two will excuse me, my date is here," he said.

"Sure, sure, talk with you later," Karen said.

Karen looked at me with wide eyes, then watched Byron walk to the door to greet Debra. I didn't have an answer for Karen and Thomas crept up behind me.

"Well, here we are." His smile was as wide as a million dollars.

"I'm so excited, Thomas," I told him.

"This is what we've been waiting on for all these years. Finally we get to find out what college our baby girl will be attending. Where does the time go?"

"Do you think the party's a bit much for her, Thomas?"

"No, not at all. She deserves it. We deserve it. We've done a hell of a job; especially you, Synthia," he said.

"Thank you, Thomas. Thank you very much."

Thomas pointed over to Stacey who was sitting on the couch with her two friends from school, Sal and Morgan, and we walked over close enough to hear what they were talking about.

"So, is this a grown-up party?" Sal wanted to know. He had an unusually profound Italian accent to be so young and a head full of hair to go along with his beautiful olive skin.

Stacey shrugged her shoulders. "I guess."

"Everyone's talking. Aren't there any toys?" Morgan wanted to know.

Stacey looked around. "There's not a toy to be found in this place. I don't know what they expect *us* to do?"

"I thought you said this was a party, Stacey?" Sal questioned.

"It is. At least it's supposed to be. That's what they said it was going to be, but I've never been to one like this before, guys."

"I'm glad I'm a kid," Sal said. "Adults are boring."

Shae
Guess who?

I didn't even want to go to the party. But, to be honest, I was lonely at home. I hadn't seen Outlaw in two days. I had his phone so I couldn't call him. But one thing's for sure, having his cell made me realize how much he was really messing around on me. There must have been at least twenty pages from different hos trying to get with him. After about the fifth page I began to think something was really wrong with me because compared to what I had, these skanks didn't have a thing, and it made me feel like maybe I was really doing something wrong to Outlaw to make him treat me so bad.

I went to the party to get away from it all and as soon as I rang the doorbell at Synthia's, I felt like hauling off to run. But I stood there and waited for someone to answer. I didn't remember the name of the guy who answered the door but I knew he'd ridden with us in the limo to my MTV gig. He was with Synthia's daughter. He introduced himself again and I walked in. It was like the whole place became quiet as I stood there. Almost as if I had on one of my costumes. But I didn't. I had on a black dress and was carrying a Chanel bag. Nothing too flashy. I just smiled at all the admiring faces and then my attention went to the couch where a group of little kids were sitting.

"Guys, guys, guys. Don't tell me that's Lil' Shae standing by the door," a black girl with the cutest eyes said. Her diamond stud earrings really brought out her facial features. Then I heard another girl, who seemed to be more comfortable on the couch than the two other kids, let out a scream, then she covered her mouth and I heard her call for Synthia. The little boy was just that. He couldn't take his eyes off me so I winked at him, then he buried his face behind a pillow. Everyone began to laugh and Karen walked over to me.

"Hey, Shae, glad you could make it."

I was still looking around a bit. "Took me a while to make up my mind, Karen, about coming. I don't even know if I can look Synthia in the eyes after finding out what Outlaw did to her daughter. But I wanted to at least show up since she invited me."

"Well, as you can see, Clarke's okay." Karen nodded over to Clarke and I kind of calmed down after seeing that she was all smiles and feeling no pain at all.

"Here comes Synthia," I mumbled to Karen. "Girl, help me get through this," I pleaded to her.

"Hello, Shae. Welcome to my home," Synthia said.

"Thanks for inviting me."

"While I have you two here together, I might as well tell you that I got a call from Warmer Productions and they're interested in optioning the rights to the book."

"A movie?" I wanted to know.

"Yes, all about your life. It's only an option but the money is good, so good that I doubt that it won't be green lit. I'll fill you in later because I'm dying to find out what college my baby girl is going to attend. You two have a good time."

Karen was so excited. "A movie? A movie? Can you believe that?" she asked me. "What's wrong, Shae? You should be glowing for all to see!"

"Karen, a movie? At a time like this in my life? Knowing that my man has been all over the country slipping girls ecstasy? There's no telling how many girls he's messed up for life. This could screw up my life to a point where I look like I knew what was going on the entire time."

SYNTHIA WENT ACROSS THE ROOM and stood right in front of her white baby-grand piano. Her face was so proud and full of joy.

"Can I have everyone's attention, please? Tonight is a very special night that I've been waiting for as long as I can remember because I get to see my baby take another positive step in womanhood." Synthia reached out to Clarke. "Come here, sweetheart, and stand by me for a second." Clarke moved toward Synthia and she was blushing out of this world. Synthia put her arm around Clarke's waist. "Your father and I thought it would be a good idea to express how proud we are of you before you let us all in on what school you've decided to attend and since I have the floor, I'll go first; if it's okay with Thomas?" Thomas held up his glass to Synthia. "Well, sweetheart, I don't know quite what to say except that I'm very proud of you. You've managed to constantly be a good student in school and, at the same time, the best daughter a mother could ever ask for. I know you might think that this little get-together may be a little too much to celebrate a decision concerning your future, but I wanted this moment to be special for you because it's really special to me. It's what every parent dreams of for their child and you've worked so hard to make it come true and I'm really proud that you did. So without any further delay, I just wanted to let you know that I love you and please keep up the good work." Synthia had become teary-eyed and before she could kiss Clarke on the cheek, a tear dropped down the side of her face. Their mother and daughter connection made me think of my mom who I hadn't talked to in a few months. Thomas walked up to the piano and gave both Clarke and Synthia a hug.

"Well, I guess it's my turn and believe me, I don't mind one bit standing here to let my baby girl know how proud I am of her," he said. I could tell that he was very comfortable in speaking in front of people. It was so effortless for him. "A lot of times fathers don't get the chance to be close to their daughters and I'm lucky enough to be a father, who over the years—and even more so recently—have become as close as father and daughter can be. I have to admit a month or two ago I didn't know if we would ever get to this point after Clarke was admitted to the hospital and we didn't know how she would be affected by the awful drug that was found in her system."

At that moment I wanted to leave because I knew who was responsible for what had happened. Karen looked at me and kind of eased my anxiety so I stood still and let his comments pass. "But we were truly blessed that Clarke made it through and it shows what kind of strength she has always had, even as a little girl growing up. I remember telling Synthia, when Clarke was two or three years old, that I sometimes wished that she had been a boy because of the strength she displayed. I thought if she would've been a boy she would have bypassed college and gone straight to the NFL because she was so strong mentally. But I'm glad that she was a girl and has grown up to be a young lady. She's my girl and I'm so thankful that Clarke is strong because her strength pulled her through when we needed it to the most, and I just hope and pray you continue to use your strength and power to knock down every obstacle that may be in your path to success and, at the same time, I want you to know that if you can't, I can, and will be here to help you get it done." Thomas placed his arm around Clarke.

"Okay, the floor is open to anyone else," Synthia said.

A man that I never met moved forward a couple of steps. I looked at Karen and for some reason she couldn't take her eyes off him. Then I heard Thomas say his name: Byron.

"Well, I would just like to say that, Clarke, it's really been a pleasure seeing you grow to this point in your life and I want you to never forget that your parents love you will all their hearts. We all do," he said.

Synthia looked around the room and one of the little girls hopped off the couch and announced in her squeaky voice, "I have something to say."

"Go right ahead, Stacey," Synthia told her.

"I just want to say that I want to grow up to be just like you, Clarke."

"Okay, it's time for the moment we've all been waiting for," Synthia announced. "Sweetheart, are you ready to tell us what school you've decided to attend?"

Clarke seemed to be relieved as shit. The look on her face reminded me of the one I had when I'd dropped out of school. She took a deep breath, looked at her father, then her mother, and over to her boyfriend.

"I am ready like you never could believe, mother," Clarke said. "But first,

I want to thank you, Daddy, Mom, Byron, and Stacey, for your kind words. You all can't believe how good it feels to be surrounded by family and friends and out of that dreaded bed resting. While I was lying in the bed, I kept telling myself that if I pulled through there was nothing in the world that was going to hold me back from everything that I want to accomplish in life. I was allowed to fight through my battle in the hospital and I definitely plan on keeping my words. So, with that in mind, I've decided to attend Brown University next year on their academic scholarship."

Synthia
What a wonderful surprise.

Thomas and I were sitting at the piano after the party. Thomas knew how to play a few tunes. They were soft. I don't know how he learned to play. He'd always loved jazz and he told me that he'd learned to play by ear on an old piano that his family had owned when he was younger. Clarke had gone out with Roland and we didn't really expect her back until later. I'd seen the look on his face; he was devastated that Clarke wouldn't be joining him for college. I looked at Thomas. The pressure of waiting on Clarke's announcement had me exhausted, but excited in a funny kind of way. "We pulled it off," I told him.

"It's fantastic, Synthia. What I've always dreamed of for Clarke has come true. Can you believe she's going to Brown? My little baby is going to Brown. She made a wise choice. I'm proud of her. And I'm proud of you, too," he said.

"Of me?"

"Yes, you. Of what you've accomplished. You've sent my daughter in the right direction and it's something special. Really heartwarming, Synthia."

"Wait a minute. I didn't do all of it on my own. You were here. You've always been here so I think we've both done a great job; married or not."

I realized for the first time in years that Thomas and I were sitting an ear-whisper apart in a happy atmosphere. Stacey was sleeping on the couch nearby. Thomas looked over at her and whispered in my ear, "Thank you."

"You're welcome," I told him.

That's when Thomas turned to me and wrapped his arms around my waist. My eyes moved down to his arms, but I didn't budge. I just looked him in the eyes.

"This feels so good, Synthia," he said.

"What we've accomplished?" I asked him.

"No, this moment."

Thomas put his warm lips on mine. My God, the man hadn't forgotten how to kiss. His kiss was just the same as the first time years ago. I forced myself to pull away from him for a moment. "I guess some things don't need to be discussed, do they?" I said.

"Not at a moment like this," Thomas said. Then he stood up, with me in his arms, and began to carry me back to the bedroom that we'd once shared.

I opened my eyes as we were walking toward my room. "Wait a minute."

"What's the problem?"

"Stacey, she's on the couch," I said.

Thomas looked back at her, then whispered, "She'll be fine."

I kissed Thomas on the cheek. "But she needs another blanket." Thomas put me down and I went into the closet and pulled out an extra blanket. I saw Clarke's old teddy bear sitting alone on the top shelf and walked over and placed them both with Stacey. When I walked back to Thomas, I asked him, "Are you sure you're ready for this?"

He picked me back up. "I'll let you be the judge of that when we're finished."

Thomas
Men talk, too.

"You did what?" Byron asked me. His question was so hard that I thought he'd burned his lips on the morning coffee.

"You heard me. I slept with Synthia last night."

"Get out of here. You and Synthia?"

"That's right."

"Wait a minute. How did this happen?"

"Has it been that long for you, Byron?"

"No, man. What brought all this on, that's what I want to know?"

"It just happened. What can I say? One minute we were talking about Clarke and the next thing you know we were having sex like it was 1979."

"Seventy-nine was a good year," Byron said. "You know what this means, right?"

"No, what?"

"It means you two have issues now," Byron said.

"We've always had issues."

"Yeah, but these are new issues."

"Wait a minute. This was a spur of the moment thing. Something like a congratulatory belly smack for putting Clarke on the right track."

Byron began to laugh. "Oh, that's what we're going to call it?"

"Nothing more," I told him.

"Thomas, there's always more. You know that," Byron said.

"Like what?"

"Like how you're going to look at Synthia the next time you see her. What you're going to say to her."

"It'll be okay. We'll act natural; probably like it never happened."

"C'mon, Thomas, get serious? This wasn't a meet-at-a-bar unexpected pickup. This is Synthia, your ex, the mother of your daughter. Never happened, my ass. You can't take it there, my brother."

"Well, I am," I told him. Synthia needed the night as much as I did and I didn't see any pending issues between us. Byron was just doing what he was used to doing and that's getting way too involved in our business, but it was a laugh because he told me that he would never change. "Trust me, Byron," I told him. "It was just a spur of the moment thing that two consenting adults decided to do."

Byron took a sip of his coffee and picked up the morning paper. "If you say so."

I wanted to drop the subject. "So, what're you doing tonight? You want to tag along to the parent-teacher conference for Stacey? I mean, since you've been helping her with math and all?"

"Sorry, can't. I'm going out with Karen."

"Karen? Again?"

"That's right."

"That's twice in as many weeks."

"I didn't know you were keeping track." Byron smiled.

"It's surprising. That's all."

"Why?"

"Because you two definitely have issues. What's going on?"

"Honestly?"

"Yeah, give it to me straight."

"I don't know, Thomas. I can't figure her out. She either can't believe I've finally gotten a good-paying job and she's positioning herself to strike again or she's genuinely sorry for what she's done in the past."

"Or she doesn't want Debra to slip in the back door," I reminded Byron.

"Exactly. But Synthia seems to think she's turned a new leaf."

"Synthia?"

"Yep, she cornered me at Clarke's party and thinks I should think about giving Karen another chance."

"That's odd. Synthia standing up for Karen?"

"Surprised the hell out of me, too. But she says that maybe she spoke too soon about Karen. Synthia said she finally had a chance to really sit down and talk to her a few times since they've been working on this project together."

"Interesting. So what do you think?"

"About what?"

"About taking her advice."

"I don't know. Maybe if it were under different circumstances."

"Like what?" I asked.

"Like, if I was still broke, working a dead-end ass job, and being *Debraless*, maybe?"

Synthia
Stepping up.

No one knew what the impromptu meeting I'd called was all about. I just got both Karen and Shae to meet me at a swanky eatery off Canal Street. I was sitting alone waiting for them to arrive thinking about how powerfully Thomas had moved me around in the bed when Karen arrived.

"Hello, Synthia," Karen said. I greeted her and Karen took off her overcoat, draped it over a chair, then sat down. I wasn't smiling or anything but I was feeling good and Karen noticed. "What'd you do, get a facial this morning? You're certainly glowing." I shook my head and told her that I really felt good and as Karen picked up her glass of water, she seemed to read me like yesterday's news. "Wait a minute? You got laid, didn't you?"

"What?"

"The same look you have on your face is one that I've been trying to achieve for months. Out with the details."

I felt so much like a young girl. But it was a good feeling. I lowered my voice a bit. "It was Thomas," I told her.

Karen let out a muffled scream. "What?"

"Yes, I slept with Thomas last night," I told her.

"Oh my goodness, do tell, do tell."

"I would never," I told her. "But one thing's for sure, after all these years—that man has still got it. What's that song I loved so much by Aaliyah a while back where the chorus is singing 'rock the boat'? Well, that is exactly what he did. You hear me, girl? He still has it."

"A satisfied customer, no doubt?"

"Yes, indeed."

"That's what I'm talking about. When's the next time you two are going to meet 'cause, girl, my motto is 'drain that thang, girl, drain it.'"

I could tell it had really been a long time for Karen. Her voice was raw and full of compressed estrogen. "No, no, it's not like that at all. It was just…"

"You enjoyed it, didn't you?" she asked.

"Heavens yes; even more than I remember." Thomas had made me feel like every bit of a woman. The way he'd held me close to his body, exploring mine like he'd never touched it before was exactly what I'd needed. It was like he didn't care what happened next; it was special. A completion to a perfect night.

"That's even more reason to make sure it happens again," Karen said. "Good sex these days is very, very rare, Synthia. Take my word for it."

"I'll keep that in mind, Karen." I had no idea how to remove the glow from my face, but I tried because Karen wouldn't stop with her sexual advice until I did. "Now enough about me," I said to her. "I asked you to come a little bit sooner than Shae because I wanted to talk to you about joining ranks with you on how to get Shae to change her ways and do something more positive."

"Don't mind me, Synthia, but deep down inside, I truly thought you just wanted to get this project done and move on with your life. I thought all the interest you were showing was strictly professional."

"I can't lie. At first it was. But you remember when I decided to make a change in my life? Well, since then, things have changed; mainly my attitude. But, I really don't feel as though I've done anything concrete."

"Hey, we've all got to start somewhere, right?"

"You're right. But that's my whole point in wanting to change. When I decided to change my life, I wanted to make noticeable changes and that hasn't happened. Matter of fact, I kind of lost a battle last night because I promised myself that I wouldn't have sporadic, all of a sudden, unplanned sex."

"Girl, never that," Karen said.

"Yes, and I learned my lesson. I should have made that promise after I had gotten some. You know… padded the hormones a bit."

"I hear you," Karen acknowledged. "Get a little leeway."

"Exactly. But I didn't. So that was one I lost. But I was thinking about what I *could* do that was realistic for me and I looked at who has been in my life lately and what has been my biggest gripe since my announcement and it's been Lil' Shae."

"Really?"

"Yes. You don't know this but I never wanted to do this book, Karen. Shae asked me several times before we took her on. I just didn't want to be a part of spreading her lifestyle around. But, I began thinking about what you told me about your past and what you would like to see Shae do with her life. I think we, together, can get this girl to change her ways a bit. Then that's change. We will be doing a service for young girls for generations."

Karen looked at me, surprised. "You're serious about this, aren't you?"

"Of course, I am."

"So how do you propose we reel Ms. Hip Hop in?"

"I don't know. Let me ask you a question first. How do you feel about her lyrics? Not just hers, but all the female rappers because I think we should start there without specifically calling out Shae and blasting her; telling her what's not right with her music. I think that's been done all ready. She needs to see herself in a group of wrongdoers who could do better; like we all are.

"Well, I can say when Tupac and Biggie were alive, I was partial to rap; even with the violence that surrounded it because the beats of the music really moved me. I would especially listen to it while I was working out. Some of their lyrics moved me, but not every one of their songs. I guess you can charge that to how old I was at the time. But here lately, nothing moves me like it used to. I mean, I do have my favorites like Ja Rule who does a great job with the duets with young ladies, and I enjoy the Roots, but besides that, I'm honestly a little sick of all these videos that show nothing but girls shaking their asses and young high school dropouts flaunting cars and jewelry they know they don't have or can afford in the first place."

"Exactly. That's my point. If we can get Shae to see what is really going on and what is really being cemented in the younger generation's minds and the effects of that, then I think I can truly say that on her level of entertainment that a difference has been made that I was a part of." I could see Karen thinking about my comment and I have to admit my mind drifted away at the thought of getting Shae to be a bit more respectful to herself and how she portrays women. "Well, I'm in the mood to change a mindset or two. Are you with me?" I asked Karen.

"Definitely," she answered.

LIL' SHAE ARRIVED THIRTY MINUTES LATER. She told us that she'd just completed a photo shoot for her record company and hadn't taken off the Prada laced negligee sent to her specifically for the cover of her CD. I was just thankful she only came in the café showing the piece from the waist up because I didn't even want to imagine what was beneath the faded jeans she had on. There were two guys with her, as usual. Karen didn't seem too happy to see them and I saw her cut her eyes at them a few times, but they sat three or four tables from us; mainly talking on their cell phones. I noticed Shae's eyes were not as wide as usual and she looked as if she'd taken a beating from the photo shoot. I didn't waste any time telling Shae what we wanted to talk to her about.

"That's the reason for this meeting?" she wanted to know. "I thought it was some good news about the movie deal or something."

"No, no, sweetheart. This could be enormous and tie in very nicely with your book; if you decided to change your style a bit. Let people see that you're not all about raunchy sex and cutoff shorts and, speaking as an older woman, I think it could do wonders for young women who are really confused about who they are right now and get mixed messages from all rappers; not just you."

Shae looked at Karen. "Confused?"

"Look, Shae, I know it's hard for you to completely understand what we're trying to say to you because you've been so successful as a rapper. And, truthfully, I wouldn't have even thought about this or approached you if I didn't think deep down on the inside that you want to better yourself. After all, who doesn't want to better themselves?" I asked her. "It wouldn't be wholesale changes, Shae. But if you could just bring out your more subtle qualities a bit more in your image and music that won't offend women and give young girls thoughts about sexuality and many of these men who look at us through your music, I think it would make a big difference. And I think if you were the first rapper to take a stand, others would follow," I added.

Shae looked around at both of us. "You just can't reinvent me. And when did I hire ya'll asses as my new publicists?"

Karen took a bit of offense to Shae's attitude. "You didn't hire us. Listen, you remember we talked about the state of hip-hop and how some of the music is not very positive; especially for some of the young kids who seem to listen to it as much as they can?"

"I remember," Shae recalled.

"Well, Shae, you fit into that category of rappers. Your music, your lyrics, aren't what we call friendly or very positive."

"And I told you, Karen, why my lyrics are the way they are. You know the reason firsthand; if you've forgotten, go over your notes."

Karen looked at me. I read her face. She was telling me that she was a part of Shae's childhood and partly responsible for what was coming out of her mouth. "You're right, Shae. But it doesn't mean you can't change. You're very talented. You don't have to sell sex to be popular anymore."

"If you haven't noticed, that's what the people want."

"No, they don't," I told her. "You might think that's what everyone wants to hear, but I beg to differ. There was a time and not too long ago, sweetheart, when you would never hear the type of lyrics that come out the mouths of these rappers."

"Synthia, what are you talking about?" Shae asked.

"I'm talking about the music that meant something. Music that made people think about their futures and the possibilities in life. Nowadays lyrics in most of the music being played are nothing but instructions on how to have sex and how to wear a thong correctly for a man while making sure he gives you a tennis bracelet or a Coach bag in exchange for sex."

"I only have one thing to say. My music sells, don't it? In the millions."

"But that doesn't make it right and you're right about the millions because every time you mention how to get sex or what it feels like when you're being sexed, millions of young girls want to experience it for themselves."

"Synthia, tell me something. Do you have something against sex?" Shae asked me point blank.

"No, as a matter of fact, I got laid last night," I let her know. After my comment we all sat around for a few seconds with smiles on our faces.

WE ALL DECIDED TO ORDER SOMETHING TO EAT and the conversation between us was less on Shae and more on a majority of topics that seemed to calm Shae down a bit. While I ate and listened to Shae, I could definitely see the capacity for her growth as an entertainer. She just wasn't completely sure of herself. Didn't have the self-assurance she needed to make a change and I found out why when we were about half-done with our meal. One of the guys she was with stood up from across the cafe.

"Hey, Shae. Are you ready to go yet? What the fuck are you over there doing anyway? You told me that this was a short meeting and you over there eating a fuckin' buffet or some shit. C'mon, we're ready to go."

I was quite embarrassed. Karen looked at me, then over at Shae. "Don't worry about Outlaw. He's trippin'," is all Shae had to say. She didn't even look over in his direction.

"Shae? Shae? Do you hear me talking to you?" he screamed again. I was hoping that a waiter or a manager would come out to silence Outlaw and his mumbling partner sitting next to him, but they were standing as though they were afraid to say anything at all. Then, all of a sudden, Outlaw made his way over to our table.

"Shae? I know you heard me talking to your ass. Look, I'm ready to go. You said this was a short meeting and it looks like to me the meeting is over. Plus, you don't need to be eatin' all this shit no way. C'mon, get your shit and go."

"Outlaw, give me a couple more minutes, okay? I want to finish," Shae said to him.

"Hell no. If you ain't out this door and in my car in five minutes, I'm leaving your ass and I mean it. Fuck this shit," he said. Then he looked at all of us and turned away and walked out the door with his partner.

"I knew I should have brought my driver with me," Shae admitted.

"Who was that, Shae?" I asked her.

"Oh, that was *my man*," she sang.

"Your man?" She nodded her head. "Let me tell you something. If he was your man, a real man, he'd never talk to you like that and particularly never in public, sweetheart."

"Oh, it's all right. He's just tired. He helps me with a lot of things," Shae said, then looked over at Karen.

"If you're referring to the thug I just witnessed standing here, he has a lot to learn."

Shae began to get her coat. "Well, Synthia, all I can say is that's my man and he's good for me. I gotta go," she said.

"Let me tell you one thing, Shae. If a man isn't in his fifties and hasn't experienced anything, believe me, he's not truly a man. And that boy who just walked out of here is not a man. A man has wisdom and is respectful; hopefully one day you'll grow to learn that and maybe one day your music will reflect that."

Thomas
No more Thomas.

Stacey plopped herself in front of the television right before I put her favorite chicken potpie into the stove, and I thought it would be a good time to talk to her about a few things that were on my mind.

"Finished with your homework, baby girl?"

"All finished, Thomas," she said.

I thought for a moment, then placed my potholder on the cabinet and walked over and sat next to her on the couch. Stacey looked at me and smiled, then began watching television again. She told me it was a show called "Zoom," which was too young for her but she watched it anyway just to pass the time.

"You know, Stacey, you don't have to call me Thomas. It's okay if you want to call me Dad, Daddy, Pops or Big Papa. Whatever you young kids say today, it's fine with me."

Stacey giggled. "Big Papa? That's funny. Are you sure?"

"Sure, I'm sure. I would be honored." Stacey's smile faded a bit. "What's wrong, sweetheart?"

"Nothing; just trying to figure out if I want to call you Dad or Big Papa," she said. "You always know the right things to say to me."

"You think so?" I was so happy to hear that come out of Stacey's mouth. I was trying my best to do the very best by her.

"Umm…hmm, I sure do. I was thinking about it at school today," she told me.

"I guess sometimes when things are supposed to happen to us, our minds let us know and it's our responsibility to say what's on our minds, right?" Stacey looked at me as though she didn't understand what I was saying to her. "I have something to tell you," I said to her.

"What is it?"

"Well, about five weeks ago, the authorities found the man who killed your mother, sweetheart." I felt so relieved to let her know what I'd been keeping from everyone because I'd just wanted it to go away. The look in Stacey's eyes after I told her was exactly why I'd been trying to avoid her knowing of the murderer's capture. Stacey's eyes were tight and moisture-filled with as much anger as any child should have to handle. But I wanted to get it all out. Tell her the truth. "The man who killed your mother not only murdered her but he killed seven other women and confessed to all of their murders. He's waived his right to a trial and the state has accepted his guilty plea." It took a while for Stacey to respond. I sat still, wondering if I'd made the right decision or not.

Her voice was low. "So what's all this mean?"

"Well, before his sentencing, the state is going to allow the family members of his victims to address him in court. They've asked if you would like to attend to say a few words to him."

I could see Stacey shiver at the thought. "You mean talk to the man who killed my mother?"

Karen
What's it going to be?

Synthia and I left the café shortly after Shae and were surprised to see her standing outside of the diner looking for Outlaw's car. Synthia went her way and I decided to go along with Shae. She called her driver to pick us up and we had planned to get some work done on the book; even though we were both pretty tired from all the food we'd eaten. I rested on Shae's couch and she was in her room. I managed to get about two hours' sleep before Shae told me that her producers for her new album needed her down at the studio as soon as possible so they could hear her over a tenacious bumping track. This time, Shae had her driver take us to the studio and we had a chance to talk.

"You would think your people wouldn't schedule your appointments so close together, Shae," I said to her from the back of the limo.

"They seem to think I do my best work when I'm stressed the fuck out and shit. They say it brings out the roughness in me."

I thought that was a pretty good point to remember and jotted it down. A lot of Shae's comments were good ones to expand on in my own train of thought to capture her voice. "So, have you decided what you're going to do about Outlaw?"

"Oh, for leaving me stranded earlier? He was just showing out; that's all."

"I'm not talking about that Shae. I mean about the ecstasy."

"No."

"No?"

"I said no. Look, Karen, I was thinking maybe you could do me a favor and forget about it. I mean I wasn't thinking. Outlaw is young, just like Synthia said. He'll stop all that crazy shit soon enough. Plus, Clarke's all right. Things are working out."

"But what he did wasn't right and I don't like the fact that somebody almost died over his silly foolishness. I swear, if he does it again and sends another girl to the hospital, there is no way I could live with myself. I don't see how you could either."

Shae turned to me. "Haven't you ever done anything wrong, Karen?"

"Sure, I have. More than you know. But it didn't involve sending anyone to the hospital or putting them in a life or death situation. I've never done things like that so change directions, okay?" We were quiet until we reached the studio. At least I was; Shae wrote down some quick lyrics and began to practice them. I was surprised; most of them had to do with what she was going through. I even got the impression she was talking about me as she rehearsed.

Thomas
Maybe he was on to something.

I was surprised to see Synthia at my door; all smiles.

"So, what brings you by?" I asked her.

"Have you forgotten that you asked me over for dinner?" she said.

I had and I'd already finished cleaning up the kitchen and placing the leftovers in the refrigerator. Synthia didn't want to eat though. She told me she'd had a big lunch so we sat down on the couch. I don't know if it was because I'd just finished talking to Stacey about her mother's killer or if Byron was right. But it did seem odd seeing Synthia again since our night of passion. I think she felt it, too.

"Thomas, is everything okay?"

"Well, I have a little situation with Stacey," I told her.

"What is it? Where is she, by the way?"

"She's back in her room. She decided to turn in early."

"At seven o'clock? What? Does she want to start wearing makeup already? I remember when Clarke went through that phase."

"No, I told her that her mother's killer confessed to her murder; along with the murders of seven other women."

"Is she okay, Thomas?"

"I guess. I really don't know, Synthia."

"Do you want me to talk to her?"

"No, let her sit a while. Stacey's a hard thinker," I decided. I told Synthia how I'd found out from the DA that the killer had confessed and the reason he said he'd killed Susan was because she was Muslim.

"Was she Muslim, Thomas? I didn't know that."

"No. Well, yes. No, Synthia, she wasn't. She was confused about it. Her parents raised her Muslim and she was fighting between Christianity and the faith she was raised by. She really had some tough questions that she couldn't answer so she went back and forth with religion."

"But she was a hooker, right?"

"Who told you that?" At the same time we said Clarke's name. "Not in the true sense, Synthia. She only did what she did to put Stacey through school. She lived a hard life."

"Well, I'm not judging. Believe me. So did you love her, Thomas?"

I didn't want to answer Synthia because her question fit right into the issue clause that Byron had warned me about. But Synthia had such a look on her face that was demanding an answer. "She made me feel awfully good, Synthia. I mean, she was great. Always smiling, energetic; even though she was kind of hustling to make ends meet. She gave me a renewed feeling; just like the one I felt with you the other night."

Synthia smiled and didn't go any further into my relationship with Susan. I heard the music in Stacey's room and thought maybe she had made her decision to speak to her mother's killer and told Synthia that I thought her telling this man how she really felt about what he did would be good for Stacey.

"So when's the sentencing?" Synthia wanted to know.

"Next week."

"Wow, that's a heavy decision to make for a little girl."

"I know. I must have come up with a thousand reasons each way. But I thought it would be best if I told her the truth."

"I think you did the right thing, Thomas," Synthia assured me. "You've always been truthful. Truthful with me, truthful with Clarke and now, Stacey. It'll work out."

I smiled at her concern.

"What?" Synthia said.

"Just thinking about something Byron said to me."

"About?"

"Some crazy analyzing mess he threw at me."

Synthia looked at me, then hit me across the leg. "You told him, didn't you?"

"Well…I."

"Thomas?"

"Well, yes, I told him. I couldn't help it. It was fantastic."

"You couldn't help it, huh?"

"No, I couldn't."

"So what did Mr. Analyze have to say?"

"He said that it was going to be different talking to you now, now that we'd slept together."

"He said that?"

"Yes."

"Why?"

"I don't know. Because he's Byron I guess."

"That's a good enough reason. He hasn't changed a bit. So what'd you tell him?"

"I told him that he didn't know what he was talking about. Then he started to spill all this 'rig-a-ra-mo' about how we now have issues."

"Issues?"

"Byron seems to think that since we've slept together it opens up old topics for us that we can't deny dealing with."

"Like what?"

"He didn't say specifically. He just said issues."

Synthia was quiet for a moment, then said, "Yeah, Karen kind of thought the same thing."

"Karen? You told Karen?"

"I had to tell someone, Thomas. You can't hide that kind of thing from a woman who is in need of some good loving as much as she is; you should know that. She read it all over my face."

"Good loving, you say?"

"Very much so," Synthia reinforced.

Karen
At least we both understand.

I hadn't been in the studio with Lil' Shae more than a half-hour before I'd thought of calling Byron. We had planned to meet for dinner, but I'd scrapped those plans hours before because I was tired and needed to rest. When he answered the phone, Byron's voice was low and raspy as I remember it to be after we'd made love and he'd fallen into a deep sleep. I was hoping I wasn't disturbing him because, who knows, he could have just finished sleeping with Debra or something. It didn't take him long to get his bearings; even though it was somewhere past two in the morning. I knew that a phone call that time of night was only for one thing; unless there is a definite attachment to a mate. But Byron had been my attachment and I hadn't completely gotten over that fact. When I'd mentioned it to Synthia weeks before, she'd smiled and told me she knew exactly where I was coming from. She even mentioned that she would let Byron know in a very subtle way. Byron wanted to know what I was up to so early in the morning and was surprised when I told him I was at the studio with Shae. I told him that I had to take a break because even though she wasn't performing, her producers and the few groupies they had on their arms were acting like she was live and onstage. I guess it was the best way to get the raw performance Shae was known for, but all the liquor and weed they were smoking was a bit much.

One thing I noticed about Shae. She didn't smoke any of the weed. She did take a sip or two of champagne but it was always after a couple of takes when her throat was dry. The music inside the studio was loud and I didn't like feeling cramped; especially with Outlaw's eyes piercing at me every time I looked up. I told Byron that the whole atmosphere was something I couldn't really get into. I did take notes though and mentioned that everyone in the studio acted like the song they were creating was just so important—like it was going to change the world.

Byron and I talked a bit about how Synthia and I were going to try to get Shae to change her image. He thought it was a really good project and would be huge if we could do it, but he told me he doubted that it could be done. I guess being up so late gave me the courage to ask him about Debra. Byron said they had gone out a few times, but with his new job and her busy schedule they'd been unable to accomplish much. I think if he had already slept with her, knowing Byron, he would have told me that to give me something to think about; so, that I would realize what I had lost. Byron asked me if I had gotten a contact from the weed in the studio when I flat out asked him if he thought we could get back together. I told him no. Why would he ask that? He said because it never had been in my nature to try to make amends. He reminded me that it had always been my style, even after arguments, to forget about everything and move on like they'd never happened. I didn't get offended when Byron asked me if I had an agenda in getting back with him. He was straight up with me and said he thought I wanted to be with him again because of his new job and he would have more than likely jumped at the chance to get back together with me, if the reason I'd left him in the first place wasn't about money. I guess he did have a logical reason of being suspicious of me.

Lil' Shae
Oh hell no?

How many times does a bitch have to twist and turn in her own bed, in her own house after working for damn near twenty-four hours without any z's? That's all I wanted to know after I got back from the studio because you would think people would respect that shit, but evidently they didn't, so I had to get out the bed without a care in the world. I was only wearing a T-shirt. I was tired and I wanted some muthafuckin' peace and that's all there was to it. When I finally made my way through the crowd of thugs assembled in Outlaw's television room, I screamed at the top of my lungs, "Can I ask what the hell is going on in here?"

Outlaw stuck his head out from a cloud of weed smoke, and a light-skinned girl who looked like she was showing him her titties or something smiled at me. There were forty-ounce beer bottles everywhere, niggas sitting on my cream Natuzzi leather sofa, one knocked the hell out on my recliner, and two more lying on their stomachs like eight-year-old boys in front of the big screen on the PlayStaion screaming like two young bitches on Christmas Day.

"Whas' happening, Shae?" Outlaw said. "You coming down to party or what?" Outlaw's eyes were glazed over and he'd just taken another sip from his beer bottle and chuckled at the girl who was trying to not let me know she was showing him her tits.

"I'm tryin' to get some sleep," I told him while I looked around at all those drunk fools up in my place.

Outlaw said, "Naww, baby. We just celebrating your bomb ass studio session tonight. Come on and partake."

With my hands on my hips, I said, "Ya'll celebrating my work?"

"Hell, yeah. It was banging hot. Wasn't it, fellas?" Outlaw said.

Outlaw almost twisted the shit around on me 'cause he knew how much I loved to hear people say they loved my work, but I wasn't having it. I was too damn tired. "Well, I need to get some sleep. I have to work again in a couple of hours. Do you mind taking this somewhere else, anywhere, but here?"

"We're already chillin' here, Ma," Outlaw said. He opened his arms wide to show me how everyone was already comfortable. "I already told my niggas they could crash the night so we can blaze all this shit up."

"Oh, hell no. I tell you what. Ya'll got to go. Straight up."

I don't know what Outlaw was trying to prove, but he tried to set it off with me. "What?" he asked with much attitude. He even had the nerve to push his little ho giving the titty show out the way and stand up and walk over to me.

"You heard me. Your friends have to go," I told him. Outlaw looked at everyone, smiled, picked up a joint off my table and lit it, dismissing every-thing I'd said to him. "Now, Outlaw. Ya'll muthafuckas have to go. Don't make me go in the back and get my muthafuckin' dogs and bring them in here on your asses. Because I will do it. Trust."

"She got dogs, Dog?" I heard this skinny bald-headed fool ask Outlaw.

Outlaw was about to dismiss what I'd said to his crew but I cut his high ass off and told him to shut the fuck up. "Yeah, I got a pit, a Rott and a got damn Cane Corso who will bite a hole in your ass. So get the fuck out, everybody."

Outlaw took another drag and looked at the girl who was face fuckin' him, then tightened his eyes while he looked at me. "Let's roll out to Harlem, niggas. Fuck this," he said.

Potentially Yours

I FELL ASLEEP as soon as my head hit the pillows. I'd never been a heavy sleeper and I was horrified when I realized someone was standing over me in the darkness. My whole body was jarred and it took me a second to gather my thoughts as I looked at the silhouette standing over me that was illuminated from the small light in the electrical socket of my wall.

"Shae, you sleep?" It was Outlaw.

"What the fuck do you think? Yes, got damn it. Why the hell you scare me like that?"

Outlaw didn't answer right back. "I just want to know why you play me in front of my boys like that?"

"You came in here to wake me up to ask me some stupid shit like that, Outlaw?"

"Yup."

"You high, ain't you?"

"Yup."

"And you stupid, too. Leave me alone, okay?"

"I live here, too, don't I?"

"Yeah, for now you do. I'm tired of them fools reaping the rewards of my hard ass work. I don't know them."

"What you mean, for now?"

"Just like I said, nigga." I turned on the light in the room. "Look, Outlaw, I think you should think about packing all your shit and leaving."

"Why?"

"'Cause things are getting serious and you're not handling your business."

"My business?"

"Yeah, your business of being my man. Don't think I didn't see that bitch in my house fuckin' your face. Now I see why you sweating me to get my tits puffed up with gel."

"Oh that? She was just…"

"I ain't tryin to hear it, okay? Plus, the pill you seasoned that girl's drink with is about to come to light and bite you in the ass and when it does, I don't want you up in here. You know how these television stations love to fuck with celebs."

239

"I thought you said you were going to handle that little situation for me?"

"I tried. People don't give a fuck about my fame. You can't always count on that shit to get your black ass out of trouble. The girl you fucked over has people who are very powerful in this city so I suggest you be gone and nowhere to be found when it all comes out or it's goin' to be your ass, 'cause I ain't sticking up for you. So, like I said, you better pack your shit and go."

"Go where?"

"Nigga, I don't know. Go south. Go back to North Carolina."

"North Carolina?"

"You heard me. It's either there or Rikers."

"Fuck that. I'm not going to prison or back home," Outlaw said. "I'm keeping my ass right here."

"Are you really as stupid as you sound, Outlaw?" I turned off the light, fluffed my pillow, and laid my head back down.

"No, I'm straight up serious. Tell me something? Who all knows about this shit? It couldn't be that deep."

"Karen, as far as I know," I told him.

"The bitch writing the book?"

"As far as I know, but I don't know how long she's going to be quiet."

"What the hell does that mean?"

"It means, she thinks the shit you did was foul and she isn't going to let it go."

Clarke
Why are they such dogs?

"I don't think so, Roland." Roland's requests were getting out of hand so I took my ear from the phone, but not so far away that I couldn't hear him. "I know we missed being together the last time you were here, but hello...if you haven't forgotten I was laid up in the hospital fighting for my life. It's called recovery. What? This weekend, no. Absolutely not, I don't want to do that...Yes, you can wait...well you're going to have to. If you don't want to, I'm sure someone at Brown will. Talk to you later."

"Trouble in paradise, baby girl?"

"Daddy, how long have you been standing there?"

"Not long. But long enough to know why you're exhausted right about now."

"Sometimes Roland can be really, really full of himself."

I could tell my father was reflecting on his days. "Yeah, guys are like that when we're young bucks."

"All guys?"

"Truthfully?"

"Yes."

"Pretty much so; especially when it comes to sex. We want what we want, when we want it, which shouldn't be the case."

"Damn shame. Nothing but dogs," I said.

"C'mon, sweetheart. Don't jump on the dog bandwagon when it comes to men, okay? I know I've taught you better than that. Remember some dogs are protective, reliable and you know they're called a man's best friend. So maybe next time *you* should choose a dog with better qualities."

"You're right."

"Some guys just don't realize these things until they're much older."

"Maybe that's the reason Susan was so into you like she was. You were patient with her."

"She told me that all the time."

"Are you over her yet?"

"Let's just say I'm dealing with it. Stacey is a steady reminder and that's a good thing because Susan should never be totally forgotten."

"Good. I admire that. I really do."

"Thanks, baby girl."

"Hopefully, I'll be able to get through tomorrow when Stacey says a few words to Susan's killer. That son-of-a-bitch."

"Oh, that's right. Does she really want to do this?"

"Says she does. And I've been thinking about it and I want her to."

"Why?"

"Because sometimes Stacey becomes distant. She holds back her feelings and I don't really know why. I don't know if it's because she misses her mother terribly or because she wants to know why this man took Susan away from her."

"Do you know what she's going to say?"

"Not a clue. I just told her to say what's on her mind. Don't forget she wants to spend time with you when this is all over with."

"You want me to meet you here?"

"No, I'll bring her over your mother's because Synthia and I are going to a movie."

"A movie?"

"That's right."

"You and Mom?"

"Yep."

"Am I missing something here?"

"Like what?"

"Like something I should know about, being that I'm your daughter."

"Nothing at all, Clarke."

"You would tell me, right?"

"Sure, I would."

"Um, hmm…"

Thomas
Order in the court.

There was no denying I'd begun to have second thoughts—once we'd stepped into the hallways of the court's thick marble floors—about my decision to tell Stacey about the opportunity to address her mother's killer. The enormous attention by the media once we walked into the courtroom was a bit overwhelming. Stacey took me by the hand as soon as she noticed what type of media spectacle it was.

We sat in the second row of the courtroom on the farthest side from the aisle on the righthand side of the court's stand. Synthia sat on one side of Stacey and I on the other side while both holding her hands. Stacey was focused and very quiet. I remember telling myself to hold her hand extra tight when they brought out her mother's killer. There were at least a hundred people in the courtroom, all silent, and finally the guards brought in Matthew with at least ten armed guards surrounding him. Four guards were in a semicircle around him, four more several feet away watching their every move, and two flanked the entrance with rifles drawn.

Matthew was shackled from head to toe and was only able to take small baby steps at a time as he was led to his seat. I looked down at Stacey and she couldn't take her eyes off him. His arms were bound together in a heavy straitjacket and his face was covered with what looked to be a stern potato bag with the eyes and nose cut out. It was dead silence in the courtroom as

the guards dropped Matthew into his chair, and his grunt from his side banging up against the wooden arm of his seat magnified the hollow chamber.

The judge appeared and didn't waste any time beginning the proceedings.
He called on the first family who'd decided to address Matthew and let us
all know that he would be going in alphabetical order, which meant Stacey
would be somewhere in the first tier because she was signed in under my
last name. The first man who approached the bench was the twin brother
of a lady Matthew had slain. We found out from the man, while addressing
Matthew, that she had been one of his first victims. Matthew confessed to
killing her in the Poconos over the Fourth of July weekend nearly three
years ago. He was struck with emotion, but managed through his tears to
tell Matthew what he thought of him and what he had prayed would
happen to him when he finally went to prison. Then there was the sister
of a victim who, after stepping on the stand, broke into tears after calling
Matthew names that didn't get even a movement from him while he sat
under the bag that covered his face. I was jolted when the judge called
Stacey's name and I kissed her on the cheek and told her to be strong as she
made her way to the stand.

Her voice was stern and sweet when the judge addressed her to state her
name and her relationship to Matthew's victim. After the judge gave Stacey
permission to address Matthew, she didn't start right away, which seemed
to be the norm of the family members prior to her. That was when it
dawned on me that Stacey was wearing the pair of diamond earrings I'd
bought for Susan and her head was wrapped in a small tight headwrap that
made her look so much like her mother. Stacey sat still and seemed to look
Matthew over. I followed her eyes and she was bewildered and confused,
then turned to the judge.

"Judge?"

"Yes, sweetheart," he said.

"Is there a reason he gets to sit there with that bag over his face?"

The judge looked down at Matthew who sat alone without any legal
representation because it was part of his deal,then at the two guards that
now surrounded him, then at the bailiff. The judge shrugged his shoulders.
"It's his choice," he said.

Stacey continued to look at Matthew and analyze the situation. "He has a choice, after killing so many people?"

"Yes, I guess," the judge said. "It's the law."

Stacey looked at me briefly, still confused, then back at Matthew. "What are my choices?"

The judge said, "I don't know what you mean."

"Don't I have a choice to look at the man who killed my mother? Don't I get to look at his face?"

The judge looked around the courtroom at all the eyes, waiting for his answer, then down to the killer. "Bailiffs, take that dreaded bag off his head," he ordered sternly. Everyone watched as they untied the bag and swiftly pulled it from Matthew's face. Stacey looked as though she was frozen, finally seeing Matthew. He looked as horrible as the crimes he committed. His eyebrows were frazzled in the opposite direction, his hair in chaos standing in the direction of the sky from when the bag was pulled from his head, and his eyes were cold and inhumane as a small embarrassed smile tried to part from his lips.

"Do you have anything to say, darling?" the judge asked.

Stacey nodded her head and seemed to make sure she had Matthew's undivided attention. Once she was sure his eyes were on her, she locked onto them like a cruise missile without blinking one time. "Mr. Killer, my mother told me to always look the person I'm talking to in the eye. My mother's name was Susan and when my father told me that you had confessed to killing my mother, I didn't know what to think or how I should feel. At first when I saw you being dragged in here with your arms tied together and your legs barely able to move, I felt sorry for you. I don't know why. Maybe because I don't think anybody should be chained up like you are. But after hearing about all the things you have taken from everyone, I'm sorry to say this, Mr., but I'm glad to see you sitting with those chains around your body so that you can't hurt anyone else. I don't know what it is but something inside of me wants those chains to hurt you so bad, not because of what you did, but because you thought you could come inside here and hide your face behind that bag and not really feel what everyone has to say to you. My father told me the reason you told the police you killed my mother was because you said she was carrying around in her purse the Holy Qur'an and you thought she was Muslim and, for some reason, in your crazy mind, you feel that all Muslims should be dead because of the terrorist attacks that happened in our city." Stacey reached up underneath the wrap covering her head and pulled down a blue veil that completely covered her face. "So how do you like me now? Normally this veil is worn out of respect in the Muslim faith but today I am wearing it to block your evil spirit and to make you realize how wrong you were for taking my mother from me. You took my mother from me and for that I will never forgive you. I know that God says we must forgive. And I know that it's difficult to do. But I will never forgive you for taking my mother from me. Sometimes I would sneak and watch television at night and see people like you, killing people, and I always thought to myself things like that don't really happen because my mother always taught me television was only entertainment. I want to know what gave you the right to decide that my mother should have lived or died? Did you not know that you had a problem, that you were sick or something long before you took my mother's life? I think you knew, I know you knew, and for that, for taking my mother's life, I will never forgive you."

When I realized Stacey was becoming upset I wanted to go up to the stand and take her down. I think I even moved forward, but Synthia grabbed me by the hand. I didn't like the hurt that was so present in Stacey's voice. It was so hard to just sit and not do anything at all. When Matthew continued to sit without any emotion at all, it seemed to infuriate my baby girl even more.

"Everything you have done can't be forgotten because I had so much that my mother and I needed to do together. I will never forgive you, for not letting my mother see how I have grown over the past six months. I will never forgive you for not allowing my mother to enjoy my next birthday and this upcoming summer with me that we planned to spend together. I will never forgive you for taking away my mother's chance to see me become a woman nor will I forgive you for taking away her chance to see me have kids or my kids ever seeing or touching her." Stacey began pointing her finger at him. "If you think your cold stares are going to frighten me, they're not. My mother told me to never let anyone who has hurt me see me cry and I have done that, but I want you to always remember that I will never forgive you, Sir, never".

LATER THE SAME NIGHT Synthia and I were sitting on the couch at my place.

"You okay?" Synthia asked.

"No, I can't even lie to you about it. Hope I didn't spoil the movie for you."

"I wasn't watching it either. How could anyone enjoy anything after what we witnessed today?"

"I felt so bad for Stacey. Do you think I did the right thing, by telling her about the chance to address that son-of-a-bitch?"

"Yes, Thomas. Stacey is strong. I always knew she was strong but she's much stronger than I'd imagined. Shit, she stood up to that bastard like an adult; she didn't even cry. I tell you what though. I cried my eyes out, the lady next to me cried, and her husband right along with us, but that little girl hung onto her mother's words and didn't shed one got damn tear. Not one," Synthia said as she wiped her eyes.

"She's something, isn't she?" I acknowledged.

"A diamond. A perfect diamond."

"I just hope she's okay," I admitted.

"I'm sure she is. She's with Clarke; just like she wanted to be. She'll be fine."

Clarke
Anytime you want to talk.

I was well aware of Stacey's trying day and we were doing exactly what she told me she wanted to do. Sitting on my bed among all of my pillows, watching television and eating everything imaginable.

"It doesn't matter to me, Stacey, but are you going to be quiet all night long?" I asked her.

"Who me?"

"Yes, you." I moved closer to her and took my nose and rubbed it on Stacey's. "I'm just relaxing; that's all," Stacey told me.

"Well, I know you had a very hectic day and if you just want to sit here and watch television, it's fine with me."

"I'm okay," Stacey admitted.

"Are you sure?"

"Yes, because I had a chance to say what was on my mind."

"Good for you. Now it's time to move on the best you can and, don't forget, I'll be there for you anytime you want to talk, okay?"

"Clarke? Who's Leon? What does he do?"

"Oh, Leon?"

"Umm…hmm?"

"He's my cousin, but more importantly he's my therapist. He helps me get over things that I'm going through at any given moment."

"Like what?"

"Like when my mother and father told me they were getting a divorce when I was younger. He talked to me about it and helped me get through it."

"Was it easy talking to him?"

"Truthfully, not at first. But I began to trust him and when I did, things actually began to feel a whole lot better."

"What do you think? Maybe I should talk to him sometime."

"You?"

"Yeah, have someone to talk to when you go off to college. What's he like?"

"Well, he's really funny and has a way of putting things in perspective like you wouldn't believe."

"Do you think he'll be able to help me forgive the man who killed my mother?"

"If that's what you want to do, I'm sure he can try."

I didn't want to ask Stacey why she wanted to forgive the asshole who'd killed her mother. I wanted to know, but I didn't want to ask. But I think she wanted me to and when I didn't, she offered the information.

"We should forgive people, right? That's what they tell us in school," Stacey said.

"Yeah, I guess."

"You know this morning, I told the man who killed my mommy that I would never forgive him," Stacey said, reflecting.

"I can understand your reasoning," I told her.

"But my mother always told me to believe in what God says and God says forgive." I was at a loss for words and didn't know what to say. "And that's what I want to do, Clarke; even though I told that man I never will." Stacey thought for a second, then said, "Does Leon let you cry if you have to?"

"Sure, sweetheart. I've shed many tears with him."

"Good, but I want you to hold me now because I feel like crying."

"No problem at all. Just like the song you made up, it's okay, it's okay," I told her, right before I reached out to her and let her put her head on my shoulder.

Synthia
So very unexpected.

The somberness of the day's activities probably put Thomas and me in the mood we were in. All night I could feel him wondering and I spent most of my time sitting on the couch next to him trying to figure out what he was thinking about. I never asked and didn't complain when he turned to me and kissed me. When I realized we were about to make love on his couch, I didn't even bother to ask when Byron would be home. Our minds were not worried about someone catching us. I know I felt like a college girl holding on to her man, not giving a damn what happened next. When we finished, we were sitting under a blanket and the room was illuminated by the light coming from the television set. Thomas turned to me and asked what we were doing. I knew what he meant as soon as he said it. I had thought about his question the night before. I thought our new *relationship* was electrifying. I can't lie, I was struggling with it because I thought of it as being an accumulation of lust and all the missed opportunities we'd had to make love—all the years we'd lived together and were divorced. I also thought our feelings could somehow be genuine and something renewed. We talked about how, after all this time, things seemed so much better between us. Thomas stumbled a bit before letting the words flow from his mouth, but he wanted to know if maybe this was our second wind of sorts.

Outlaw
I got this.

After my episode with Shae and long ass after-party with my peeps in Harlem, all I wanted to do was get high and think about what I was going to do about my little situation. The only people left from the party were two freaks that I had strung out on X and my partner J.B.

"Damn, Outlaw, pass that shit, nigga. You hittin' that blunt like you an addict or some shit," J.B. yelled over to me while he lay on the mattress I had sprawled on the floor.

My room that I'd rented in Harlem was in a brownstone. It was most definitely a place where I could get away from Shae's ass when she wanted to trip. The brownstone had lots of rooms in it and was like an open house. Most of the peeps that rented there were never at home and it was damn near like the whole fuckin' place was mine.

"So what the hell is wrong with you, nigga?" J.B. wanted to know. Muthafucka always wanted to be up in my business. He was the first nigga I'd met when I came from Charlotte and I thought he was cool 'cause he had some rappin' skills that I'd peeped down on 125th when Shae was in the hood getting her hair did.

"I just got a lot of shit on my mind, nigga," I told him.

"Like what? What the hell you got on your mind, with the life you livin'?"

"With the life I'm living? What you mean by that shit, yo'?"

"Like I said. Your life, nigga. Shacking with the number one female rapper in the business, fuckin' her, living her lifestyle. Like I said, what the hell you got on your mind 'cause the way I see it, I know a lot of niggas who would love to be in your shoes."

"I'm just on fire 'cause of the stupid shit Shae threw in my face."

"Last night?"

"Yeah."

"Oh, man, she was heated when she came in the room. What's up wit' dat?"

"That's what I'm saying, yo'. She was buggin' about niggas being over so late, talking 'bout I should just move back to North Carolina."

"For what?"

"'Cause, she thinks that I'm goin' to catch a case for slippin' some X in that ho's drink on New Year's Eve."

"Did you do the shit?"

"Hell yeah, I did it."

"Nigga, for what?"

"For what?"

"Yeah? Why you do the shit?"

"Nigga, because of the reason you layin' up in that bitch right now and she ain't sayin' nothing, that's why," I told J.B.

J.B. looked down at the girl he had been going in and out of the whole night, then asked, "This bitch on X?"

"Fucked up," I let him know. "That's why I be doin' the shit. So I don't have to hear their mouths while I fuck'em and I can do them as long as I want. Now what?"

"I thought she was just high or something. But she don't know what I'm doin' to her?"

"Don't know shit."

"This is wild, too wild." J.B. began to gently slap her face.

"What the fuck you doin', nigga?"

"Tryin' to wake her up. I don't like fuckin' no ho that don't know I'm fucking her. What kind of shit is that?"

"Well, she ain't going to wake up, J.B. That shit has to wear off."

"So how the fuck you let Shae find out about this shit, and ain't you trippin' that she might turn your ass in?"

"I don't really know, nigga, but Shae ain't crazy. I already told her what's up if she does."

"See, man. I told you a couple of weeks ago you was losing focus, dog. All we supposed to be doing is getting our lyrics tight and approaching Shae with 'em. I don't know about you, but I'm tryin' to get paid."

"Nigga, don't worry. I got this. I got this."

Karen
Something to tell you.

When I picked up the phone to call Synthia I had one thing on my mind. To tell her Shae's boyfriend was the one responsible for Clarke damn near losing her life. I had waited as long as I could and while we were working on the very last chapter of the book over Shae's place, just listening to how her thug of a man was talking to her only solidified my decision.

There's no doubt young couples have difficulty. I know I'd had my share when I was Shae's age. I couldn't trust and was out for the take. But Outlaw was totally ridiculous. He was disrespectful for no apparent reason. There were phone calls to other girls in front of Shae and he treated her like she didn't deserve his utmost respect. After all, she'd told me, after one of their heated arguments, that she was tired of footing the bills for his clothes, phone, drawers, sneakers and toothpaste.

Synthia was really hyped when I finally reached her on the phone. Of course, I gave her an update on the book, then she jumped right into a conversation about Thomas and how intimate they were becoming. I just couldn't refuse to partake in the conversation. When Synthia took a deep breath concerning all the details, I told her that I knew I was right about them getting even more serious as time went by.

"I have to admit, you were right, and here lately, being together has really been something special and I am not just talking about the sex," she admitted. "It's become emotional for us both."

"That makes the relationship the best, Synthia. You're finally having the best of the best. I'm so happy for you."

"It's been like this since we both witnessed Stacey address her mother's killer. I'm telling you, as we sat their hand in hand, it was like we instantly bonded."

"So what now?" I had to know.

"Funny, that's the same thing Thomas wants to know."

"So?"

"As I see it, we have two options. I can take this thing on and jump into an all-exclusive relationship with Thomas again. Or sit back and see where all of this newfound emotion and lust will take us." I let Synthia know that those were not bad options; especially since I didn't have any options. "But they're difficult options," she said.

"Meaning?"

"If I get emotionally involved with Thomas again and then things don't work out, then, hell, I'm right back where I started and this whole thing becomes nothing but a heated fling. But if I sit back and wait, play this thing out, see how it works, it may be for the better. Damn it, I'm too old to be going through this," Synthia said.

"At least you're going through it," I let Synthia know. "After all this time, Byron still doesn't trust my motives and I really do think he's playing his cards with Debra."

"I hate to say this but why don't you just seduce him?" Synthia chuckled.

"What?"

"Give Byron what he likes the most. We both know Byron has always been crazy about you in the bed. He told me all the time."

"He gave you details of me in the bed, Synthia?"

"Sure did."

"You two were close friends, weren't you?"

"Too close. That's why I needed a little distance."

"Seduce Byron, huh?"

THE VERY NEXT DAY I was over Shae's.

"Shae, we need to talk," I said to her. The only reason I was there was to pick up some of my pages. Shae had to approve them for the final manuscript. "Have you made up your mind about Outlaw yet?" Shae puckered her lips and shook her head. "We can't keep going around in circles with this. I just want you to know I called Synthia last night to tell her, but our conversation got twisted somehow. But I'm telling you, this has gone on too long."

"Whatever," Shae responded. "I'm not bringing my man down like that."

"C'mon, Shae, Outlaw doesn't even respect you." I was at a point with Shae where diplomacy and tact were not going to work. She wasn't from that side of the tracks. She needed to hear the true non-sugar-coated facts. "And you might not like what I have to say, but he doesn't respect you because you don't respect yourself."

"Don't start, Karen, 'cause I already told you, my life is my life and there is nobody that can change that."

"Oh yes there is, Shae."

"Who?" she snapped.

"You."

"Whatever."

"I know you care, Shae."

"What?"

"If you didn't, you wouldn't have told me in the first place. You would have continued to let *your man* drug as many girls as he wanted without saying one word to anyone."

"I told you in confidence, Karen, because I was afraid of what it would do to my career if someone found out. But no one has and you're the only person still worried about the shit."

"Because it's not right and I know you feel the same, Shae. I see it in your eyes; that you don't like what he's doing. I would be upset also if my man was sleeping with other women."

"Don't matter what you see in my eyes, okay, and we both know you ain't got a man," Shae lashed out.

"Look, I'm looking out for your best interest. If the media finds out that you knew all about the drugs, you are as much as responsible as he is."

"Well, I don't know what to tell you, Karen, because I don't know anything about it, okay?"

"Girl, have you lost your mind? What kind of hold does Outlaw have on you? What's he have on you, Shae, to let him continue what he's doing? It has to be something, I know it has to be, because you're much smarter than you're acting."

IT TOOK ME ANOTHER TWO HOURS to drag it out of Shae. She let me know the only reason she hadn't told me was because she was afraid I would begin to pressure her to divulge this part of her life in the book. I quickly understood why her lips were sealed. Right before she'd won her first recording contract, money was tight and Outlaw had talked her into doing a porno film with two underground adult film producers down in Charlotte, one of which was his cousin. A fast-talking country bumpkin' who thought he was the answer to any problem. A hundred and twenty-minute exclusive featuring Shae with five different men doing everything imaginable in front of the camera was shot and the film was scheduled to come óut close to the time of Shae's signing her record deal. She and Outlaw went back to Charlotte, paid off the producers for the masters of the tapes, which Outlaw kept instead of burning like Shae had suggested, and when he found out that Shae agreed with me that what Outlaw was doing with the X was wrong, he'd threatened to turn the tape into the highest bidder for the world to see.

Thomas
Moving in that direction.

It was one of those early evenings that I relished. Dinner was cooking: Chicken Parmesan along with steamed broccoli. Stacey was doing her homework nearby and jazz lightly played in the background while I sipped on red wine.

"Thanks for helping me with my math, Big Papa," Stacey punched.

"Baby girl, I only answered a few questions and I suggest you get those checked. Maybe I need to go back to school so that I can keep up with you. You know your math is getting to be very difficult."

"No, you don't have to go back to school. I think your answers are right." Stacey closed her books, moved them aside, and looked over at the stove.

"Just give me a few more minutes and we'll be all set." All I needed to do was pour the sauce. "You know, sweetheart, I didn't tell you after court, but I was really proud of you. You are a very strong lady."

"Mommy told me to always be strong."

"Well, you're doing an excellent job."

"I've been thinking, maybe I should talk to someone like Clarke did when she was younger, like Cousin Leon?"

I took the food over to Stacey. "Clarke mentioned to me that she thought it would be a good idea."

"I don't really know too much about psychiatrists, but maybe he'll be the best person for me. I don't even know if I will like talking to him, but I do want to try."

"Well, I can set something up. But in the meantime, I don't want you to ever forget that you can talk to me about anything you want. You understand? And that goes for Byron, Clarke, and Synthia, too." When Synthia's name came out of my mouth, Stacey giggled and refused to tell me why all through dinner.

THIRTY MINUTES LATER BYRON WALKED IN THE DOOR and by the look on his face I could tell he was pissed about something. Evidently Stacey could tell also.

"What's wrong, Uncle Byron?" she pried.

"Same old thing. I don't even know why I get upset anymore when it takes me close to an hour to hail a cab. I should just take it as a fact of life, being a black man living in the city."

"What if Harriet Tubman thought like that?" Stacey said. "If she did, maybe you'd be complaining about how hot the sun was smacking you across your head while you picked cotton." She giggled.

She always knew how to make a point. Byron and I looked at one another in amazement of her knowledge. "Maybe it's time to break down and buy yourself a car," I told him.

"A car? In New York City? Never…"

Stacey stood up, holding her dinner plate, and Byron bent down so she could kiss him on the top of his head. "Well, better luck next time. I'm going to my room to watch some TV."

"Hey, did you finish your math?" Byron's tone of voice reminded me of my own father's when asking the same question.

"Big Papa helped me."

"He did? I'll be back in an hour to check it, okay? You know, just in case."

I gave Byron a glass of wine. "Here you go. A toast to you," I told him.

"To me?"

"I heard you passed your final exam for the job, brother. Congrats!"

"Are you serious? Now that's a load off."

"You had doubts?"

"Sort of. You never can tell with tests. You know what I'm saying?"

"Well, worry no more. It's a done deal and you're officially a Con-Ed sales rep. Just wear the badge proud."

After Byron reflected and took a couple of sips of wine, he asked me how things were going. I told him okay.

"No, no. How are things really going? I saw you and Synthia leaving here arm in arm the other night, getting into a cab."

"Yeah, I was taking her home." Byron had an exploring expression on his face. "What?"

"So how are things going?"

"To be honest?"

"Yeah."

"Out of control. I don't know how to explain it. But this is not in a bad sense. It's great, much better than I ever remembering us being together."

"Just think, if Synthia wouldn't have gathered up enough courage months ago realizing things weren't right in her life, we probably still would have been trapped in that silly web of same ol' without giving it a second thought," Byron reflected. "I would probably still be going back and forth with Karen, working a dead-end job. Damn, I don't even want to think about it."

"Now that's a very scary thought. Particularly, how things have panned out."

"Oh, don't mention it. I can't even imagine still selling suits and living in the back of the shop."

"I can say one thing for certain. If Synthia and I agree on becoming an item again I'm going for the whole package. That's how much I'm really feeling this."

"Meaning?"

"Marriage, man."

"Either this drink is really strong or I didn't hear you correctly?"

"You heard me right."

"And she knows about this?"

"Our feelings have been renewed. She knows that. Even Clarke asked me what was going on between her mother and me. It's no hiding it, it's written all over our faces."

"Sounds like love to me," Byron admitted.

"I want to give her so much. I know I can't give her all the years back that we were divorced and barely speaking. But I damn sure want to try. I put her through a lot of mess, and it all could have been avoided; especially when I slept with the cheerleader, man."

"Yeah, I remember that," Byron's voice trailed off.

"It took the sparkle out of her eye, Byron. But the sparkle that I used to see is back and, damn it, I want it."

Karen
It's true what they say.

I definitely needed to stop fooling myself when it came to Byron. I missed him and didn't know how much until I'd literally dissed him and thrown all the time we'd spent together away without any regards to anyone's feelings down the road, including my own. The enormous amount of time I'd spent with Byron sunk in on Synthia's advice that I seduce him. I smiled at the thought. Waves of ideas flowed through my mind of what aroused him; even what I enjoyed doing for him. Sometimes, I'd told him I didn't enjoy them so he could think of me as a good girl, instead of a stone-cold freak. So souped up on Synthia's advice, I called Byron. I wanted to play on the phone and it didn't take him long to join the game.

"…oh, that makes it really good, Karen. You know you're right, a Jell-O bath is making a brother wonder about its endless opportunities," Byron whispered into the phone. "You know I've always been a freak," he claimed.

"One thing's for sure, Byron."

"What's that?"

"You could really get your mouth full," I told him.

"As I remember it to be, it was your favorite thing to be on the receiving end of."

"You know, just thinking about it makes me want to feel your tongue."

"I see things are getting a little hot," Byron purred into the phone.

"Hot…and nasty, baby. So…hot. Oh, I wish it wasn't so late," I let him know, then he wanted to know why. "So you could come over, so I can make you eat your words, literally." Byron became silent. When my voice trailed off the phone, I knew he was on the other end wondering what I was doing, so I didn't want to disappoint him since "Kitty" was in need of attention, so I just went with the flow. "Byron?"

"Yes."

"Are you serious about kissing me all…over my body?" I asked for *Kitty*.

"No doubt about it, nice and slow and not missing a spot."

"You wouldn't believe how bad *Kitty* needs that, Byron. You do remember *Kitty*, don't you?"

"Yes, I remember."

"Well, she says hey…"

"Hey…" Byron sang.

I said as slow as I could to him, "Byron, I really, really, really need to feel your lips on my body, baby."

"So bad that you can show me how much you need it at this very minute? So bad that you can release all your tension as we speak?"

"Uh…huh…Ummmm…" I purred while *Kitty* enjoyed the moment. Oh Byron, Byron…Oh…" There was silence and I could tell Byron was on the other end thinking.

"Karen?"

"Yes…?"

"Did you…"

I cut him off. "I'm not goin' to tell."

"Why not?"

"You really want to know?"

"Sure, I do."

"Okay, how's this. Would you rather me tell you or show you?"

"If you tell me, does it mean you won't show me?"

"Yes."

"When do you plan on showing me?"

"I'll leave that up to you."

"I think I'll wait on the show."

"You always did like to watch, Byron. Whew, I can honestly say this has been one hell of an enjoyable conversation."

"What brought this on?" Bryon asked.

"For me it's seeing Synthia and Thomas running around like two teenagers in heat. I think it's great they're looking at possibilities."

"Yeah, it kind of makes a brother want to venture off into the whole commitment thing again."

"Debra should be pleased to hear that."

"Didn't I tell you?"

"Tell me what?"

"There is no Debra. She decided to take her long-lost lover from college back. It seems he finally divorced his second wife and thinks that she's the only woman for him because *his past* tells him so."

"You know you didn't tell me that, Byron?"

"I know. Anyway, when's my show?"

Synthia
The nerve?

I went to the recording studio to meet Shae and Karen, expecting a joyous gathering with the news I was carrying. What I got was a rude awakening to what they call thug life; blatant ignorance and disrespect that made me want to call somebody's mama so they could literally spank some ass.

I arrived while Shae was in the recording booth finishing up a take on her last song for her new CD under the watchful eyes of producers. I'd always known that producers were actually the ones who made it happen for the artist but I was surprised to see that they were the facilitators and consumers of most of the liquor and weed being passed around while they worked.

Karen was sitting in a lounge, wondering what was so pressing, so after I told Karen that Warmer Productions green-lit Shae's movie and that her book contract with Shae stipulated twenty-five percent of any proceeds from movie rights, we walked in to see Shae hand in hand and told her the good news and began signing contracts. Karen was the first to sign her contract and while I dug into my carry bag to pull out Shae's agreement, I was forced to look up because the aroma of marijuana and liquor hit me square in the face. When I saw the guys who strutted in the recording booth I tried to register where I'd seen them before. Then it dawned on me they were the fools who had gotten loud with Shae the day we were eating lunch. I guess so many people ran in and out of the recording booth when Shae was taking a break that she didn't bother to look up until Outlaw began to clear his throat.

"Shae? Don't you see me standing here?" he wanted to know. He looked over at his partner with a smile, then I noticed the smirk he gave Karen.

Shae looked up. "Hey, Outlaw."

"Look, we need to talk to you for a quick second," Outlaw requested.

Shae looked at me, then Karen and all the paperwork in her hand. "Outlaw, I'm busy."

"Too busy for me?"

"Ah…yes. Can't you see I'm signing some important papers?"

"Later for that. I wanted you to listen to our demo. Remember I told you about the demo I was working on?"

"Yes, I remember and I told you when I get a chance I would listen to it. Why don't ya'll go back in the room and chill for a while, then when I'm done recording, I'll see if I can get to it."

I looked at Outlaw and could tell he'd definitely missed out on home training. I thought for a second about how his mother must feel about him. He looked as though that once upon a time he was a good kid. As though at one time in his life he'd loved animals and remote control cars. But now he was trying his best to look hard. Like someone owed him something for breathing. Then I thought he probably used his shocking tone of voice with Shae because he never knew his mother and didn't know how to talk to women. Or even worse, he didn't give a damn about women period; mother or not. He didn't scare me though. None of the young boys who acted in such a way ever had. Whenever I had to, which was very rare, I'd put them in their place and wouldn't think twice about it. For some reason the younger males walking around seemed to look hard and intimidate folks, but I didn't fall for that scam. Shae continued to sign her contract, as Karen and I looked on and then I heard Outlaw take a deep breath. He stormed out the recording booth and into the control room. Instantly our ears were being punished by a thunderous pounding of music under Outlaw's watchful gleaming eyes; listening to the worst song I had ever heard in my life.

SUCK MY DICK BITCH
Til' I tell you to quit
SUCK MY DICK BITCH
I think you need a hit

SUCK MY DICK BITCH
I told you—my shit is thick
SUCK MY DICK BITCH
It don't get no betta than this

The lyrics just got worse and the pounding of the bass through the speakers was so revolting that I stood up and asked one of Shae's producers to turn the music off, then walked back into the quiet recording booth under everyone's shocked face, picked up my paperwork, and laid it back across my legs.

"Bitch? What's your problem?" Outlaw wanted to know.

If I'd tried to explain how much his words hurt me I would've failed miserably. I didn't have to say one word to Outlaw because Karen stood up and so did Shae.

"Fuck you, you young stupid ass nigga," Karen said. "You need to take that sorry ass song and stick it up your ignorant ass!" Karen looked as though she was ready to go to blows if need be.

"Outlaw... what is your problem?" Shae wanted to know.

"Bitch, I told you I wanted you to listen to our shit. I know it's bumpin' and I want you to give it to your people on your label so we can get on. That's my muthafuckin' problem, now what?"

"Outlaw, get the fuck out," Shae demanded.

Outlaw's friend was even embarrassed and tried to get Outlaw to leave.

"Bitch, we ain't going nowhere," Outlaw told her.

"You just ought to, with your ignorant ass," Karen chipped in.

"Fuck you, ho."

"No, fuck you, druggie..."

Things paused briefly and I noticed Shae look up at Karen who turned to me.

"Synthia…" Karen said. "This…"

"Uh, unh, Karen. Don't worry about it. I'll do it later," Shae said.

Karen looked at Outlaw. "You're a sorry ass punk," she said.

Outlaw looked at Shae hard, then demanded his sidekick to follow him and they walked out. I gathered up my things without saying a word to anyone, went into the lobby, called Thomas. He insisted that I stay put until he came with his driver to pick me up.

Karen
The shame of it all.

I asked Shae's driver to drop me off at my place because, after the episode with Outlaw in the studio and seeing how hurt Synthia was when that fool called her a bitch, it really put me in a mood to want to break something. When I got out the car I was quite sure Shae understood that she had twenty-four hours to tell Synthia what Outlaw had done to Clarke or I was going to the police first, then to Synthia. I didn't have much to break at my place so I called Byron and was determined to take all my frustrations out in the bed without a care in the world.

"What the hell is this about?" Byron wanted to know. He was straddled behind me and asked me the question after I told him to spank my ass.

"What? You don't like it?" I asked him right before I bared down on him. I could feel his body say, "Oh shit!"

"I didn't say that," he told me. And slapped me on the ass. First the right side, then the left.

"That's the best you can do?"

"Baby, I told you when you talk like that you make me…"

I knew what was coming next so I made sure I was going there, too.

TEN MINUTES LATER Byron was lying across my bed and I was standing in a towel drying off.

"Was all that for me?"

"Unh…unh. For me," I told him.

"Oh, you missed it that much?"

"Nope. I mean I did. But I needed to release and that's for real. I had a really bad day." Before I could tell Byron what had happened, the phone rang. It was Shae and she wanted me to know that she'd finally decided to turn Outlaw in and asked if I could come to see her.

Byron told me that he understood that I had to go. But he told me he felt used and I asked him if I could tell him the truth about something. When he answered yes, I told him—he was, but not to worry because I would fill him in later as to why. He wiped the sad look off his face when I assured him that I wasn't finished with him and he seemed to like that.

When I finally made it over to Shae's it was the first time I'd ever seen her drink. She had a whiskey sour in her hand and I suspected she'd downed a few more before I'd arrived. To my surprise J.B. was there and he quickly apologized for what happened earlier in the studio. Shae wanted to turn Outlaw in. She felt bad about what he'd said to Synthia and it made things worse, to know he was the person who'd come close to killing her daughter.

Shae had paged J.B. and offered him a deal. She knew that he was aware of where Outlaw was hiding the porno tape of her because surprisingly Shae and J.B. had been sneaking around behind Outlaw's back when he was busy with his playmates. Shae knew that Outlaw let J.B. watch the tape and offered J.B. a record deal with her independent label if he gave the tape to her so she could finally burn it. Shae was in no shape to go with J.B. out to Harlem to get the tape. I was so energized and ready to take care of Outlaw's ass for once and for all that I decided to ride out to Harlem with J.B after he assured us that Outlaw would be over his new friend's house whom he'd met a week earlier.

Synthia
I really needed to relax.

I was wiped out after the studio fiasco. Thomas talked me into going to the movies with him, Clarke, Stacey and Byron. We saw *Ali*, which I enjoyed immensely. Afterwards, we went to a nearby pizzeria.

"I think this was a good, spur of the moment activity," I told everyone. Stacey had a smile on her face the entire night. Clarke kept her arm in mine most of the night. I think she realized our days of spending time together were rapidly depleting. For some strange reason Byron looked washed out, while Thomas was his natural, handsome cool self.

"I think so, too," Thomas said.

"Did everyone like the movie?" Stacey asked.

"I certainly did. Who wouldn't enjoy Mr. Smith in all his splendor. Jada sure has molded that man nicely," Clarke cooed.

"I really liked Jamie Foxx. I think he and Will work well together. Not to mention the photographer's camera movements were excellent," Stacey pointed out. "But I would have focused more on Ali growing up if I was the director." We all gave Stacey a glancing over. "What?" she asked.

"Girl, you sound just like a movie critic," Clarke pointed out.

"Sounds like we have a critic on our hands," Thomas said.

"Unh, unh. A movie executive, thank you very much," Stacey made clear. "Did you guys know there is no one of color in the movie industry that can greenlight a picture?"

"I knew that," I told her. "I'm so impressed."

"Greenlight?" Byron mumbled.

"Yup, not one black person in America can find a movie they like and give the go-ahead to get it made at a studio," Stacey informed us.

"I didn't know that," Clarke admitted.

"Not many people do," I told my daughter. "But we're a large percentage of moviegoers, which doesn't make sense, but our Stacey is on her way."

"That's right. Hollywood isn't going to keep me out," she boasted.

"That's the spirit, sweetheart," Thomas said. Thomas looked over at Bryon, who seemed to be in a daze all night long. "Hey, Byron, you okay?"

"Yeah, sure," he said back.

Thomas said, "Anyway while Byron daydreams over there, I want all of you ladies to know you all are my angels and I don't know what I'd do without you." We all purred at Thomas. "I really do mean it," he said and I believed him, too.

"Dad, what're you going to do with all these women in your life?" Clarke asked him.

"Take care of all of you, the best I can." Then he grabbed my hand and it erased every moment of my bad day.

Karen
Just go in and get it.

Shae's driver took us to Harlem. He parked around the corner from the brownstone and I went along with J.B. to get the tape. He said it would only take us a couple of minutes to get it, then he wanted to grab a few things because Shae had agreed to let him stay with her until the authorities had Outlaw. J.B. opened the door to the brownstone. I stood with one foot inside and one out with the door wide open.

"Hurry up and get the shit and let's go," I told J.B. and he ran upstairs. I could hear him rummaging through drawers and throwing things into a plastic bag. It must have taken him only a couple of minutes before he came huffing back down the steps, and as soon as I stepped away from the door so that we could hurry back to the car, a gun fired and J.B. fell to the floor.

"Bitch, you better not move," Outlaw said to me. "Get your ass back in here."

I was frozen at the sight of J.B. lying in front of me. The next thing I know, I'm upstairs without any clothes on, tied up lying on a bed.

"So, ya'll talked this nigga into doing some foul shit, huh?" Outlaw said. "I knew J.B. wasn't shit. Punk ass nigga." Outlaw looked down at J.B. and shook his head. J.B. hadn't moved since being shot and I just knew he was dead when Outlaw dragged him upstairs into the bedroom. "Damn, Karen, I didn't know your nipples were so long," Outlaw said and there was nothing I could do because my hands were tied above my head and my legs were super tight, tied to a radiator heater. Outlaw leaned over me and started to run his tongue across my tips. I tried to move a few times and after he slapped me I just let him get his kicks. "Shit, we need some music up in here," he said.

"Outlaw, you better let me go," I told him.

"Bitch, what? You have a problem telling me what to do. You know that?"

Outlaw walked away from me and turned on his tape player. It was the song he'd played for Shae at the studio and it was so loud that I could barely hear what Outlaw was saying.

"So you didn't like my music, huh? So you didn't like it? Well, now you're going to suck me until you tell me you like it, then I'm going to smoke your ass right here." Outlaw took off his shirt and began to dance to the music, then pretended to give me a strip show. I screamed twice and after each time Outlaw punched me in the face with his fist. When he unzipped his pants he walked over to my face and tried to stick his body part in my mouth.

"Open up, Karen. Bitch, I said, open up," he demanded. At that point I was not going to let it happen and every time he came close to my mouth I tried to bite him and didn't care if he hit me again or not. "Oh, I know what we need," he said. Outlaw went to a shoe box and opened it. "Damn it, out of X," he said. He looked at me and thought for a minute. "That's okay. Since you wanted the tape of Shae so bad, you can lie here and watch it while I go get me some more X." Outlaw leaned over me again and ran his tongue over my nipples and left me to watch the tape.

LIL' SHAE
Where ya'll at?

I was drunk, but I knew Karen and J.B. should have been on the way back so I called my driver to find out what was taking them so long. When I found out that my driver was still sitting in the car waiting for them I told him to drive around the corner to see if he could see anything and he told me that he'd just noticed Outlaw walk down the brownstone steps all by his lonesome. After I threatened to fire my driver if he didn't go to the door and at least try to find out what was going on, he refused so I began to get nervous and I called Synthia because I didn't know what else the hell to do.

Byron
She's where?

I got a call from Synthia right before my head hit the pillow. There was no doubt I was spent after what Karen felt she needed to do and on top of that, the pasta I'd eaten at the pizzeria covered my body like a blanket. The urgency in Synthia's voice was the culprit of my putting on an old pair of jeans, baseball cap, sweatshirt and my sneakers. She told me that Karen, for some reason, had gone to Harlem with a thug to retrieve a tape from the guy who'd drugged Clarke. All of it was a bit much to digest because I was groggy so I took down the address, grabbed my jacket and made my way to Harlem.

I was having my usual luck getting a cab. There were plenty of cabs rolling by, but, of course, they wouldn't stop for me. While I waited with one hand up, whistling for service every minute or so, I would speed dial Karen's cell phone number, but there was no answer. I must have waited ten minutes at close to one in the morning to pull down a cab and while I waited I noticed a white man from the corner of my eye come out of a pub having trouble finding his balance. He stood up as straight as possible, raised his hand, then hollered, "Taxi." Miraculously the lights of a cab sitting on the street that I thought was parked for the night beamed in my eyes and went right past me to pick up the *drunk*. When I turned to watch the cab back in, I was so fed up that I ran a few feet toward the man and the cab. I put my hand on the car door right before the man, who reeked of alcohol, threw himself inside. I put up my right arm while I maneuvered my way between him and the opening, then pushed the man back and jumped into the cab and shut the door.

"Take me to 121st in Harlem," I told the cabby.

The driver's eyes were engulfed. "What are you doing? I didn't stop for you," he admitted.

"Well, you should've. Let's go," I told him.

"Look, I don't do Harlem. So get the fuck out," he said.

"I'm not going anywhere. Take me to Harlem."

The driver slammed the car in park, reached under his seat and before I knew it, had my door open with a pistol in my face. I looked out the door and right behind the cabby, I could see the drunk who was in shock and didn't know if he should call out for help or run. "Get the fuck out," he said.

There was nothing left for me to do other than get out of the cab and when the cabby noticed that's what I was doing. He took a step back, nodded to the drunk, instructed him to get in, and then called me a "stupid ass nigga" and I wasn't taking it. I turned around so fast that it even surprised me, snatched the pistol out his hand and pointed it directly into his chest. "Get in the back."

I heard the drunk gasp.

"Do what?" the cabby asked me.

"Get in the back. We're going to Harlem. There is a very special person that might need my help and I need to get out there now." The cabby wouldn't move so I pointed the pistol at him so real he thought I would pull the trigger any second. He asked me to take it easy and did what I said. I moved around to the other side of the cab and before I got in I asked the drunk if he needed a ride.

"Ah, yeah?…Sure, why not," he said, confused.

"Well, c'mon, let's go," I told him and he hopped in the front seat with me. After I'd pulled off, the drunk was making me sort of nervous because he kept meddling with the distance counter, telling himself that he knew they were all rigged.

"Do you know how much trouble you're in?" the cabby said from the back.

"Look, I don't mean you any harm, man. I just want to go to Harlem and that's it."

The drunk looked over at me. "Hey, that's where I'm going, too."

"Did you tell him that before you got in the cab?" I wanted to know.

"Sure did. He said no problem at all."

"Ain't that a bitch?" I looked back at the cabby.

The cabby said, "Look, if you were a cabby you wouldn't take a nigga to Harlem either this late."

"You sure are using the word nigga loosely, aren't you?"

"What's wrong with that? I hear you guys calling each other that all the time. I picked up two earlier today, only took them seven blocks and it was nigga this, and nigga that. Just nigga, nigga, nigga."

The drunk turned in his seat and began to shake his finger and head at the cabby.

"You have a lot to learn. Where are you from, man?" I wanted to know.

"It doesn't matter where I'm from. I've only been here two weeks and all the cabbies told me to never take a black man to Harlem," he said. He sounded like he was from Poland or something.

"Well, guess what?" I saw his identification on the dash. "Baron, we're going to Harlem tonight," I told him.

The drunk looked over at me. "Can you drop me off at 125th?"

We were making it to Harlem in good time and the whole time I tried to explain to the cabby that all Black men didn't rob cabs. He was confused but I swear I felt it was my time to at least let one of these guys know the truth. To my surprise the drunk helped me explain it to Baron and by the time we'd reached 121st we were all friends on a first-name basis.

When I got close to the address Synthia had given me, I turned off the lights on the cab. I looked over at Ron, the drunk, who seemed at home, then back at Baron who had wandering eyes looking out the window.

"Do me a favor. Will you guys wait here for me?" I asked. Ron looked at me and smiled. I made eye contact with Baron in the rearview mirror. "C'mon, man, like I told you, if I wanted to shoot you, I would have done it by now. I need your help."

"Okay, okay. But hurry up and I'm driving my cab," he decided.

After I told them where I was going, I got out the cab, gave Baron a hundred dollars and let him know I would give him the pistol back as soon as I returned. While I walked to the address, I heard Baron scream at Ron to leave his got damn distance meters up front alone.

I took the venture up the dilapidated brownstone steps. It was dark leading to the door and I had to focus my eyes to adjust to the darkness. After I made my way up the steps I tried to listen for any movement inside and what I heard was music and what seemed like a woman screaming. I went back to the cab.

"Call the police," I told Baron.

"What? The police?"

"Yes, the police. Didn't your friends, who told you about the niggas, tell you how to call the police, Baron?"

"Look, I'm here illegally. I can't call the fuckin' police. I have warrants in my motherland."

"For what?" Ron asked.

"Robbery."

"Ain't this a bitch," I said. "Look, call the police, Ron. There's a woman inside there screaming for help." My information seemed to perk Ron up a bit. "Baron, pull down the street a bit and keep this cab running because I might come out of there in a hurry," I told him.

"Okay, okay, just hurry the fuck up," Baron said. "Harlem makes me nervous."

The drunk picked up Baron's microphone and keyed it. "Nine-one-one, I have an emergency." When Baron's home base station answered, Baron snatched the handset from Ron and began to speak.

I STOOD AT THE DOOR OF THE BROWNSTONE, looked back at the cab, and flashed a flashlight at Baron. When he flicked his lights back at me, I knew the police had been called. I turned the doorknob on the door and to my surprise, it was unlocked. I paused before I stepped inside, but the screaming was clearer now. I was inside for a couple of minutes before I made it close to where the music was coming from. The door of the room was shut. I took my pistol out, counted to three and kicked the door in, and saw Karen lying on a bed tied up next to a body on the ground with a porno playing on the television and some very bad music blasting in my ear.

Karen screamed. "Byron, hurry up and get me out of here!"

"What the hell is going on?"

"Untie me, Byron, hurry up! We don't have a lot of time!"

I untied Karen and she put on her pants and shirt, and I was standing down looking at the body at my feet and the porno on the television.

"Grab the tape, Byron," Karen told me.

"What?"

"Get the tape and let's go," she said.

"Who is this on the ground, Karen?"

"He's dead."

"I can see that."

Karen was tired of talking to me. She went over to the VCR, took out the tape, and we were about to make our way out the door when she screamed. I looked down and the young buck on the floor had grabbed her leg.

"Karen, don't leave me here," he said.

"C'mon, Byron, let's pick him up and go," she said. Luckily he didn't weigh that much at all. I would have guessed about a hundred fifty-five pounds. We were moving much too slow, with Karen holding his arms and me with his legs down the steps, so I put him over my shoulder and moved like crazy to get out of the place. When we reached the front door, got down the steps and were on the way to Baron in the cab, we heard screaming coming from down the street.

"Hey, hey got damn it, come here!"

"It's Outlaw!" Karen screamed. "C'mon, Byron, let's go."

When I started to run, that's when the weight of the fellow I had on my shoulder began to bother me. Then I heard gunshots whipping past my ear. Baron must have heard them as well because he put the cab in reverse to meet us.

"Get in, damn it!" he screamed.

Karen hopped in the cab first, I placed the guy on my shoulder inside, then I felt a hot burning sensation in my body as we drove away.

Lil' Shae
Do what I have to do.

After what everyone had done for me, how could I not answer every question the police asked me during their investigation of Outlaw. Come to find out, there were at least three girls still in a coma from the ecstasy he'd laced in their drinks from places I had toured and another in Texas who had died. I wasn't surprised that they were going to give him the chair for his actions because they don't play that shit in Texas and the only concrete evidence they had was me because he'd admitted to me that he was giving girls X.

The media found out anyway and there was no way I was not going to testify; especially after Karen told me she had been one of the girls I looked up to when I was a shorty visiting in Brooklyn. I was so happy that J.B. made it back. He took a bullet to the chest and they say it was a miracle that he made it. I wasn't going to go through with giving him the recording deal at first, but after I got the tape back I decided to work with him anyway. Plus, I still liked the way he licked my nana. You don't find that type of shit often.

Synthia
Who would have known?

Four weeks after all the drama had unfolded with Shae, things in my life were beginning to get back to normal for whatever that really meant. The bullet that Byron had taken only turned out to be a graze wound on his arm. Clarke had left for Brown and called me what seemed like every day to let me know how much fun she was having. To my surprise Shae's first three concerts were benefits for sexually abused women, and she'd invited Karen and me to a sold-out concert at the one in only Madison Square Garden. Karen and I were backstage waiting to catch a glimpse of Shae before she took the stage.

"I think this is great," I told Karen.

"A benefit for abused women. See, I knew she had it in her," Karen said proudly.

"Hello, ladies!" Shae said as she stood in front of her many handlers before taking the stage. We all exchanged hugs. "Thanks for coming. I really do mean that."

"Thanks for the invite. Easy now, my youngest is in the audience," I told her with a smile on my face.

"She is?"

"In the front row," I told her.

The stage manager walked up to Shae, right after her theme music, to help her to the stage. It was time.

Before she walked away, Shae said, "Listen, I was wondering if you two were still interested in helping me change my image a bit. I really think it's time."

"Why sure, sweetheart," I told her.

"Of course, I'll pay you. Just a little tweaking here and there."

I told her, "Don't worry about paying me, Shae. I'll do it because you're right and you're trying to reach your full potential. I'd be honored."

"Well, you got to pay me, sista gurl," Karen said. "I don't have it like you two yet. Not yet!"

"Deal," Shae said. Shae turned and looked at the stage when clouds of smoke began to rise and loud explosions filled the arena. "But let's not get started tonight, because I'm about to rock this bitch!" Shae said and she walked away and put the microphone up to her mouth. "All right, my niggas! Are you ready to lick my punany!" she screamed.

"Oh, my goodness," I said to Karen. "Stacey's in the front row." I laughed. "Oh, her sweet, sweet virgin ears. She'll be ruined for life after this."

SIX WEEKS LATER Thomas and I were on a double-date with Karen and Byron. We were at a restaurant that had invited Thomas to enjoy its very first night of business. The setting was cozy and I loved that they'd only invited thirty couples or so to partake in the opening. I was having such a wonderful time sitting around our table with plenty of food and drink.

"This is so wonderful," Karen said.

"I needed this night like you wouldn't believe."

"Thank God that bullet only pierced me. I would hate to think I could have missed out on this night," Byron said.

All of a sudden Otis Redding began to echo through the establishment. Thomas raised from his chair and asked for my hand.

Karen
Um, um. Um.

Byron took my hand as soon as Thomas and Synthia had hit the dance floor. It felt so good to have a man, my man, on completely truthful terms.

"Wow, it is so good to see them back together," Byron said.

"They seem really happy, don't they?"

Byron took a sip of his drink. "What about you? Are you happy, baby?"

"Sure, I'm having a wonderful time," I told him.

"No, no, I mean with your life?"

"Yes, we're dating again and my career is taking off and now I have options that are leading me to new options."

"It's amazing how things work out," Byron said. "Now, if I only knew how things are going to work out for us."

"Us? As in the future?" I wanted to know.

"Yeah, I was thinking since *potential* has finally crept into our lives. I think we should take full advantage of it, don't you think?"

"You mean, actually give this another try?"

"Yes, and living together again," Byron told me.

"As a couple?"

"As a married couple," he said. Byron smiled and opened his suit jacket and pulled out a stunning ring.

I couldn't even scream, I was so surprised.

"I don't want to ask you sitting down, baby. I want to ask you while we dance together. Will you dance with me, sexy?"

"Sure, I'll dance with you, Byron, forever," I told him.

Synthia
With all my heart.

"Look at those two," I said to Thomas while we danced.

Byron and Karen were dancing and kissing at the same time without a care in the world. The sound of Otis blaring in the background made the entire moment that much more special.

"I'm really enjoying this, sweetheart," Thomas whispered in my ear.

"So am I, Thomas."

"I can't believe how fast life is moving. It seems like yesterday that we were bringing Clarke home from the hospital."

"And now she's in college. Whew, I get chills just thinking about it," I said. "What a ride it's been, but I'm so glad I traveled down the road with you."

"Do you really mean that, Thomas?"

"With all my heart. So are you ready to work our magic with Stacey like we did with Clarke?" Thomas wanted to know.

"Ready as I'm going to get. I think it will be so much fun."

Thomas said, "I think so, too." Then he kissed me on my forehead. "What do you say, we get married and do this right this time, Synthia?"

"Married?"

"Yes. I've done a lot of thinking about everything you've said over the last couple of months. I've realized that I'm no good without you, sweetheart. And not just concerning having a partner to go out and do things with. My entire life is a hell of a lot better when you're a part of it and I just want you by my side forever." Thomas kissed me again. "Put your hand in my suit jacket," he told me. I was hesitant. "Go ahead, it's okay." I did and pulled out a ring and we stopped dancing as I looked at it. I was lost for words. "So you'll marry me, Synthia?"

I smiled and kissed him on the cheek and thought about the possibilities of what we now had really flourishing into something special. But marriage was difficult for Thomas and me. What we had now was something I'd never felt before and I wanted to keep it that way. "No, I can't, Thomas. Not right now," I told him.

"But what about all the talk about us living right? Changing in a positive direction? You seemed so adamant about that."

"I know, Thomas, and I still am, but I put everyone through so many changes when I decided that I wanted to change and I don't even know if it was such a nice thing to do. Going through all of this has made me come to one conclusion."

"What's that?"

"Even if *potential* is there, some things never change and I don't know if we should want them to or ask that they be." My decision wasn't exactly what Thomas wanted to hear. But I looked at the ring again, then placed it on my finger.

Thomas noticed me. "I thought you said you wouldn't?"

"I did," I let him know. "But I like this ring and I didn't say that you couldn't move back in, did I?"

AUTHOR'S NOTE

All right, ya'll, this is how my acknowledgments actually went down.

I was sitting at my desk wondering what and the heck I was gonna do next since I was finished with this book. I was either going to start on another West Owens novel— (if you haven't read *Money For Good,* please pick it up) or something totally different, which is always fun. Then my phone rang.

I answered.

"Franklin White."

A rushed voice on the other end came through my wireless connection. "Franklin?"

I looked into the phone because I couldn't catch her voice. And I was hoping it wasn't any unsuspecting-surprising-Baby Mama Drama.

"Who's calling?"

"It's Charmaine."

Whew, Charmaine is my fantastic editor at Strebor Books. *By the way, if you didn't know Strebor Books is coming with it! Now you know!*

So I asked in my best Tony Soprano accent, "How you doin', Charmaine?"

She said, "Look, I need your acknowledgments for *Potentially Yours*—like yesterday..."

I said, "Say what?"

"Yeah, we're in production and I need your acknowledgments."

"And-you-need-them-today?"

"Unh-unh, I said yesterday. Talk to you lata."

"But...."

Click all up in my ear.

So here they are and if I left anyone out—truly believe a brutha didn't do it on purpose and don't look at me so mean the next time I see you out and about on the streets because a brutha was working under a tight deadline and you know all I got is love for ya!.

First, Franklin would like to thank GOD for allowing me to bear the challenge of telling another story. Writing ain't easy, ya'll—let me clarify that...making a living writing ain't easy...and that's my word.

Thanks goes out to my editor Charmaine Parker for constantly staying on me and making my prose right and tight.

To Zane since back in the day we both knew it would happen! Continue to be blessed.

To Zelda Miles, my first line of defense and editor who keeps my work on track.

To Marvette Critney for keeping franklin-white.com nice and tight.

To my family. Family know who they be!

I have to shout out my mama, Ann E. Griffin. Thanks for instilling in me early in life that anything can be accomplished. Did ya'll know my mama was the First Black City Treasurer of Columbus, Ohio? Ya'll really need to put her up in that hall of fame down in City Hall...hint...hint (Somebody get the mayor on the line for me.) Richard Griffin, thanks for taking good care of my mama To my pops, Carl White Sr. Thank you for always being there and constantly teaching bout the way of the world. And what a world it is! (Side bar) My father is part of the reason black folk now have the opportunity to live anywhere they want these days—he has fought housing discrimination for over thirty years—in my eyes he's done no less than Malcolm, Martin or any other leader in the community...much love and respect...Thanks Sue; thanks for taking care of my pops...To my twin sister Sandy Graves—gurl, stop calling me every five minutes. I know your phone bill is sky-high J...hehe...Always remember I know what you're thinking at all times—that connection is for life and beyond. To my nieces Brea and Cleo, Nephew Bidea, my girl, Miea and the rugrats, Trey, Morgan, Langston. Ya'll keep a brutha sooo busy and it's all good! Claretta Allen, Reva Walker, Emma Moore, Jeff White, doing major business in Philly, Danny White, Uncle Phil, Deanna Moore, Pudin, Brandon, Chaka Chandler, Pastor Todd and Mrs. Todd, Meliea, Tonya and Rick, thanks for the phone calls! Aunt Donna, Kaloa Hearne, James and Carol Brown. For those of you out in Fort Wayne, Indiana, check out the White's School Of Arts and get your Tae Kwon Do on! Ask for Tyke White and get your workout and discipline on...he works wonders with kids!

Karla A. White—Rest in Peace.

Central State Connection, Roy Johnson, James Parham, Terry Castleberry, Arthur Thomas, Ed Clay, Lois Benjamin, Joyce Gregory, Hugh Douglas, Frank Tatum—Ya'll better watch out for my Marauders!

To my Friends who are friends The Poindexter clan: Terrance and family out in Cali—Love you brutha, Ziggie, Patrick, Nell, please continue to keep in touch. Waydis, Boxton, Lisa Durroh and Family, Frank Tatum, Lee Craft, Toni Jones, Foley, Lisa Starks, Karen Wilson, Kim Mills, Kendra Story, Alvin Dent, Ronald Steward, Mark Stinson, Garland Williams, David Dungy, Rick Carter (keep them emails coming), Michael Washington (see you in L.A.!), Randy Clarkson, Sandy Jackson, Lamonte Waugh, Lisa Durroh and family, Eric Troy and family, Eric and Sheila Shepard, Darryle Melson, Eve Melson, Rosita Page, and holding it down in Brussels: Maricruz E. Andeme. I promise I will venture there to do a signing.

Big Up's 2 to my New York City Connection. Reggie English, Bill Bolden, Sheryl Jones, Ernestine Callender, Tonya Anderson, Wilton Cedeno, Vaughn Graham, Pam Mason, Joann Christian. Harry Morrison, you think I didn't hear you when you said I should be a writer!

To every single Book Club! Thanks for continuing to read my work! Keep the emails coming! Much love goes out to Emma Rodgers—I will never forget how you helped me when my first novel was released! I still can't believe that cover! Thank you very much and good luck to you!

All those writers who I've met during this journey, Walter Mosley, Bebe Moore Campbell, Eric Jerome Dickey, Zane, Kimberla Lawson Roby, E. Lynn Harris, Victoria Christopher Murray, Sheneska Jackson, Yolanda Joe, Tim McCann, Thomas Green, Patricia Haley-Brown, Sharon Mitchell, Marcus Major, Colin Channer, Sister Souljah, Brian Edgeston, Lolita Files, Irene Egerton Perry, Vicky Stringer, Bridgett Stewart, Travis Hunter, Pearl Cleage, Margaret Johnson-Hodge, Brandon Massey, Tracy Price Thompson, Venise Berry, Phill Duck, Tonya Marie Evans, Evelyn Coleman, Parry "Ebony Satin" Brown, Michael Baisden, Curtis Bunn, Dr. Yvonne Butler, Jimmy Hurd, Nikki Jenkins, Janice Pinnock, TJ Butler.

Support our black bookstores!

Check out the website Franklin-White.com

Peace. Courage.

Franklin White

ABOUT THE AUTHOR

Franklin White is the author of the *Blackboard* bestselling novels *Fed Up With the Fanny, Money for Good,* and *Cup of Love.* He is the former features editor at *Upscale* magazine and lives in Atlanta, Georgia.

Printed in the United States
By Bookmasters